DEATH DEALERS

ALEX FOSSOR, NECROMANCER I

M.G. GALLOWS

For Myles, Ellen, and Paula,
who helped make this real

TABLE OF CONTENTS

ONE   9

TWO   20

THREE   33

FOUR   41

FIVE   50

SIX   62

SEVEN   69

EIGHT   78

NINE   87

TEN   97

ELEVEN   107

TWELVE   118

THIRTEEN   127

FOURTEEN   134

FIFTEEN   145

SIXTEEN   155

SEVENTEEN   162

EIGHTEEN   170

NINETEEN   177

TWENTY   191

TWENTY-ONE   201

TWENTY-TWO   211

TWENTY-THREE   222

TWENTY-FOUR   231

TWENTY-FIVE   240

TWENTY-SIX   248

TWENTY-SEVEN   257

TWENTY-EIGHT   271

TWENTY-NINE   282

ONE

I was on my way to fetch a corpse.

It would mean a late night on a workday, but I needed the money, and the Gallows needed the meat. Besides, Piotr said the job wasn't far from Hauer's, a condemned hospital I'd chased some ghost-hunters out of earlier that night. Barring sleep, I'd have it bagged and ready for delivery with enough time to shower, pick up the frat boys, and make it to the church on time.

Still, I took a cautious route, avoiding the highways and their frequent police patrols. It meant crossing old residential neighborhoods, ragged homes with patchy lawns, tall trees and cracked concrete driveways. I passed the occasional driver, but the crowds of costumed trick-or-treaters had gone to bed hours ago. The city was asleep.

My destination was West-Side Noodles on Samson and Pine Street, smack-dab in the industrial park that dominated the southwest end of the city. Most of the factories processed food; fish sticks, fruit cups, milk products, that kind of thing, so the chill October air smelled a little sour.

The noodle shop was one door down from the street corner. A sun-bleached poster in the window, flanked by a pair of construction paper jack-o'-lanterns, declared it was open all night. The interior had a small dining area with a few occupied tables. A hot meal was hard to find in the dead of night. No one looked my way as I approached the counter.

An older Asian man poked his head out of the kitchen. "What would you like?"

I scanned the menu. "Wantons, and a coffee."

"Who's it for?"

I dug a crumpled five out of my wallet and handed it over. "Robert."

"Be right back," he said.

I watched through the serving hatch as he put a few wontons into the bottom of a styrofoam cup, ladled hot broth over it, and poured me a cup from the world's saddest-looking coffee maker. He'd written *'Robert'* on both in green.

I was half-way through my midnight meal when a solid-looking black guy entered, dressed in a mix of Army fatigues and street clothes. From his bearing and crewcut, I guessed he was fresh from a military tour. He assessed the room with a glance, then crossed to the counter.

"Spicy noodles, for Philip," he said, as if he'd ordered it a hundred times. He looked my way while he waited, noted the name on my cup, and gave the slightest of nods. When his order arrived, he took it and left.

It was a little more professional than what I was used to. My paranoia put up a red flag, but it does that for everything. I finished my soup, returned to my truck, and by the time I got it started Philip had slid into the passenger seat.

"Lincoln Street," he said. "Turn left at the lights and keep going."

My knowledge of the city's gangs wasn't thorough, but I knew about the Lincoln Street Mambas. Not one of the big dogs, but they oversaw protection of the nearby river docks, where firearms came in and out of the city. Lucrative stuff.

Considering my job description, I expected our destination to be somewhere private, like a basement, or the back room in one of the shuttered businesses we passed. Lincoln had seen better days, but not in decades.

"We're here."

He pointed at a squat apartment building, with dark wood siding and brick walls. It wasn't massive, maybe twelve flats, but from the muffled pulse of music and rapid fire lyrics, every room was having a party. A pair of guards watched the front door like it was the best nightclub in the city.

"Second floor, Room Six," Philip explained.

I shifted in my seat to face him. "This job requires *privacy*."

"I know what I'm askin'. But Piotr says you're good. We need it clean, and we need the body gone, *before* the party gets out. We got the gear you need upstairs."

Grinding my teeth, I tried again. "I don't perform for an audience."

He held up a hand. "I hear you, but judge the scene first. If it ain't your noise, I'll find someone else. No strings."

No strings, I thought. *Right. I walk into a building that's wall-to-wall with his gang, and he'll just let me walk if I say 'no'.*

I weighed the pros and cons in my head. "Fine. I'll look."

He led the way to the front of the building. The music from inside shook the door on its hinges. The bouncers weren't just big guys with mean looks. I could see plenty of guns on them, and hints of body armor under their heavy coats.

A little overdone for guard duty, I thought. *In the heart of their own turf?*

But they greeted Philip with casual familiarity and a quick set of gang signs. They didn't get serious until their eyes fell on me. "Who's this?"

"Old friend from the service," Philip said. "You remember me tellin' you 'bout Robert Trimble, right?"

One of the bouncer's faces lit up. "No shit? You're Robbie-T?" He offered his hand in a more traditional handshake.

I tried to keep my tone casual. "In the flesh."

"Damn, Phil told us about that firefight you guys got into overseas. That is some prime Hollywood shit."

I managed a wry grin. "If he says he saved my ass more than I saved his, he's full of it."

Philip laughed. "C'mon, Trimble. I'll introduce you to Josh. Where's he at, Brute?"

The bigger of the two gestured with his boulder-sized head. "Pacing around upstairs, scopin' out the girls."

The music was deafening inside, and party-goers stuffed the building to the ceilings. The Mambas were diverse for a gang; black, Latino, whites, even a few Asians. Probably triad leftovers from the Yakuza's push into Uptown, a few years back. All big, tough hombres with colors and tattoos, and everyone had at least one gun in a proper holster. Blunts, booze and hookers were being passed around, but I didn't see an ounce of cocaine or any other hard drug. As far as gang parties went, it was almost prudish.

Maybe that was the point. Everyone was armed, and it was like they were waiting for something bad to happen. The gangster equivalent of whistling by a graveyard.

My price tag rose with my anxiety, but I didn't turn back. Philip cut a path through gangsters offering respect, and girls that looked happy to see him. Maybe he tipped well. A few gave me colder stares, since I was a stranger, but I kept my face neutral and followed my client.

The second floor was clearer. Through the open doorways, I saw groups of men watching Halloween horror flicks, discussing issues that weren't my business over coffee tables loaded with bongs and booze. Apartment Four looked like it was in the middle of a porn shoot, a quintet of bodies tangled on the living room floor in front of a trio of cameras.

The sixth flat was closed. A skinny guy, barely out of his teens, stood nearby trying to peek at the show next door.

"Josh," Philip barked, and the kid jumped so high you'd think he'd won the shirt in a tournament.

"Fuck, finally," Josh turned his gaze on me. "Who's this?"

"He's your gravedigger, so be cool- the fuck is this?" Philip grabbed a silenced .22 pistol sticking out of Josh's belt. He pocketed the silencer, pulled Josh's waistband up a few inches, and pushed the weapon into the holster against the kid's back.

"You stow your tools proper, 'fore you get your dick shot off," Philip growled under his breath. He stepped past Josh towards Apartment 6.

"Whatever," Josh muttered. I tried to follow Philip, but the kid stepped in front of me. "Watch yourself, white boy. These ain't your streets."

I considered giving him guff, but thought better. In my business, respect and professionalism are everything. That goes double for freelancers, who have nothing but their reputations to speak for them, and no one to watch their backs if they fuck up.

Kids like Josh lived in an environment where they had to prove themselves, so they were always hungry for opportunities. Every stranger and wrong look was a challenge that he was ready to answer.

"What, you deaf? Got nothing to say to me?" He talked like I didn't have one-fifty and a foot on him. Trying to save face after getting scolded in front of me.

"Josh, we ain't got all night," Philip called. "Let's *go*."

The kid held his glare on me for another few seconds, then turned and walked away like I was a nobody. I rolled my eyes and joined Philip. Maybe he had the gang's colors, but he was all swagger.

Apartment Six was empty, and had been for some time. Heavy curtains covered the windows, and stove lights in the kitchen cast a harsh glow over a murder scene. A corpse lay on a pile of blood-stained newspapers, next to a broken chair.

Philip bolted the door behind us, then he and Josh watched me approach the body. It was a black adult male, with his hands bound with plastic zip cuffs. He wore frayed khakis, no shoes or shirt, but he had tattoos of dancing skeletons in top hats, drinking rum and smoking cigars. From the calloused hands and perpetual squint, I guessed that he had spent most of his life working under the sun.

Not a local, I surmised. Someone from a warmer climate. He had plenty of bruises, but a bullet hole in the back of his head had ended him. There was no exit wound. The bullet had bounced around inside his skull.

Mashed potatoes, ala cranium.

"I hope you can do this," Philip said, but he kept his glare on Josh. "We pay the girls downstairs for their time, but not their silence."

I surveyed the rest of the scene, taking in as many details as possible. Blood spatter dotted the kitchen. No way to tell why they'd beaten him. He could have been an innocent store clerk who refused to pay protection, or a sicko caught flashing kids at the local park. My bet was on a rival gang member, but in my line of work, asking questions wasn't professional.

"You got the money?" I asked.

Josh made a face. "Nah, you get your cash when the job's done."

At least he knew that much. "Three grand."

"Grand- three *grand*?" He stammered. "Are you fuckin' playin' me?"

"One male, six feet, two hundred pounds. That's fifteen. Everything else, blood, fingerprints, hair, spit, semen, feces? That's another five."

"That's *two-*"

"And a grand for a rush job in an occupied building."

14

He tensed up, like he was gonna try something stupid. I guessed Josh wasn't used to outsourcing *or* negotiating. But the apartment was full of Mambas, why not get them to do it? Why was I even discussing price with *Josh?* Philip looked like he was in charge, but he said nothing. Perhaps the young gangster was being put through some kind of 'smoke the whole pack' punishment, after he'd lost his temper and shot the guy.

Josh fumed, but he wrangled in that fast-boil anger of his. "Yeah, you better be *thorough*. If this place ain't clean enough to eat off of, it'll be you on the floor next to this Haitian motherfucker. Thought he could sell his Stig on our turf."

"Shut *up*, Josh," Philip said. "No details, you hear me?"

"I ain't telling him nothin'!"

Stig? I'd never heard of it. But drugs had a lot of street names. "Right. Go enjoy the party and keep the door locked."

"Nah. We ain't leaving you alone with this."

I rubbed my face. "You called Piotr, right?"

Josh looked at Philip, who nodded. "Yeah?"

"So he only gets the best. He gets me because I do the job *right*. And I can't do the job with people sweating all over my workplace, get me?"

Josh opened his mouth, but Philip put a hand on his shoulder, and at last I saw the familial resemblance. Brothers, or cousins.

"That's fine," Philip said. "Long as it's done before sunup. Gears' in the bathroom."

"One hour," I told him.

"That's all?" He didn't look convinced, but herded Josh out. Once they had gone, I locked the door. Philip had a key, but I trusted him to keep his distance.

Alone, I gave the corpse a second look-over. Dead and gone, for at least an hour. The last of his soul had bled out, with no trace of a ghost. He may not have wanted to die, but he'd accepted it. I could respect that.

15

I splayed my fingers over its torso and focused on my magic. Welling up from the depths of my soul, it gathered into a cold gray fog that swirled around my fingers. When I'd built enough of a charge, I made a clawing gesture and invaded the corpse with my will.

It convulsed as I assumed control over dead nerves and muscles, forging a connection between dead flesh and living mind. The sensation was a bit like a numb limb regaining its sense of feeling. With stiff, mechanical effort, it sat upright and rose to its feet.

I'd intended to deliver him to the Gallows, but I couldn't risk it. Instead, I willed it to move, and it shuffled into the bathroom. There were chemicals arranged on the sink counter, along with a rubber apron, safety goggles, and breathing mask, all from the local hardware store.

"Cute."

I found it hard to believe the Mambas had never disposed of a body before, because it would take weeks to melt down a body with the chemicals they'd provided.

The corpse sat itself in the bathtub, and I returned to the kitchen, gathered up more of my magic, and watched blood, hair, and incriminating DNA turn into an ash-gray powder so fine it scattered under my breath. If I wanted to, the spell could chew through wood and carpet fiber too. Anything organic and dead was fair game. I'd gotten pretty good at mitigating unintended damage, after I'd desiccated my couch trying to scrub some spilled soup.

With the kitchen cleaner than it had been in years, I returned to the bathroom and drew up enough power to break down a full-sized adult. He would have to go down the drain.

Then I heard something that made my heart do a backflip.

Silence.

When a house full of gangsters and their music goes quiet, you notice. I went to the apartment door and peeked outside. Josh was hovering near the stairs.

"Josh!" I waved him over. "What's goin' on?"

"Cops," he breathed. "How much more time do you need?"

I resisted the urge to get grouchy and did some quick mental planning. "I need a hat."

"A *what?*"

"Don't argue," I said. "A hat. And no colors. Go."

He looked at me like I was crazy, but slipped into another apartment and returned a minute later with a beige bucket hat.

"Thanks." I shut the door before he could ask anything else. The patio doors looked out over a rear parking lot full of cars. The coast was clear.

I stuck the hat on the corpse's head, and tugged it low over the entry wound in his skull. With my necromancy, I tried to approximate an expression of drunken giddiness in his face. The blood washed off in the sink, but I couldn't hide the bruises on his face.

I hopped the balcony railing and dropped to the sidewalk with a grunt. While I shook the ache out of my ankle, I willed the zombie to join me, and grimaced as it flopped into the pavement in a rib-cracking belly flop.

But it could still move, so I willed it to stand and put my arm around it. "Heh. C'mon man. Gotta go. Gotta go, gotta go."

Imitating a pair of drunks, I walked us around the building. A single patrol car was sitting near my truck. A tall black linebacker and a short Latino power-lifter in police uniforms were chatting with Philip at the apartment's front doors. From their tone, they knew each other on friendly terms. The black cop entered the building to a chorus of cheers from inside.

The Latino touched the radio on his shoulder. "Ten-Ninety-Seven, dispatch. Nine-Ten on the noise complaint."

He followed his partner in, and the music resumed its booming rhythm.

I seized the moment and urged the corpse forward. We shuffled across the street towards my truck. I was about to open the passenger door, when someone cleared their throat behind me.

"Hey."

My grip tightened on the corpse, and I turned us around. A light flashed in my eyes, but I could just make out the outline of the Latino cop, like a bicep with legs. Me and the corpse couldn't weigh any more than his morning workout routine.

"You two with the party?" He asked.

"Yeah." I squinted against the glare. "My buddy had a bit too much to drink and took a flop. Time to get him home."

The light turned towards the corpse. I urged it to lift its head and flinch away from the light.

"Ha, urgh, ah," it managed, as I worked its lungs and mouth.

The cop tilted his head, then chuckled. "Oh yeah, he's gone. You're okay to get home?"

"Sure," I said. "Just stopped by to pick him up."

He nodded. "Go on, then."

I grinned and led the corpse to my truck. "Easy does it, buddy."

The cop joined his partner inside while I buckled the body in. Maybe they were on Philip's take, but I doubt things would have been so clean if they had realized I was smuggling a corpse out.

Philip and Josh emerged from the building as I was climbing into the driver's seat.

"Yo Rob, you dropped your wallet," Philip said. He handed me a money clip loaded with bills, a disbelieving smile on his face. "Don't know how you pulled *that* off, and I don't care."

Josh stuck his head close to mine. "Listen. We're tight, alright? But if any word of this gets out? If the motherfuckers on

Bodega find out their boy got iced? We'll know it was you. And that fat Russian won't be able to protect you from us."

"He's Ukrainian." I turned the key and got the engine going.

"Hey. How'd you do it?" Josh asked.

I wiggled my fingers in the air. "Magic."

Philip started laughing as I drove away.

TWO

I headed north for the city's center, and when I hit a red light at a quiet intersection, I reanimated the corpse. It crawled through the back window of the cab, and flopped onto the cargo bed, hidden from sight under the camper shell.

The core of the city was divided by the Bogachiel River from east to west, and the 101 Highway going north to south. The difference between the two halves was night and day. Uptown was northeast, modern, all polished glass and bright, clean streets. Nothing north of the river was older than the Reagan presidency.

Downtown, my destination, was southwest, with older 'goth deco' buildings casting an oppressive shadow over neglected streets. It felt more east coast than west, a gloomy place of sunless alleys, wrought iron, and leering gargoyles.

I turned a corner on Old River Avenue and approached the Oakview Parking Garage. A burly security guard watched me from the toll booth as I came to a stop.

"Fossor," he grunted.

"Kolisnyk."

He hit a button, and the barrier started to rise. "Don't make me come find you."

"Bless your heart."

I entered the garage, descended two levels, and parked near a big box truck. I could hear footsteps clomping around in the back, so I folded my arms and waited.

The back door rolled upward, revealing a heavyset man with thin, greasy black hair and a maroon tracksuit. He hopped from the truck and aimed the biggest assault rifle I'd ever seen my way.

"Fossor," he growled.

"Piotr," I said. "That a S.A.W. or are you happy to see me?"

He broke into a rumbling, deep-throated laugh and leaned the weapon against the truck's bumper. "Friend's nephew's birthday present. Ammo sold separately! You have my finder's fee?"

I took out the roll of bills and tossed it to him. "Five hundred is yours, and I'll take that big TV you've kept in there forever, but I'm keeping the extra grand because that building was full of people you didn't warn me about."

One of his thick eyebrows perked up. "Eh, yes. But you came through! I knew you would." He unrolled the money and flipped through it.

"I've worked with you for a year, and you still count your share."

"You treat money like toilet paper. I am a businessman. Ha!" He stuffed the money in his pocket and climbed into the truck. The interior was wall-to-wall with unmarked boxes, satchels, and other cargo. A black market candy store.

"How's your mom doing?" I asked.

"Good, good. Finally settled in that little place on Baker Street. Now she can see trees, and not just brick walls. Not that she will ever let *me* forget."

He slid a flat cardboard box the size of a tabletop towards me, and we carried it to my truck.

"Eugh! You brought the body here?"

I shrugged. "The building was hot, remember?"

He made a series of disgusted sounds, punctuated with some Ukrainian vulgarities, while we shoved the TV in beside the corpse. "I tell myself I am done with bodies when I come to America."

"I'm used to it."

He wiped his hands. "You're paid to be. Go on, get it out of my sight."

"See you around, Piotr."

He gave me a Polish two-fingered salute as I headed out.

☠

My neighborhood, Sutcliffe Street, used to be a housing block for a military base during World War II. After they moved the base, Sutcliffe endured a few decades of abuse and neglect, before being rezoned as off-campus housing for the nearby college. The semester had started, so cars crowded the street, and there were lights on in most of the homes despite the hour. College students can't sleep. It's a law, I think.

I wasn't a student, or a member of the college staff, but I got the place on a discount. No renter had stayed more than half a semester, so my landlord thought it was haunted. Being a necromancer, I'd have paid extra for it, but the house was empty of spirits. If there were bad vibes in the house, they accepted my presence.

I arrived home a little after 3 AM, and parked in the back driveway, next to a white Keller Funeral Home work van. I opened the back of my truck and cast another animation spell on the corpse, so it could help me carry the TV into the house.

My place was about the size of a pack of gum, but it was mine. A living room and kitchenette covered the south side of the house. The north side had a master bedroom and a small office or child's room. A bathroom and laundry space were sandwiched between them. I had a TV and an L-couch, but no other chairs or tables. A terracotta planter sat near my front door. I'd failed to grow dill in it, and meant to throw it out, someday.

I set the TV down and rolled a throw carpet away from the trapdoor in my kitchen. A cramped, cool basement waited below. The corpse descended the ladder while I stripped down to my waist, put on a pot of coffee, and followed it down.

The basement was lined with plastic sheeting, and the concrete floor had a drainage grate in the center. A modern water heater was installed in the southwest corner, hidden behind a shower curtain I'd erected. A sturdy metal table sat in the center of the room, with a wheeled stand loaded with tools bought from butcher surplus, or lifted from a hospital or two. I'd learned to respect splurging on the right tools. My early attempts at home butchery with improvised means had been messy, to put it mildly.

While I donned a raincoat, gloves, and a plastic face guard, the corpse laid itself on the table and went limp. I grabbed a knife and got to work.

Despite our size, the human body doesn't have much in terms of usable meat, but if you know what you're doing, you can get your money's worth. I opened the torso, draining its organs and fluids into a tub under the table. Next went the extraneous parts, feet, hands, head, genitals… I won't say I wasn't a little envious of what he was packing, but it wasn't like it would do him any good anymore.

After that went the skin, which was always a pain in the ass. It doesn't want to let go, so you have to take it off in strips. Once I'd freed the body of big arteries and other nastiness, I didn't need the delicate tools anymore. I revved the bone saw and used it to remove the limbs at the joints, then sawed each one into portions. When I finished a section, I wrapped it in plastic and deposited it in my freezer upstairs.

The mouths I had to feed could eat everything, bones, skin and all that, but if you had a choice, would any of that stuff be first on your list? Or last?

When I'd finished, I sat on the slab and fed my fast-decay spell to the unused portions. Skin shriveled, bones crumbled, and guts dried into raisin-like cords, before it all turned into powdery ash. While I worked my magic, I read from my favorite book—a handwritten journal from the life of a two hundred-year-old undead wight—and sipped black coffee. A garden hose hooked to my kitchen tap helped wash the substance down the drainpipe afterward.

Sleep gnawed at my mind, but dawn was already shining through my windows. I took a quick shower, downed another cup of coffee, and put on my good suit.

A busy night, but a quiet one. Just the way I liked it.

☠

A crowd of people in somber attire had gathered outside Saint Mary of Bethlehem Church. I parked in the rear, and opened the side door of my work van to free my four co-workers.

"Put on your game faces, guys."

Donnie Edwards was the first to emerge. He was an inch or two shorter than me, but had a similar build and big forearms from squeezing those little workout grip-trainer things.

"It's gonna rain. I can feel it in my bones."

"You're full of shit, Donnie." Frankie Halsey was the shortest, made worse by a constant hunch. Only an outsider would assume he was the group's unpopular tagalong.

"Guys," I piped in. "Best behavior, huh? Respect for the dead."

"Is that a joke?" Max Jensen asked. His long red hair hung over his dark blue eyes. He didn't look very dignified for a funeral usher, but at least Deb had managed to even it out.

Jeb Rainsford stepped out last. He was taller than me by an inch, but skinnier than Donnie. He gave Max a clap on the shoulder. "Relax, Max."

The four wore their old prom tuxedos, but at least they looked respectable. My suit was secondhand from a thrift store.

I knocked on the church door, and Dietrich Keller—my boss, and a man five years my junior—let us inside. Dietrich was a funeral director and mortician, so he wore a tailored suit that matched his pay grade. His dark hair and blue-gray eyes reminded me of a storm cloud.

"You're early," he said.

"Couldn't sleep. Any coffee around?"

He led us through a rear corridor to a banquet hall. The day before, Dietrich and I had hung heavy drapes over the windows, and decorated the tables with small bouquets of flowers and pictures of the deceased taken at various points of her life. Dietrich had prepared a snack table against one wall, with an assortment of unappealing grocery-store pastries. Dietrich was a decent funeral director and a talented mortician, but he was shitty at catering.

"Don't go nuts on the snacks," he said. "You know your jobs?"

"Max and I watch the coffin for the viewing," Donnie said. "At eleven-thirty we'll wheel it out into the church for the service."

"Frankie and I will hold the fort here," Jeb promised. "At noon we grab the hearse and bring it to the front doors."

Dietrich nodded in approval, then left to check on the chapel. I helped myself to a cup of coffee, loaded with cream and sugar. Donnie took his black. Max folded his arms over his stomach, glaring at the food.

I leaned over to Donnie. "Is he getting enough to eat?"

"Who? Max? He's fine, just restless. We all are. We don't get out much, y'know?"

"Mmh."

Donnie sipped his coffee, then squared his shoulders. "Hey, Alex, do you think my boys and I could take a field trip? There's this band planning to-"

"No," I said, loud enough that everyone heard me.

Max cursed. "Told you he wouldn't."

Donnie deflated a little, but leaned closer. "C'mon man, the Gallows is dead. Dead like 'nothing to do,' dead. And the other thing. Look, that's not the point-"

I held out my arms. "You're up here now, aren't you? It cost a ton to get those IDs from Piotr."

"C'mon, this is *prison labor*."

"You wanted to contribute," I said. "That doesn't mean it's a license to run off and party. I'm making a delivery tomorrow. Once everyone's leveled off, we can talk."

Donnie winced. "You said that back in *April*. You can't leave us hanging down there, man."

My turn to wince. "I can't go making my own supply. I just need you to stay cool for a few more weeks. Maybe a month. We're on probation, remember. Deb is still on edge about this scheme you four cooked up. Don't give her a reason to hang us all up by the balls."

He sighed but nodded and kept quiet.

Dietrich returned to the hall. "Alright. We're ready. If anyone asks, the bathrooms are through those doors. No one goes in the kitchen. The viewing room is this way."

Donnie nodded and gave Max a push. Max growled at him, then walked away, brooding. Dietrich and I opened the main doors of the church, and attendees filed in.

Dietrich didn't schedule who viewed the body, so the deceased's immediate family said their goodbyes first, followed by a steady trickle of relations. Afterward, they went into the banquet hall to hug their relatives, sit at tables and talk, or just stare into their coffee.

In my short time working for Keller's, I had seen grief in many forms. Grown men breaking down in tears over their deceased mothers, women rendered numb by the prospect of carrying on without their husbands, children struggling to process the dead thing in the coffin as the family member they knew.

And sometimes I saw the darker side of death. A daughter who spat on her father's coffin. Brothers that came to blows over an old unspoken grudge. A man who confessed to a string of infidelities while his wife died a slow, lonely death from cancer.

But usually I saw sadness, or a kind of painful hope. I saw respect for the dead from people who didn't know how to express it, but tried their best anyway. Death is a thing of inevitability and mystery, and our species can't help but be honest before it. We're afraid, confused, and we need reassurance, but we know it will never come.

So we cling to each other as tightly as we can and hope the pain fades with time. If that doesn't define who we are as human beings, I don't know what does.

☠

The clock told me it was almost eleven-thirty, so I went to fetch Donnie and Max. They stood guard outside the viewing room, ready to move the casket. Donnie looked almost dapper, straight and still like a loyal doorman. Max was his opposite, nervous, hunched, and rubbing his lips.

I didn't know the deceased's name, but I'd helped Dietrich dress her for the casket. A woman of advanced age with curly silver hair, dressed in a sky-blue Sunday church dress and matching shoes. She held a pair of thick spectacles in her folded hands, leaving her face uncovered, as if she'd climbed into the casket to take a nap.

"They're ready," I said. "Release the brakes on the gurney and bring her into the chapel."

Donnie nodded, loosening the brake with the tip of his shoe. "You give any thought to that field trip?" He asked. "You know we don't ask for much. You can chaperone if you think you gotta. We'll pitch in some gas money."

"I'll think about it, but-" The words froze in my throat.

Max was bent over the body, and not in a way that suggested trouble pushing. I cursed through clenched teeth and yanked his head back by his hair. Dead flesh flecked Max's teeth. He let out a gargled hiss and gnashed his teeth at me. I jabbed his forehead with my thumb, giving him a jolt of my magic that made his body stiffen like the corpse it was. He fell flat, like a plank of wood.

"What are you doing?" Donnie gasped.

"Get him up!" I snapped.

The door opened and Dietrich poked his head in. "We're waiting."

I put myself between him and the coffin. "Sorry, Max tripped. Give us a second."

He made a disapproving face but stepped out and closed the door. I inspected the corpse and found a clean bite above the ankle. I closed the coffin's lower half-lid and locked it, leaving only her upper torso exposed.

Donnie got a dazed Max to his feet, and I pushed my van keys into Donnie's hand.

"He wouldn't be this hungry if you were staying near your soil, which means you've been sneaking out. Get him back in his grave!"

I shoved them towards the door. Donnie let out a chorus of hushed curses, but he ushered Max out. If they were smart, they'd be in the Gallows before the service was over.

I gave Dietrich a low whistle, and he came over. "Max sprained something. Gimme a hand?"

He nodded, and we moved the coffin into the chapel.

The church service was quiet, somber, and best of all, uneventful. Before it ended, I slipped out and found Jeb and Frankie waiting near the hearse.

"What happened?" Jeb asked. "What did Max do?"

"He took a bite out of the body!" I snarled under my breath. "Have you guys been going out without telling me? Yes or no?"

They exchanged glances.

"Yes," Frankie said, head bowed.

"Goddamnit you guys. Has this happened anywhere else? Anything else you wanna share?"

"We went to the bar," Jeb said. "No longer than an hour. We-"

"N-nothing happened," Frankie said. "Max just hasn't eaten in a while."

"None of you have," I said. "But you wouldn't be hungry if you stayed in the Gallows!"

My burner phone started ringing. I dug it out and muted it. Piotr knew better than to call me during the day, and I didn't have time to deal with *three* problems.

Jeb put himself between me and Frankie. "We know the risks. But the Gallows is a tomb, Alex. It's no way to live."

I clenched my teeth. "You're *dead*, you're not entitled to it!"

29

His face was a mix of hurt, anger and resignation. I turned away, hands on my hips. The strain of a long sleepless night tugged at me through my caffeine life-preserver.

"They'll be out in a moment," I said. "Get the engine started. We'll do this job, and I'll stop by tomorrow."

Frankie perked up. "You got a delivery?"

I glared. "Just keep your teeth together."

☠

It was almost six when the funeral finished at the East Pine Cemetery. The casket stayed closed, no one saw the bite mark, and neither Jeb nor Frankie gave me any guff.

While the mourners departed, I used a bit of magic to scrawl my magemark on her tombstone. Two quick slashes in an anchor shape. It shimmered pale blue-green before it faded out of sight.

All mages can make their own mark, no matter what type of magic they wield. It's like a signature, but distinct as a fingerprint. Depending on how much magic you put into it, a mark can last a few seconds or forever, as long as they're written on something solid. They'll turn invisible to normal humans after a few seconds, which was handy, because there were a fair number of graves in East Pine alone that glimmered with my mark.

It wouldn't stop someone from doing anything, but if they thought the graves had been 'claimed', maybe they'd leave them alone. I had never met another necromancer in my life. To my knowledge, we're rare, but I knew our reputation. Let the buried rest, I say.

Dietrich found me as I was loading the last of the equipment into the yard truck. "Any word from Max?"

"I sent him home. Sounds like he was hungover."

"We can't have employees hungover for a funeral, Alex. It's hard enough dealing with the hungover mourners."

"I know." I shrugged. "College kids."

Frankie mumbled something, but Jeb shushed him.

Dietrich sighed. "I can cover for Donnie if he took Max home, but Max isn't getting a full paycheck for this. If he wants to keep this job, he's gotta respect it."

"I'll talk with him."

He nodded, the matter settled. "Can I give you guys a ride home?"

Dietrich dropped us off on Dowry Street, close to the Gallows and where Donnie had parked my van. Before he departed, Dietrich leaned out the window. "Don't be too hard on Max. They won't be young forever."

When he had left, I turned to Jeb and Frankie. "I'll be around tomorrow, don't know when."

"Right," Jeb said.

Frankie looked at me, then Jeb, and shrugged. "Sorry, Alex."

I was still plenty angry at Max, and at Donnie, who I suspected was the mastermind behind their escapes. But I didn't feel like lecturing them anymore. "Max aside, you guys did good today. But don't go risking yourselves or Deb's sanity anymore."

Once they were underground, I got in my van and headed home. I was halfway there when I remembered Piotr's call. Food and sleep called to me, but I couldn't leave him hanging forever. I dug out my phone, and saw that he'd tried to reach me another half-dozen times. Piotr had never spammed my phone before. I dialed his number and put the phone to my ear.

"Finally," he said. "Where in hell have you been?"

"Day job. That thing most people have?"

"Nevermind. I have an urgent one." I was about to protest, but he fed me the address. "Did you get that?"

"Yeah, but-"

"Hurry! I have been waiting for hours!"

His panic had me on edge, but I had never said no to Piotr before. So I hurried home, changed into my street clothes, and took the pickup back to Lincoln Street.

THREE

I hadn't gotten a good look the previous night, but Lincoln Street was a neighborhood one could only affectionately call a slum. I passed plenty of run-down homes and apartment complexes, places that looked older and less impressive than Sutcliffe Street. No college had adopted Lincoln. The city had moved on, leaving the locals to eke out a living with bottom-rung jobs in the nearby factories.

I didn't see anyone on the streets that wasn't on full alert. There's a stereotypical idea of what a street gangster looks and acts like; the colors, the swagger, a piece stuffed into a low-hanging waistband... During the party, the Mambas had fit the look.

But as I passed through Lincoln Street, the bravado had vanished. Men moved in groups of two or three, overlapping patrols of backup and cover. They dressed in combat-ready body armor and dark military fatigues. Their firepower was modern American combat rifles, not old Soviet surplus. A few groups had big dogs, who barked at the end of their chains as I drove by. Philip had instilled some military discipline into the Mambas.

It hit me why my cleanup job the night before was so important. The Mambas weren't competing with a rival or dealing with an intruder. They were fighting a war, and it had them spooked. They occupied their own neighborhood like it was contested territory.

The dead guy could have been a spy, or a prisoner of war being squeezed for info. When he didn't talk, Josh had killed him in a fit of rage. Or maybe he was a messenger sent to deliver an ultimatum, and Josh had broken the rule about shooting them. To avoid retaliation, Philip needed the body disposed of without even his own gang learning about it, just in case someone was a snitch.

Getting myself shot had become a real possibility, and I debated turning around. The Mambas did nothing to suggest I was an intruder or threat, just an annoyance. One or two reported my progress over their phones to whoever coordinated them.

Screw it, I thought. *When I find Piotr, he's going to get a piece of my mind.*

The address he'd given me belonged to a quaint little bungalow that stood out like a sore thumb in the otherwise bleak part of town. It was bright yellow, with a healthy green lawn. A man stood guard, obscured in the shadows, holding an AR-19 with practiced discipline.

"Philip," I said, recognizing his broad shoulders and crewcut.

His expression killed any hope I had for friendly conversation. Not a day had passed since I'd met him, but his calm strength was a thin mask over red-eyed grief.

"This way," he said.

He led me up to the front door, and Piotr was inside. Sweat stained the chest and armpits of his tracksuit. "Hurry, hurry!"

The interior of the home was downright pleasant. It was clean, decorated, and smelled like baked bread and hand lotion. An old lady's home, I realized. I'd carved up my share of bodies for Piotr, but I didn't relish the prospect of disappearing someone's *grandma*. I followed him through the living room, and into the basement. The victim lay on his side in front of a TV set, a plate of cookies and a spilled glass of milk at his side.

"Hurry," Piotr said.

"What's the deal, Piotr?"

He wiped his brow. "I don't normally get involved, but he was a client. You know him."

I knelt and rolled the body over to face me. Josh Wilkes' eyes had rolled up into his head.

In death, he didn't look like a wannabe gangster, full of angry bluster. He looked like a kid.

I met Piotr's gaze. "What's going on?"

"His cousin, the man upstairs, found him this way. They want him removed before his grandmother returns from a trip out of town. He also does not want the gang to know anything is wrong."

I ground my teeth. "They're fighting a war, aren't they?"

Piotr muttered something in Ukrainian. "Yes. But there is more." He gestured at the body.

I inspected the kid without touching him. No gunshot, no signs of blood or violence. It was like he'd just dropped dead. I glanced at the cookies and milk. His grandmother wouldn't skip town and leave him a batch of poisoned cookies. Would she?

I mean, I'd seen worse. It was part of the job. But death by cookies didn't add up.

"The arms," Piotr said.

Both arms bore a distinct puncture mark past the wrists. One had a blue substance smeared into it. The other looked swollen and red.

"Drugs?"

"Provided by their enemy," Piotr said. "Something I do not deal in, myself. They call it Stig, er, *Stigmata*, from the delivery method."

"Two chemicals, pumped into either arm?"

"Coming together in the heart. Boom." He made a fist over his heart and spread his fingers. "I am told it is like living death. Oy. Whatever happened to Mary Jane and Magic Mushrooms?"

I shook my head. "Maybe they want to get high on Jesus."

"I am no fool, Alex. I know you have some tricks. The other clients, sometimes they talk, say you have body one moment, gone the next. Cleaned like new. Think you can make him disappear without the men outside knowing?"

I rubbed my face. "It's not that easy, Piotr. I don't make things vanish. I'm just good at covering my tracks."

"Can you get rid of the body? With chemicals? Tools?"

"Not here," I said. My magic could have done it, but the whole situation didn't sit right with me. I'd take any excuse I could to get out of Mamba's territory, body or not.

Piotr cursed in his native tongue and wiped a layer of sweat from his face. "Then we need to get it out of here. The big one has made many not-so-subtle threats on my life if I can't deal with the problem. I won't get far in this business by making enemies of my clients."

"So you made yourself a pawn, and you're pulling me in with it."

"Yes, may my mother forgive me. If they learn this drug poisoned him, there would be a frenzy. This boy's grandmother is important to them. They would burn down half the city to ease her pain, and not care who they hurt."

"Alright," I growled. "Go upstairs, get Philip to tell his people that Josh has to get out of town for a few weeks, I don't care what the excuse is, as long as it doesn't involve me. Then go get my truck and bring it into the alley behind the house."

"Good idea." Piotr went upstairs, spoke to Philip, and they departed out the front door. Their footsteps made audible thumps down the wooden porch steps.

When the coast was clear, I charged my magic and cast it into the body, preparing to reanimate it for the walk into the backyard.

The energy seeped into him, twisted, and recoiled back at me like I had stuck a fork in a power socket. I jumped to my feet with a yelp. Josh's body convulsed, then went still again. My fingers took on a gray, deathly pallor and stung like I'd pinched a nerve, but after a few moments of shaking my hands, the effect proved temporary.

Drugs alone hadn't caused that. My magic had clashed against someone else's. Another *necromancer's*. And they were strong too, if my spell could get feedback like that. Anyone who poured that much juice into a corpse had some kind of long-term investment in mind, because it hadn't faded yet.

A million scenarios played out in my head, including the possibility that they had cursed the body. Grave traps were as old as grave robbing. But I hadn't burst into flames or contracted the plague, so I decided it was just nothing but two power sources meeting and causing a bit of feedback. Yeah. That's all.

But that meant I couldn't animate the corpse. So I knelt, lifted the body over my shoulder, and carried him upstairs. Magic was an easy fix, but I'd spent a few years on a farm, and I worked as a mortician. Lifting a few hundred pounds of dead weight isn't easy. You put on muscle, and you learn the right areas to balance and leverage a body.

The back door was in the kitchen. The yard beyond was spacious, decorated with garden troughs on metal tables to spare grandma's knees. I turned off the kitchen lights and kept an eye out for Piotr.

Headlights rounded the corner, and I heard the crunch of gravel as he parked. I ducked out the door, rushed across the yard, and Piotr opened the gate. I put the body in the truck and slammed the tailgate shut.

"Okay, get out of here," Piotr said. "Make sure that body doesn't turn up in the river!"

"You owe me big this time, Pete."

"Yeah, yeah. Just go!"

I jumped into the driver's seat and drove out of the alley. I wanted to hammer the gas pedal, but I kept a law-abiding speed, and my face neutral. Philip was talking to a few of his men as I passed. He nodded once. His stoic face looked set to crack. The rest of the group watched me, confused that some nobody could get an acknowledgement from their boss. Nothing I could say would appease them, so I drove on.

When Lincoln Street was behind me, my body unclenched, but my mind still raced with uncomfortable possibilities. Whoever the Mambas were fighting had a mage, and he was making their lives a living hell. No wonder they were up in arms.

I was so distracted I didn't notice the flash of lights in my rearview until I passed the West-Side Noodles shop. A police car tailed me, close enough to kiss my bumper. Even as I spotted him, another appeared to block my path.

My foot hit the brakes out of reflex. The part of my brain accustomed to a life of crime screamed for me to escape. To run, put the city behind me, and never look back.

The cops stepped out of their cars with weapons drawn, and shouted orders. I forced my fingers to release the wheel, turned the engine off and tossed the keys out the window. They yanked me from the truck, planted a knee on my spine, and slapped cuffs around my wrist before I could speak.

Kissing asphalt, I asked, "What seems to be the problem, officer?"

They stuffed me into the backseat of a patrol car. When they found Josh's body, an officer radioed it in. Minutes later, more units arrived, along with an ambulance. The EMT's checked Josh for a pulse and then carted him away.

There goes my payday, I thought.

They tore my truck apart looking for more evidence, which they wouldn't find. Score one for me. I told myself to relax, to think of my next step. It wouldn't be easy, since they already had the body. So what would I tell them?

I saw the kid stumbling around, looking sick, I mused. *He asked for help. I got him in my truck and headed for the hospital. I didn't know he was dead 'til the cops pulled me over.*

I'd play dumb as long as I could, and then? A nickel at Seagate, with good behavior.

But the cops had been waiting for me. It hadn't been a random stop, someone tipped off someone. I dismissed Piotr and Philip as potential squealers. Piotr didn't sell people out, and Philip had looked beside himself over losing his cousin. Maybe the Mambas' enemy had caught wind of it.

Must've been the body, I thought. The feedback *had* been a trap, alerting the mage to my presence. He'd tipped off the police, letting me take the fall for murder. It was an efficient way to get rid of me without exposing his or herself.

A thirty-something beat cop climbed into the driver's seat of the squad car. "You're a sick bastard," he grunted.

I kept my mouth shut and stared out the window as he drove.

"Nothing to say?" He asked. "No emotion for killing some kid?"

I was running on coffee, cheap catering, and surrounded by bad juju. Exhaustion was creeping on me, but I could ignore a bully, even one with a badge.

Then he stamped the brakes. I lurched forward and smacked my head into the metal grating that separated us.

"Whoops," he said.

I shook my head and glared at him. He wasn't filming us, or he wouldn't have been so blasé about provoking a suspect.

"Got something to say?" The challenge in his tone was obvious.

I inhaled and charged my magic. Necromancy works better on the dead, but if you give a living brain a gentle jab to its fear center, it can have a noticeable effect without risking permanent damage.

"Shut up and drive." The words turned to fog on my breath.

The cop jumped like I'd screamed it at him. "Wh-what?"

I turned back to my window and said nothing. His hands shook on the wheel, but after a few minutes, he got the car rolling again.

Whoops. I'd meant to give him a shiver, not a shock. Instead of seeing me as a petty thug he could handle, I had become a potential psycho who might chew his throat out.

That would sound great at my trial. *'I don't know how, your honor, but I suddenly believed this man was the devil himself.'*

At least he'd shut up.

FOUR

Our destination was the 8th Precinct on Sunset Row, just south of Downtown. The squat brick building had a fortress-like atmosphere, a bastion of law in a part of the city known for its dangerous neighborhoods and gang turf.

My driver decided I wasn't safe enough to move alone, so he got two of his buddies to come help. They herded me into an interrogation room, cuffed me to the table, and left. I could hear the one I'd stung with my spell muttering to them through the door.

I kept my face blank and surveyed my surroundings. The table and chairs were bolted to the floor. A mirror dominated the wall before me, likely a two-way just like in the movies. A caged lightbulb hung overhead, a little too bright and buzzing to be comfortable under.

Two officers entered, dressed in plainclothes. One of them was young and athletic, an African-American with short black hair and brown eyes. He had a natural charm to him, a million-dollar smile that could disarm a tense situation, or make a woman blush if he aimed in her direction. He wore an honest to goodness tanned leather duster, like a noir gumshoe. It was a little silly, but it didn't appear to faze him.

Behind him came an ice queen. Tall, pale as snow, and built like a mixed martial artist. She wore a gray sharkskin suit that looked too expensive for everyday police work. Her blond hair was pinned taut behind her head. Vivid blue eyes glared at me behind a pair of tinted glasses. Everything about her told me she was in charge, and ready to tear my head off.

Needless to say, it was kind of sexy.

"Mr. Fossor, would you like to make a confession now? It'll make things easier for you." Her voice was frozen honey.

I shrugged and stayed mute. She glanced at her partner and he tagged in.

"Alex Fossor, I'm Detective James Runner, this is Detective Lorensdottr. We have questions, you have answers. I'm not gonna lie, you're on shaky ground. Play this smart, and it means a chance for parole in a few years. Play it dumb, and you get life."

I licked my lips, nodded, and asked, "Can I get a cup of coffee?"

Lorensdottr whirled back to the table, hands on her hips. "Look smartass, you want us to spell it out? We found you with a body in your truck. As soon as we get your prints, we'll have everything we need to charge you. So cough it up."

Funny, she didn't say what she could charge me with. No sign of violence, no probable cause, no motive, no murder weapon. My fingerprints could confirm I touched the body, but a decent lawyer could argue that I had tried to help him get to a hospital.

I played obtuse, to see if they'd let anything else slip. "So, no coffee?"

Detective Lorensdottr—what was that name, Icelandic?— looked like she wanted to explode, and kill me with the shrapnel. But someone knocked at the door, and her wrath turned on the interruption.

Another plainclothes detective, tall, dark, and handsome, stood outside with a manila folder in hand. The moment he saw Lorensdottr the color drained from his face.

"Jefferson! What the hell do you think you're doing?" She stepped out and shut the door, and I heard her snarling through it with the fearless, ball-ripping anger that comes from someone with a collection.

"Smells blood now," I said.

Detective Runner shook his head as he stifled an unprofessional chuckle. "He's Narcotics, we're Homicide. We don't always get along. Look, Alex, right?"

I nodded.

"You don't look stupid. So before my partner comes looking for a second course, we'd like you to cooperate with us. We know you're not working alone. The cops don't walk Lincoln Street often, but we keep eyes and ears on it. A truck matching yours passed through last night. Tonight you come through again, with a body. Maybe not the first."

He sat down and splayed his hands on the table. "The gang that runs Lincoln, they call themselves the Mambas. Bad news boys. We know they're fighting someone, and they're losing. In the past six months, they've retreated from their holdings on the docks all the way to their home turf. They're getting desperate. Maybe desperate enough to shoot people who don't deserve it."

I chewed on my tongue for a second, glanced at the door, and then at him. "Who are they fighting?"

He leaned away. "I'm sure you know."

Damn, he wasn't green enough to take the bait. Still, he had confirmed some of my suspicions.

While I considered my next move, I felt a ripple of energy through me. It started in my gut, a sour feeling that turned into nausea. It wasn't a stomach ache. I was sensing magic. Some-

43

thing powerful. And I *recognized* it. The necromancy I'd felt in Josh Wilkes.

The cops had his body. Could they have brought it to the 8th? Had some hapless cop sprung the curse that had missed me?

I waited to hear a scream, or for an alarm to go off, or for cops to rush in and gun me down, convinced I was the one responsible. Runner watched me the whole time, waiting for a confession, or for his partner to come back.

Lorensdottr was faster. She slammed the door behind her as she entered. "Anything?"

Runner shook his head.

"I don't think we need to waste our time tonight," she said. "A few days in lockup will let him stew on what's coming. He'll be more willing to cooperate, then."

I met her steady gaze with my own.

"Fine. Alex Fossor, you're under arrest for the murder of Joshua Wilkes. You have the right to remain-"

Another, more urgent knock interrupted her.

I knew Lorensdottr wasn't a mage, because when she glared at the door it didn't turn to ice. "Book him," she snapped and opened the door. "What?"

An older man with a curly mustache and a bald pate waited on the other side. He met her furious gaze with steady indifference, and the way she tensed up told me he was her superior. She stepped through and shut the door, gently.

"Alex Fossor," Runner said. "You have the right to remain silent, anything you say can and will be used against you in a court of law, do you understand?"

I sighed and nodded. A few more cops ran by the door, silhouettes behind cloudy glass. Some of them stopped near it, but I couldn't hear what anyone said on the other side.

Runner rattled off my Miranda rights, slow and clear, and made sure I understood. Yeah, the police on-scene had given

44

me the same, but Runner wasn't a bored beat cop going through the motions. He knew his procedures, and he followed them like a cat on a fence.

But before he could finish, Lorensdottr returned. A kaleidoscope of emotions rippled over her face. Her SO watched from the doorway.

"Let him go, James."

Runner blinked. "I- what?"

"Do it."

I was so shocked I almost recoiled when Runner uncuffed me. "What's going on?"

No way I'd gotten bail. No way the mayor had called to give the bad guy his freedom against all sense and justice. I could only offer a dumbfounded look as Runner helped me to my feet.

Lorensdottr's lip curled. "Get him out of here!"

☠

Being released from police custody doesn't mean you get to just leave. They took me to a waiting room, stuck a foul-smelling cup of coffee in my hand, and ignored me for an hour. Then some uniformed cops led me through booking. They photographed me, took copies of my fingerprints, got down all my vitals, where I work, who I work for, my driver's license, my registration, where I live. Everything they could get out of me without a warrant.

They put the fake ID Piotr gave me to the test, and the whole time, none of them would tell me anything. If I spoke, they shushed me, or barked another order.

When it was all said and done, they escorted me out of the building and left me on the curb. My truck, I was told, was in the impound lot. They'd mail me when I could retrieve it.

"Mr. Fossor?" Detective Runner stepped out of the precinct building, waving my wallet. He stuck it in my hand and gave me a look like he wasn't sure if he should congratulate me or punch me out. "You should know that my partner and I will check in on you, so don't make yourself scarce."

"Wait," I said. "What's going on? No one will tell me."

He frowned and glanced back at the precinct. "The body they *allegedly* found in your truck... vanished."

"Vanished?" It took a second to hit me. No body, no evidence, no crime. It was practically my job description.

Runner shook his head. "Nevermind. Go home. We'll be in touch."

When he returned inside, I checked my wallet. Nothing was missing, though I suspected they had made copies. I'd know if they detected the forgery when they came to arrest me. At least I'd left the gravedigging cash at home.

I considered the wave of angry magic that had washed over me in the interrogation room. The necromancer must have re-animated the body and walked it out of the precinct. But why? Maybe they'd made their point, and cut me a break? Whatever the reason, it had won my freedom, but I worried about where they'd taken Josh's body. I was still working for Philip, technically, and if the body reappeared he would be after me. As much as I liked Piotr, I didn't expect him to stick his neck out over it.

I shook my head. It was too much to fathom wandering the inner city streets in the dead of night. I needed to get home, call Piotr, and get some sleep, so I walked north until I found a corner store with a payphone out front. After calling a cab, I leaned against a brick wall and paced the parking lot.

Less than a minute later, a taxicab straight out of the Forties rolled into the lot. It was a big, heavy brick of a car, with rounded edges and circle headlights.

It was *not* the cab I had called for.

An Indian man stepped out of the driver's seat. He was handsome, clean-shaven, and dressed in a red silk *sherwani*, an Indian button-up coat that hung down to his knees. It was like he'd stepped away from a formal party.

"Alex Fossor," he said, with a hint of smug amusement. "I wish we could meet under better circumstances. You're under arrest."

I took a step back. "I'm *what?* Who are you?"

"My name is Agni Chakrabarti," he said. "I serve as Sheriff in this city, and all of North America, for the Rimbault Society."

"The who?"

"The Rimbault Society, Alex. Surely you've heard the name, at least."

I scanned my memories. "The Society. Yeah, the Visatori I used to run with had some choice words about you guys. High and mighty mages with a bug up their asses. Like to flex their magic on the dregs on the bottom. Let everyone know they're the big shots."

His smile didn't falter. "Unflattering, but accurate. And also not the entire story. The Society devotes itself to protecting the Untold—everyday humanity—from exploitation by the Versed. What you call 'mages'."

"The Edicts. Sure, I know about them, too."

"Do you? Could you recite the seventeen for me?"

I frowned. "What is this, a classroom?"

"If that helps. The Society teaches its members the Edicts before they're permitted to begin their apprenticeships. I can't vouch for the Visatori's methods, but surely they instilled some measure of discipline in you?"

I frowned. "They didn't care for the Edicts. A lot of them stamp on Visatori beliefs."

"Perhaps, but that's the nature of progress," Agni said. "The Edicts exist to protect the Untold."

"The way they explained it, it just gave the Society permission to meddle with others. The Visatori lived for centuries without need of some oversight committee."

"If that were true, they wouldn't live like fugitives," Agni said. "Even before our Society existed, the Visatori accrued a rather unkind reputation, one that their Romani cousins suffered the blame for."

"That's the nature of racism," I muttered. "One side deciding the other isn't welcome. They'll invent any excuse to get rid of them. Like the Edicts."

Agni smirked. "I see your intentions are good, even if you've had plenty of indoctrination from their perspective. But you're not with the Visatori anymore, Alex. This is a Society-protected city. You're under our jurisdiction, whether or not you welcome it. So please, the Edicts? All seventeen."

I scoured my memory for the list the Visatori had recited, so they could pick apart all the contradictions between what the Society preached and practiced. "Wisdom, Discipline, Life, Sanctity, Consent, Responsibility, uh, Defense... Temperance, Diligence, Respect, Hospitality... Silence, Industry, Fraternity, um, Truth, Preservation and Self-Reliance."

Agni nodded as I finished. "The Society prefers the more gender-neutral 'Fellowship' over 'Fraternity' these days."

"Whatever. I read your list. Are we done?"

"I'm glad to see the Visatori didn't abandon you completely unprepared. I suppose that explains why you haven't violated those rules until tonight."

"Violated? I've done nothing!"

"That's not what the evidence suggests, Alex."

I took another step away from him. "What evidence? The magic in that body?"

"The *Necrourgy*," Agni said. "Yes."

"I use that magic all the time."

"We're not interested in you animating a few bodies here and there. No matter how abhorrent some of us find it."

"So why?"

He tilted his head, as if disappointed. "Alex, the boy is dead."

"I didn't kill him!" I shouted.

"And yet here you are, and here I am."

Panic rose in my gut. I only knew about the Society second-hand, but the Visatori had never said one good thing about them.

"I'm afraid I'm going to have to ask you to come with me," Agni said.

"Where are we going?"

"Uptown. Get in, please." He opened the rear passenger door for me.

"No way. I'm not going-"

I hadn't finished the sentence before I plopped down in the back seat of the cab, with no memory of getting in. Agni climbed into the driver's seat. Confused, but too scared to sit still, I was halfway out the door when I blinked back into my seat. The door slammed itself shut.

"Try to sit still, Alex." Agni smirked in his rearview mirror. "Running doesn't help your case."

I shouldered open the door, but he blinked me back into my seat.

"Let me go!"

He sighed. "Perhaps some perspective would help."

The cab vanished, and I was falling.

Out of the *sky*.

FIVE

The city spread out far below me. I couldn't think, couldn't reason, couldn't stop or slow my descent. I screamed until my throat hurt, and all I heard was the wind whipping past my ears. The biting cold felt like razors on my skin. I had enough time to reflect on how much I did *not* want to die before the asphalt rushed on me-

And I landed on my ass in Agni's cab, bounced to the floor, and let out a hoarse croak.

My heart danced around in my ribcage. I had never felt so relieved to be alive, and white-knuckled the door handle as I pulled myself into a seat.

Agni met my gaze through the rearview mirror. "I have your attention now?"

With a shiver, I leaned away from him, unable to muster an ounce of defiance. He nodded, satisfied, and continued his leisurely drive through the city's center.

"Who, *what* are you?" I croaked.

"Versed, like you," Agni said. "As Sheriff, my job is to enforce the Edicts in North America, and I've served for, hm, thirty years, give or take."

Thirty years? He didn't look a day older than me. But that info didn't shock me. Mages could live a long time. Most of the Visatori I knew had stopped aging around thirty, and the oldest—Nana Valerie—was around a hundred and twenty. She looked her age, but she'd been sickly most of her life. I knew mages could live longer. Two or three centuries, if they were healthy and smart.

I shuddered. "How old are you, Sheriff?"

"Ninety-seven next month," he said.

"Does that explain the car?"

"Indeed."

Despite its age—including its outdated opinion on seat belts—the taxi's engine rumbled like some kind of dragon lounging on a hoard of treasure. The trip was so smooth I couldn't feel the road under us.

"Isn't this embracing a stereotype?" I asked.

He smiled. "Please, Alex. You know better."

I was silent for a few minutes, but my curiosity peaked again. "How did you do that?"

"Tilemetaforurgy."

"Tile-*what?*"

"Teleportation," he clarified. "I can project objects, including people, from one place to another at my whim. And that wasn't my maximum range."

"I've never seen magic like that before."

He shrugged. "My art is more common than you think. But Necrourgy? *That* is rare, and dangerous. It is Society policy to deny apprenticeships to Versed with such talents. The potential to breach the Edicts, even accidentally, is too high. But I have to admit, for your age, you show appreciable skill."

"Why do you call it 'Necrourgy'?" I asked.

He met my eyes in the mirror. "That's the correct parlance. Necromancy, from *necromantia*, means to learn prophecy from the dead. 'Necrourgy' means to craft, or work, death."

"Doesn't sound as cool as 'necromancy'."

"The Society tries to avoid romanticizing our abilities," Agni said.

"But you call yourselves the *Versed*," I grumbled. "Even though we don't get our magic from *books*."

He smirked. "Touche. Here we are."

The cab parked at the foot of a skyscraper in a large plaza dotted with modern art. I had seen it before, from a distance. It was the tallest in the city, a landmark to navigate by. 'Breckenridge' was written in large brass letters in the plaza's name-sign.

Agni stepped out of the taxi, and I was teleported into step alongside him, with no sensation of leaving my seat.

Uniformed guards waited to permit us entry. The lobby was enormous, and showed off the wealth of the place. The floors and walls were warm, brown marble. Fountains and greenery decorated small waiting and reception areas, and four glass elevator tubes rose into the ceiling high above.

"Sir," the shorter of the two guards said. "Council is already in session. The Archmage says to come right up."

"Very good." Agni walked to the nearest elevator, hit the call button, and waited with his hands clasped behind him. I fidgeted, glanced at the guards, and wondered if they'd tackle or shoot me if I bolted. But with Agni around, they didn't have to worry. One step out of line, and I'd be teleported to whatever part of the building he chose.

Or he'd send me *above* the skyscraper, and let gravity show me the way.

When the elevator arrived, he stepped on board, and I followed a few heartbeats later.

"Fortieth floor, please," he said.

The idea of Agni even using an elevator seemed ridiculous to me, but I suspected he was drawing the moment out just to keep my stress level at a rolling boil. My sweaty hand had a death grip on the arm rail. My legs felt like rubber. I wasn't ready when the doors opened into a wide hallway lined with soft lights and guards.

The men wore unusual robes, black with dark red trim. A red sash hung from one shoulder, bound by a brass brooch shaped like a fist holding three lightning bolts. Along with a modern sidearm and earpiece receiver, their weapon belts sported an ornate dagger with a silver blade, and a shiny black stick I realized was a *wand*. It was a hybrid of archaic and modern style, like a Shaolin monk crossed with a Secret Service agent.

"These are the Keepers," Agni explained. "They are my eyes, ears, and hands. Enforcers of the Edicts."

I had never seen a Keeper before, but I could imagine each being something akin to Agni, a decades-old veteran of hunting wayward mages, more than prepared for anything I tried to throw at them.

"Keepers. The Visatori mentioned them," I said. "Magic cops."

"Crude, but accurate."

A set of tall double doors waited at the end of the hallway. Dim green glyphs danced over their surface. Agni produced a brass key from his coat, the kind that opened locks about two hundred years ago, and touched it to the door. I felt a shift in pressure, a *'whumpf'* that made the doors rattle.

The glyphs vanished, and he motioned for me to enter. "Remain silent until the Archmage addresses you. Uncivilized outbursts will not be tolerated."

The room beyond was a Greek amphitheater the size of a basketball stadium, far too large to occupy the building Agni and I had arrived from. Rows of descending seats circled a stage in the center. Thirteen thrones on raised pillars overlooked the stage.

As my eyes adjusted to the dim lighting, I saw people gathered in the audience. Hundreds of them. There was energy in the air, a kind of distant buzzing sensation in the back of my neck, like standing too close to an electrical power box.

Every single human being in the room was a mage.

Until that moment, I'd never seen more than twenty in a group. To see so many, and feel the power they gave off, was like nothing I'd encountered before.

There was a clear delineation of hierarchy and rank. The youngest were consigned to the nosebleeds, furthest from the stage. They looked indistinguishable from someone you'd see on the street, albeit with more expensive attire. Some wore odd adornments or trinkets, which I assumed were enchanted.

Older mages sat closer to the stage. Like Agni, most remained in their physical prime, but their archaic fashion sense gave them away. They no longer saw a reason to follow contemporary fashion trends, at least among their fellow magi. Cloaks, robes, and tunics were the norm. Their reliquaries were bizarre, ranging from tribal fetishes of bone and fur, to regal scepters of gold and precious gems.

Eleven of the thirteen thrones were occupied by men and women that looked to be in their early seventies, which meant they could have been centuries old. Each owned a staff that floated next to them like a badge office, forged from purest gold, silver, thick plates of iron, or ancient wood, with gemstones the size of fists, or primal runes etched into stone. One staff—belonging to a woman dressed in a yellow slicker and ornate gas mask—was made from *liquid,* a bubbling column of green that stretched and coiled like a sunbathing snake.

A man stood center stage, addressing the elites. He had a disciplined air about him, broad and straight like a soldier. I would have said he was in his late fifties, but who knew with mages? His attire—a light gray suit with a maroon shirt and tie—looked more modern and fashion-conscious than anyone near him. His staff was deceptively simple, iron bound in wood stock, which gave the impression of an old musket rifle.

"This insistence on a vote is not only premature but rash," he said. "The passing of Robert Lacroix has diminished our number to twelve. We have no tie-breaker for a vote."

A man dressed in a Regency-era waistcoat rose from his throne. "Irrelevant. There has been a breach of the Edicts, and the accused has been brought to account. This issue is not so black and white that we cannot proceed with confidence, Archmage."

Several members of the throned circle nodded.

The old soldier—the *Archmage*—turned his gaze my way. "Bring forth the accused."

I blinked and found myself on the stage, in the very center of the room.

Every eye turned on me.

Holy crap.

It wasn't just an arrest, it was my *trial*. Under the scrutiny of all that power, it was a struggle to stay on my feet, and keep my bladder in check. Sweat stained my brow and T-shirt.

The Archmage approached, with a lack of fear most politicians can't muster. I could see he had a trimmed beard and immaculate hair, brownish-red with streaks of silver. His eyes were the color of smoldering wood; dark brown with hints of burning embers within.

"Alex Fossor. You stand accused of murder with intent to reanimate. A breach of the Edict of Life. How do you plead?"

I had to step back to avoid falling. "Innocent!"

Snorts and derisive muttering came from the audience.

"You'll have to do better than that, son," the Archmage said. "The evidence is compelling. Our auguries have confirmed you were in the vicinity last night, and encountered the victim there. Tonight, he is dead. Murdered by Necrourgy. Do you deny you wield this aspect of the Art?"

"N-no, but you can-"

"That same body then vanished from police custody, did it not?" He interrupted. "Sparing you from their persecution. Very convenient."

"I didn't reanimate him. And I didn't kill him! I sensed 'Necrourgy' in his body, stronger than my own! I didn't want to risk the feedback, so I didn't try again."

More derision, more scowls. Half the audience had already made up their minds, come hell or exonerating evidence.

"Necrourgy is one of the foulest expressions of our Art," the Archmage spoke. "It is inherently destructive. Few develop the capacity to wield it, yet you would have us believe you happened upon another? One our augurs cannot detect?"

"It's the truth," I said, fists clenched.

"Then identify them."

"I didn't see them. They left their magic in the corpse."

"A corpse that has disappeared," he said. "Conveniently."

I swallowed back my surprise. They didn't have it?

"You found *me*," I insisted. "Have your charming Sheriff hunt it down."

I heard a few chuckles from the back rows. I wondered if any of them had met Agni under similar circumstances to my own.

The Archmage stroked his beard. "The body is warded from our sight."

"You think I could do that?" I asked. "From all of you? God-damn, before tonight the most powerful mage I knew used her gifts to find missing *car keys*. Her granddaughter could make rocks float. Where could I possibly learn how to shield myself from people like you?"

His eyes bored into mine. I could only guess at what someone of his age and power was thinking. I jumped when he clapped his hands and turned to the audience.

"A breach of the Edict of Life. Evidence beyond our reach. A Necrourge whose circumstances are far too convenient to be coincidence. The sentence is death. What says the Council?"

"Wait-" I said, but my teeth snapped shut, held by an unseen force.

The twelve Councilors—those seated on the thrones, and the Archmage himself—considered me with naked hostility, or pensive dislike. Some turned to their attendants, cliques of personal advisors in the audience behind them, who spoke in hushed tones.

One by one, they dolled out their vote by either conjuring their magemark, or abstaining. Six marks appeared, including the Archmage's, a heart of flame adorned with a crown, which hovered over his staff.

He shook his head. "As I feared. We have brought ourselves to an impasse."

"Unacceptable!" A haggard crone of a woman, with long gray hair and tribal tattoos on her bare, wrinkled arms, rose from her throne. "This mage feeds the dead to an army of wights below the city! His actions put countless lives at risk!"

The blood ran from my face, but I couldn't speak to argue with the woman.

Agni appeared to speak in the Archmage's ear, and the old soldier put on a patronizing smile. "A dozen is hardly an army, Councilor Boudicca. And the Necrourge's methods in dealing with the wights, however unsavory, are not in breach of the Edicts."

The woman let out a disgusted snarl and sat down. The staff at her side—a primitive-looking twist of gnarled wood and leather-bound bones—rattled in anger.

The Archmage held up his hands. "Councilors. Until more compelling evidence comes forward, or we appoint a new Councilor to the thirteenth seat, a vote is clearly meaningless.

I elect to contain the suspect until either of those events occur. All in favor?"

A flurry of magemarks appeared. There was no questioning the result.

"Very good. Sheriff, remove the defendant."

My mouth could work again, and with it came my bluster. "Listen here, you sons of-"

The floor fell out from under me, and I plummeted through the pitch-black darkness.

I screamed, thinking I was in freefall over the city again, but there were no lights or stars. I couldn't see my hand in front of my face. But the air was room temperature, so at least I wasn't *freezing*. I let myself fall, or float, in silence.

After minutes, or hours, of weightlessness, a light appeared below and swallowed me. I slammed into the very stage I'd left. The impact wasn't hard enough to break bones, but I nursed the impending bruise on my noggin as I rolled onto my side.

The amphitheater was empty. I had landed behind the Archmage, the only one still present. He was speaking into a cellphone as I came to my senses.

"-but this isn't up for debate."

"Walter, you can't just sic your dogs on him," I heard a woman say over the speaker. "Let me handle it."

"Sorry, I've made my decision. We'll talk later."

"But-"

He tucked the phone into a pocket and turned to smile at me. "Need a hand, son?"

I didn't move when he offered one.

"Rest easy," he said. "The dog and pony show is over for now. Just you and me. I'm Walter Breckenridge, First Councilor, Archmage of North America, yadda-yadda."

I accepted his hand, and he hauled me to my feet with ease. "You already know me, I noticed."

"You, and about every other Versed on the continent," he explained. "Privacy is for people of no consequence."

"Or enough power to demand it?"

He smirked. "Sometimes. But the Edicts are important, and we need to be fast to catch transgressors."

I frowned. "Not fast enough to catch the real culprit.".

Walter shrugged. "We're not convinced you aren't, remember."

"So, what? I'm 'contained'? Do I sit here waiting for you to kill me, or is Agni going to kick me into his terminal velocity funhouse for a few days?"

His smile broadened. "You've got spirit, son. But mind where you wave it. Some of my fellow Councilors have slain armies in their day. They won't think twice about stepping on you, and they've had plenty of time to learn how *without* breaking the Edicts."

Despite my fear, the part of me that turned acidic in the presence of such self-important authority was boiling over. "Most of my life, you guys never noticed I was crawling around underfoot. You didn't care. Then your Sheriff shows up and suddenly I'm an ant under your magnifying glass. All so you guys on top can remind me I'm at the bottom. Who the hell are you to rub your noses in people's lives?"

"We're *mages*, that's who the hell we are. And you're a mage too, son. One of the Versed. You may not like it, and you're as backward as they come, but it's high time you started acting like one."

"How's that?" I asked. "By confessing to a crime I didn't commit? By dancing to this song you guys keep singing about Edicts and laws? To give you all the illusion of control?"

His grin didn't falter. "Illusion?"

I was on fire. All of me at once. I screamed, my skin blistered, my muscles charred, my fats sizzled. I tore blackened flesh from my cheeks as my eyeballs boiled-

59

Then the pain stopped. I was whole again, unharmed save for a gash below my eye, where I had cut myself with my own fingernails. I could still smell the burned flesh and hair.

Walter loomed over me. "That was no illusion, son. Only the truth. And Necrourges like you—brazen, self-righteous and volatile—rarely last a century before you breach the Edicts. Sometimes gleefully. So tell me, 'necromancer', why *shouldn't* I crush you underfoot?"

My mind reeled for an answer. I combed over my sparse knowledge of the Edicts and found it by accident. "Destruction doesn't serve knowledge!"

He flinched as if I'd slapped him, then broke out laughing. A deep, honest laugh that echoed across the amphitheater.

"The First Edict," he said, as he caught his breath. "Wisdom. We wield the Art in pursuit of knowledge. The only Edict that is, sadly, more philosophical than enforceable." He clapped me on the shoulder. "I think I like you, Fossor. One day you'll trip. I've never heard of a Necrourge who didn't. But not today."

I rubbed at the gash on my face. "So, what now?"

"My opinion on the matter can't take priority, I'm afraid. The Council wanted you contained, so you will be." He made a fist and opened it, revealing a ball of fire the size of an orange. Before I could react, it streaked into my chest.

I jumped back and clawed at the flesh over my heart. I could feel an unfamiliar warmth in my ribcage. "What did you do?"

"If you try to leave the city, you will die," he explained. "And if the Sheriff discovers evidence to convict you, you'll know it, when you drop dead where you stand."

Holy crap.

Walter checked his watch. "That's all the time I have for now, I'm afraid. Sheriff?"

Angi materialized beside me. He grabbed my arm, and I plopped down in his big taxi outside of Breckenridge Plaza. The *Archmage's* tower. Agni got the engine started, and we sped away from Uptown. I put my head between my knees and tried to get my brain around the epic clusterfuck I'd been dragged into.

SIX

It was too much.

The Rimbault Society had come out of nowhere and peeled my life—my entire world—apart on a whim. Every secret I'd kept, they had laid bare. They'd dashed any misconceptions I had of freedom, or privacy. They could snuff out my life with a thought, and justify it as their civic duty.

This must be why mages keep their distance from normal people, I thought. A young mage like myself could twist reality in ways that would horrify people. But if some unprepared normal, an 'Untold', were to encounter the Archmage? They would go mad from the revelation.

"You look pensive," Agni said. "It can be a sobering experience, to understand actual power."

My lip twitched. I had to clench my fists and remind myself that I hadn't stood before some divine entity. "It's disgusting. You're lording over everything and everyone. You're not *gods*."

"Easy, Alex. You would do well to keep your perspective 'ant-sized' for now."

"So I won't know it when you smite me?"

"You *were* ignorant. Now you know how the world works. The Rimbault Society is everywhere. Economies, governments, we're there, doing our best to protect the Untold from magical abuse."

"And making yourselves stupidly rich, while you're at it?"

He smiled. "Money is the least of our resources."

I sighed. "Where are we going?"

"That depends on you. The Archmage has given you a rare opportunity, one few people appreciate. You say you are innocent-"

"I *am*."

"So do you expect someone else to prove it for you? Will you sit at home, feeling sorry for yourself, until the worst comes to pass?" He stared at me through his mirror.

"You think I should... what? Find the necromancer on my own and expose him?" I asked.

"The stakes are high and stacked against you. If you want that to change, do you think it will come from the people who just voted to condemn you?"

I licked my lips but didn't answer. My mind churned over the evening's revelations, but by the time I climbed out of Agni's cab in front of my house, a modicum of a plan had formed.

"Don't dawdle, Alex," he said. "My Keepers and I will search for that body. If we find it, you'll know." He put a fist over his chest and splayed out his fingers. "Boom."

I watched him speed off. He hadn't reached the end of the street when the entire taxi vanished.

When I staggered into the house, the clock on the microwave told me it was four in the morning. My bed was calling to me, but I was too wired to let myself sleep. Instead, I put on a strong pot of coffee and stuffed myself with whatever I had in the fridge. Food and caffeine would have to replace sleep. I jumped in the shower, shivering under the cool water, then pulled on a fresh pair of jeans and a threadbare superhero T-shirt.

63

I think I was pulling my socks on when exhaustion caught up with me. One moment I was getting dressed in the darkness of pre-dawn, and the next I was blinking against the gray morning light. My microwave informed me it was almost *eight*. My untouched coffee had gone cold in the pot.

I pushed to my feet with a growl. No time to make a fresh pot.

"Time to go," I said out loud. "Find the mage, clear your name, get the hex removed, make sure Piotr and Philip aren't out for your blood after losing Josh's body. You gotta… I gotta feed the Gallows. Damnit!"

I'd have to take the work van. Dietrich wouldn't approve, but I was sure he'd understand, once I told him my truck was evidence in a murder investigation. I grabbed some grocery bags from a drawer and swung open the freezer.

There was a knock at the door.

My first thought was that Philip had tracked me down. I shut the freezer and crept to the front. It didn't have a peephole, which was a glaring mistake on my part, so I had to crane my neck against my front window.

Detectives Runner and Lorensdottr were waiting on my porch. Runner still had that ridiculous duster on, but both looked like they'd gotten plenty of sleep. The jerks.

I opened the door. "Officers?"

"Mr. Fossor." Runner flashed me that million-dollar smile. "Good morning."

"Not really. You here to give my truck back?"

Lorensdottr rolled her too-blue eyes behind her tinted glasses.

"No." Runner said for her. "But we wanted to ask you a few more questions. May we come in?"

A little early for a check-in, I thought. They really wanted to peg me for something.

Maybe it's the freezer full of human flesh, my brain offered.

I told it to shut up.

"Sure." I ushered them in and shut the door. "Want some coffee?"

Runner sat on my couch. "Sounds great."

"No thank you," Lorensdottr said. She folded her arms, as if afraid to touch anything.

I set the grocery bags on top of the freezer, then started a new pot with fresh grounds and bottled water from my fridge.

"The man likes his coffee," Runner said.

"Tap tastes like piss," I admitted. I dug a 'World's Greatest Accident' mug out of my cupboard. "You want anything in it?"

"Frothy soy milk and chocolate shavings?" He asked with a smirk.

"Sure. You want a shot of testosterone, too?" I asked. Lorensdottr snorted.

"Two sugars, one cream," he reiterated.

I loaded his mug, then made one for myself with more than double of both. 'Real men drink it black' is bullshit. I drink my coffee however the hell I want, testosterone jokes aside.

"Food of the gods," I said, offering him the mug.

Lorensdottr stepped forward and eyed her partner. "If we're done with the pleasantries?"

He shrugged, and sipped his coffee with a look of surprise on his face.

"You didn't get what you wanted last night? Fire away, detective." I sat on the opposite end of the L-couch from Runner.

"What were you doing that had you up late last night?"

"Out for a drive," I said. "The city is peaceful at night. Meditative."

"You don't strike me as the spiritual type."

"I'm a man of hidden depths."

"Do you often frequent the more unpredictable parts of the city?" She asked, without missing a beat. "The Lincoln Street Mambas don't let just anyone wander their turf."

"Lincoln? I was on Samson and Pine. It's an industrial park."

She pursed her lips. "What were you doing there, then?"

"West-Side Noodles. They're open late."

Her eyes were frosty behind her glasses. "What do you do for a living, Mr. Fossor?"

"They already asked me at the station," I said. "Gave 'em my boss's number and everything."

Her smile was insincere, but still attractive. "Humor me."

"I'm a mortician's assistant at Keller's Funeral Home."

She nodded as if that made sense. "What does that job entail?"

"The Kellers run a family business, not one of the big chains, so I do a bit of everything. Dig plots, move caskets, decorate, cater, prepare pamphlets, anything that funerals involve, I've experienced, even if it's not my job description."

"Like working with corpses?"

"Dietrich Keller is the mortician, but I help him prepare, dress and move bodies, sure."

"Do you have any other co-workers?"

"Dietrich has three brothers, they're all funeral directors with assistants of their own."

I hesitated. "We hired some new gofers, dropout college kids. Don, Jeb, Frank and Max. We were on the job yesterday at Saint Mary of Bethlehem for a burial service."

She nodded. "Mr. Keller hired these men?"

"That's right."

"Do you like being a mortician, Mr. Fossor?"

"It's alright. Death is steady business, to put it grimly."

"Thinking of running a mortuary of your own?" She asked.

"No."

"Why?"

"I'd need four years of anatomical, physiological, and business management study, plus at least a year's apprenticeship to become a fully fledged mortician. I never went to college. And there's a big dropout rate. Dietrich said he almost did. I would have."

An eyebrow perked over her glasses. "Why's that?"

"Undertakers have to bury children," I said. "Prepare their bodies, build a casket to their size..."

She broke eye contact and stared at her shoes.

I drank my coffee. Truthfully, I had never buried a child in my time working for Dietrich, and he said he'd never done it before. For what it was worth, I hoped he never had to. Or anyone else, for what *that* was worth.

Runner broke the silence. "So, you live here alone?"

"Yeah."

"Rent?" Lorensdottr asked. I nodded.

"Pretty nice, for this part of town," Runner said. "My apartment is half this."

"I get it at a discount. The landlord says it's haunted." They both looked at me. I shrugged. "Some people take it seriously."

They laughed. Well, Runner laughed. Lorensdottr strolled into the kitchen and surveyed the space. My heart seized as her eyes lingered on my freezer. The moment drew out like a blade being pulled from my chest, but she moved past it to the fridge instead.

"Do you mind?" She asked. When I shrugged, she opened it. "At least you don't live on takeout."

I let myself exhale. "I like to cook."

She left the kitchen, and the trapdoor creaked under her foot. If she noticed, she didn't so much as flinch.

"Help you find something?" I asked.

She looked into my bedroom. "Just curious."

"Well the TV shows say you need a warrant to search a person's house."

Her face froze over. "I think we've seen enough for now. Those friends of yours, they got numbers we can reach them at?"

"Try Dietrich. You're pretty thorough about this, eh?"

She frowned. "We go where the leads point."

I rose to my feet. "So, I've answered your questions. I think I've been cooperative. What is going on, exactly? Those cops on Samson were waiting to ambush somebody. Why?"

"We're not at liberty to discuss an ongoing investigation," Runner said. He set his empty mug on the table.

"Especially not with a person of interest," Lorensdottr added.

Great. Stonewalled. So much for quid pro quo. "Then I'll call an attorney while you show yourselves out. I'd like to see what he has to say about this whole situation. As far as I can see there is no investigation, just cops bullying random citizens over bullshit charges."

"Now listen here-" Lorensdottr started.

"It was an anonymous tip," Runner interrupted. "Someone contacted Narcotics, told them a shipment of Stig was being moved in a truck matching yours."

"Stig?" I asked, then quickly added, "What's that?"

Lorensdottr grabbed Runner by his coat. "We'll be in touch, Mr. Fossor."

I watched them go from the porch. They entered her car, an unmarked gray mid-size, and sped off. When they were out of sight, I shivered.

That was close. It wasn't the end of my troubles, either. Lorensdottr had it out for me. She'd be back with a warrant and a forensic team, as soon as she could get them.

Which meant I had to get the meat in my freezer to the Gallows *yesterday*. I loaded the grocery bags, jumped into my work van, and left in a hurry with one eye on my rearview.

SEVEN

I parked the van in my usual patch of gravel, in the alley behind Dowry Street.

Dowry was a middle-class neighborhood southeast of Uptown, made up of shoulder-to-shoulder townhouses. It was clean, with trees planted in decorative gaps along the sidewalks. I always thought if I'd won the lottery, I would buy a place on Dowry.

I cast a covert eye, scanning the windows. Don't mind me, folks. Just a gravedigger, dropping off six bags of butchered drug dealer. Putting the macabre thoughts aside, I walked to the back door of the Dowry Street vent station.

The building looked like any other house on the block, but inside it had a system of automated machinery to move fresh air into the subway tunnels below the street. It was the easiest way into the Gallows.

I knocked once, then twice. A second later it opened.

A curvy, forty-something woman emerged, dressed like a homemaker from any sitcom made in the sixties, beehive hairdo and all. Deborah St. Germaine had lived in the Gallows longer than anyone else, one of its original inhabitants. "Alex?"

"Heya Deb," I said, hefting a bag. "Got a delivery. Wanna help me move the TV in?"

"Oh, thank heavens!" She said, putting a hand to her chest. "It was getting to be a bit too much with those boys asking to share Bill's set all the time."

I smirked. "Sorry I haven't been around. Work is slow, you know?"

"Hush," she said. "I know you weren't holding out on us."

"How's Max?"

"He's hanging on, but he's grouchy. I feel terrible for that woman's family."

"Hopefully, this will help." I tried to step past her, but she stopped me in the doorway.

"You promised this would *not* be a problem," she said.

I shrank back a little. Deb wasn't a tall or violent woman, but she was a den mother to the Gallows. She had given her all to looking after its inhabitants, keeping them safe and the rest of the world safe *from* them.

Wights also get stronger as they age, and she'd been undead for more than seventy years. She didn't look it, but Deb could flip over a car if she got it in her head, and it wouldn't even muss up her hair.

"I did," I said. "But let's not talk about it *here*, okay?"

Past its deceptive exterior, the vent station looked like a factory, with lots of warning labels on everything. The machinery was hidden behind sound-proofed walls, and I'd never seen it, but it took up most of the interior space.

We descended well below street level and navigated a dimly-lit maze of concrete corridors. A freight elevator, big enough for ten or more people, waited at the end of our path. We set the TV and bags aside for the slow ride to the very bottom of the city.

"Donnie and his buddies have been sneaking out," I said. "Max is starving. That's why this happened."

Deb sighed. "Norton has suspected for a while, but he hasn't caught them in the act."

"If I'd known, I wouldn't have taken their side when they said they wanted to get jobs."

"I didn't want to accuse them of something we couldn't prove. I only had suspicions."

"And Max getting sick? Hungry?"

"This past year, you've given so much towards improving the Gallows. It doesn't feel like a cage anymore, at least to an old maid like me. But seeing more of the outside world only made their isolation more difficult for them. I mistook Max's mood for restlessness, not hunger. They want to go out, like all boys their age."

"They're not boys. They're old enough to drink, and it's not them I'm worried about."

"I know. Hopefully, some food and the sports channel will help."

The lift stopped in pitch darkness. I pulled open the gate, and Deb turned on an electric lantern hanging from the low ceiling.

The sewers at that level were some of the deepest in the city, abandoned as modern tunnels were constructed above them. The smell was less like damp sewage, and more like an old cave. Sometimes, I swore I could hear a distant tapping behind the mustard-colored brick, though Deb assured me the tunnels had been bricked up decades ago.

The short hallway ended at a solid steel door, with 'Hazardous Materials' painted on it in faded red stencil. Deb knocked, and a middle-aged man with a potbelly opened it from the other side. He had the look of an aging biker, still pretty solid, but his bare arms showed off sagging skin and faded tattoos.

"Alex!" Bill Weber's voice came out as a breathless rasp. "Finally showing your face."

"Bill, how is everyone?" I shook his hand, calloused and yellow from a lifetime of labor and cigarettes.

"Quiet. Come on in," he said. "Is that a TV? Look at the size of that sucker!"

He hefted it out of our arms by himself, and we entered the Gallows proper. It was an old cistern, about the size of a hotel lobby, dotted with pillars that rose to an arching ceiling. Thankfully, it no longer received runoff from the tunnels above.

Metal catwalks lined the walls about five feet off the ground and connected to bricked off tunnels, or storage rooms that had been refurbished as private dwellings. The central drain in the ceiling overflowed with power, TV and internet cables. They hooked into a frantic web of extension cords, splitters and Wi-Fi boosters, granting the Gallows electricity and internet connections siphoned off Dowry's networks.

A bar and dining area made up a corner of the cistern, with a handmade counter, a few scavenged tables, chairs and stools. Two old freezers and a refrigerator hummed behind the counter. Someone—I suspected Donnie, or Miguel—had nailed up a wooden sign that read 'Fossor's Finest Cuts' in bright red letters. Deb had pinned paper pumpkins and witch silhouettes to a corkboard under the sign. Miguel and his sister Ximena had scattered orange and yellow silk marigold petals and painted sugar skulls over the counter.

My arrival had stirred the wights from their rooms. There were a dozen, and I knew them all, at least in a professional sense. Donnie and his frat-boy crew were the youngest inhabitants. Bill, Deb and Henry were its oldest.

"Brought us a snack."

Ichiro Takano was a wiry Japanese man with tattoos up one side of his body, from his knee to his shoulder. He was missing his left pinkie, and the right was only a stub above the knuckle.

He scratched his head and cocked his ear towards the empty air beside him. "No, we'll watch it later. We're hungry now."

"Hi, Alex. A new TV? It's a big one." Roger Pedanski chuckled, but he never took his eyes off the grocery bags. He was a lanky, wild-haired electrician, and it was thanks to his skills that the Gallows had its electrical conveniences.

"Alex, I am sorry for Max's actions." Norton Mwela stood at attention like a soldier. He was the tallest, an African immigrant with cropped dark hair and eyes.

"It's not your fault," I said.

"It is. I promised I would watch over this place. I don't know how they are getting out."

"Just the same, leave them be. I don't want any of you fighting one another. I'll be the bad guy here, okay?"

He sighed but nodded.

"We can't expect them to sit on their hands. They're still adjusting to all of this." Henry Offerson said. Physically, he looked to be the oldest, having 'died' in his late seventies, but he was still decades younger than Deb. There was always a book in his hands, because 'death' had been the retired English professor's chance to read to his heart's content.

"They should respect their responsibilities," Norton argued.

"That's easy for us to say, we didn't die when we were college students," Henry replied.

"Hello Alex," Ximena Celestino whispered, while the two men argued. Her frumpy sweater, dress, and black wig hid the burns that scarred most of her body.

"Hey Xim," I whispered to her. "I like your skulls."

"Thank you." She offered a smile, but it was followed by a wide-eyed shudder. She withdrew to the safety of her shorter brother Miguel, tugging at her wig out of sheer anxiety.

I turned to address the crowd. "Everyone eats today."

Some looked reluctant, others resigned, but they all nodded.

73

"Time again, huh?" Miguel asked. Unlike his sister, he wore bright Hawaiian shirts, cargo shorts and sandals. "This sucks. I don't need to eat. I don't feel hungry. I haven't left my room in weeks."

Ximena tugged on his sleeve, and he held up his hand in surrender.

I turned to Bill. "Hey, go show Donnie and his boys their new TV, then ask Donnie and Max to come meet me."

"Right-o." Bill said. He hesitated, eyes on the grocery bags, then hurried off.

Guess it has been a while, I thought, and loaded the freezer while everyone stood by and made small talk. When I was done, Deb grabbed a portion and hurried to her room. The others followed suit.

No one was greedy. None of them took more than they needed. It didn't come from a spirit of communal sharing. Perhaps what they were doing was evil. Or wrong. Or unnatural. Whatever you want to call it. They knew it. I knew it. Eating human flesh? Does that sound right to you?

But that doesn't mean they enjoyed it, that they *wanted* to, or that it gave them some kind of buzz. It was a balm. It dulled the hunger, but never satisfied it. An insane act to keep them sane.

Ximena approached, with a plastic-wrapped bundle tucked under her arm. "Thank you, Alex."

Before I could reply, she scurried away after her brother. I felt a pang of guilt. Thanks, for bringing her a hunk of human being? So she could eat it and hold off the hunger, so it was more bearable to lurk in their glorified sewer, and exist. Just exist. For as long as she or any of them could.

Being undead was a miserable existence.

Donnie arrived, dragging a sick-looking Max with him. "See? He's here, man. Ta-dah." He grinned at me. "Thanks for the TV. I know we ain't exactly earned it-"

74

"You can thank me by keeping near your phone," I said. "Something happened last night, and now two homicide detectives are hounding me. They want to talk to my co-workers, and that means you. I need you ready if you get a call."

"What do I tell 'em?"

"The truth. I'm your buddy, your brother from another mother."

He smirked. "So lie to them?"

"You know what to do, smartass."

"Okay." He tilted his head. "I'll do it for a field trip."

I rolled my eyes. "Give me a goddamn break. After sneaking out? After the TV?"

"Look, hear me out. Once Max eats, he'll be fine. And it isn't just to have fun. Some of us haven't been up top in a long time. We need things. Clothes, books, toilet paper. The rest are too polite to ask, or they think you'll say no."

"The cops are watching me, I can't be your chaperone. And there's more, the Society has tabs on this place. They know you're here."

"The who?" Donnie asked. "We haven't seen anyone down here."

"Mages. Big league ones, and I don't think they have to be *here* to watch us. But my arrest was thanks to another necromancer who tried to make me take the fall. I've got to deal with him, or shit's gonna hit the fan."

He nodded. "So we scratch each other's backs. One day. That's all I'm asking."

"You're really gonna blackmail me?"

Donnie shrugged.

I rubbed my eyes. "Goddamnit, fine. *One* trip. Tomorrow. Today, you sit by the phone and be the best goddamn friend I ever had for those cops."

He smiled and made a little cross over his heart. "Hope to die."

"You'll want to if this goes south, Donnie. And first things first," I pointed at Max. "He eats."

"Right away," Donnie promised. He hopped the counter, grabbed a slab from the freezer and set it in front of Max. "C'mon man, lunchtime."

Max sneered. "I don't want it."

Donnie's eyes darted from me to Max. "Y'gotta eat. Yeah, it sucks. And your guts hurt 'cause you took a bite from an old lady full of embalming fluid."

Max groaned, and it turned into a growl. "I don't want it! I want to go home. I want to see Maddie. I wanna get out of here, goddamnit!"

I looked at Donnie. "Who?"

"His ex. From before."

"She's not my ex," Max snapped. "You *make* me sit down here. I can't even see her!"

Donnie grabbed his shoulders. "Hey man, stay with me. You can't be spinning your wheels hoping for tread on that action. If she won't return your calls, you gotta move on, man. There are bigger fish in the sea. Even for zomb-"

Max shoved him against the counter. "I'm sick of your shit, Donnie!"

I grabbed Max and gave him another corpse-jolt to the forehead. He bounced off his seat, fell on his butt, and kicked at the ground, letting out a disgruntled cry.

"Eat, Max, 'cause *I'm* sick of *your* crap. If you want to ruin your chance to go topside *with permission*, that's your choice, but I'll bury you up to your neck if you keep this up."

His face stretched in a grimace, clenching his fists until the knuckles creaked. I didn't so much as blink. After a few seconds, he shuddered and relaxed, black tears rolling down his cheeks.

"You make sure he eats that," I said to Donnie. "Every ounce. If he doesn't calm down, he stays with his dirt, field trip or not."

"Every bite," Donnie said. As I walked away, I heard him muttering. "Jesus, Max. I fucking swear if you fuck this up..."

I rode the elevator to the surface alone and fumed all the way home. By then it was mid-afternoon, and I could feel the weight in my steps as I walked up the front step. Maybe there were crosshairs on my head, but I *really* needed eight hours of-

Something clicked behind me. "Hold it, you *bastard*."

Confused and angry, I turned. A woman had a gun aimed at my head, with a look of nervous wrath about her.

"Tell me what you've done with my brother!"

EIGHT

My muscles tensed as the woman waved a gun in my face, but my brain was too tired to panic. It wasn't the scariest thing I'd faced in the previous twelve hours.

My year had been going so well, too. What the hell?

I inhaled. "I don't know who-"

"Don't lie to me!"

Her hands were shaking. If I couldn't talk her down, she was liable to splatter my brains across my front door by accident.

"My name is Alex Fossor," I said. "Why don't you tell me what is going on?"

"I was at your trial. I know you're involved. What did you do with him?"

I looked past the barrel, and did a mental backflip. The woman was *gorgeous*. Shiny gray eyes like silver mirrors. Thick, curly brown hair that hung off her shoulders. A leather jacket and tailored trousers hugged an hourglass figure you'd only see in the movies.

I only got a quick glance, I swear.

Under normal circumstances, I would have remembered seeing her at my trial. But learning the Illuminati was real, run by wizards, and wanted to execute me, was a lot to take in.

Still, that meant she was a Society mage. One of the 'Versed'. Why hold me at gunpoint?

"What's your brother's name?" I asked.

Her brow furrowed. "Jesse."

"Last name?"

"Kendall. But he doesn't use it."

"What's he look like?"

Her frown deepened, but the confusion relaxed her grip on the gun. "He's your height, gray eyes and brown hair like mine. Crooked nose from a fight years back."

"Okay. I don't know anyone by that description, but do you mind if we go inside?"

She flinched. "I'm not interested in what you want. I came to find my brother. Start talking!"

Damn. Even her voice was attractive. I detected a soft London accent, and a lyrical undertone, like every word was on the cusp of a song, despite her agitation.

"I gave you one. Whether it's the answer you want doesn't matter, 'cause it's the truth and I'm too tired to lie right now. I'm gonna open my door. We can talk somewhere warm, eh?"

I entered the house, ignoring her as she tripped over a response, and waited in the kitchen. She took a hesitant step into my home, checking her corners like a cop.

"You look hilarious," I said with a smirk.

She huffed, then relaxed her shoulders and shut the door behind her. "I could have shot you."

"That would fix some of my problems right now. Why don't you have a seat and tell me what's going on? Maybe we can help each other."

She perched on the edge of my couch, holding the gun in her lap. "My name is Jocelyn. I'm trying to find my brother. I-I think he's in trouble."

"What kind of trouble?" I asked.

She gave me a wounded look. "The kind that gets people killed." The word turned into a sob and she buried her face in her gloved hands.

I let her cry for a minute or two. She let it all out in one go, removing her gloves and opening her jacket to reveal a blouse with a plunging neckline. I tried not to watch as she tugged a kerchief from her cleavage—yes, really—and dabbed her face dry.

"I'm sorry," she said. "God, this is embarrassing."

I shrugged. "Crying is good. Relieves stress. A good orgasm would do the same, but I promised my mom I'd get married first."

Jocelyn snorted, grimacing the way women do when they're both amused and mortified by the opposite sex.

"Laughter works, too," I offered. "How about some coffee? Tea?"

"Coffee, please. Strong as you can make it."

With a nod, I took my time grinding the beans and searched for a suitable mug while she composed herself. I didn't have any 'missing sibling' mugs, so I settled for 'How I Like My Men.' I get my stuff at garage sales and thrift stores. Sue me.

I set the cup on the coffee table and slid it within reach, then retreated to the far end of my couch. "Why don't you start from the top?"

Her eyes wavered as she took a sip. "Bloody hell, that's good." She put the gun on her lap and held the mug in both hands.

"Is that piece legal?"

"More than that antique I saw on your fridge," she smirked.

Huh. Good eye on her. "It's an heirloom. I don't like guns."

"Hm. Being a Necrourge, I imagine you don't need a gun to throw some pretty nasty darkness at people."

I shrugged. "Eh, I don't like using it on the living. The last guy I hexed, it went a little overboard. Might have trouble sleeping for a while."

"Who was it?"

"Er, a cop. I think he was trying to goad me into confessing something. So I pulled his fear trigger."

"Oh yeah? Let's hear."

I frowned. "You want me to cast on you?"

"I'm a Fonourge. A voice mage. I know how to protect myself from mental influence."

I smirked. "That Society naming convention is a little odd. Why not 'fonomancer'?"

"Because it's inaccurate," she said.

"Well, I'm sticking with necromancer, because I talk to the dead." I rolled my eyes, breathed out some cold fog and said, "Boo."

It wasn't a potent effort. My heart wasn't in it to terrify her, and I didn't want to make the same mistake I'd made with the cop.

Jocelyn leaned back, eyes wide, and giggled. "That's a tingler! Not bad, but you put a bit too much personal menace in it. You want them scared, but not scared *of* you, know what I mean?"

"No."

She chewed on her lip. "Think of it like a dream. In a dream, you feel a weird emotion and your brain conjures all kinds of scenarios to explain it. Fear, sex, the point is to make the emotion first, and let the target create the cause. Otherwise they know you're the source of their fear."

"I don't think I can do subtle. Necromancy is... predatory."

She pursed her lips in thought. "That explains the shivers. For me, playing with someone's mind is like playing a harp. Nice and gentle. Lemme show you." She licked her lips and flashed her eyelashes. "Is it hot in here?"

The words flowed off her tongue and cupped certain parts of my anatomy. The idea hit me like inspiration, or an epiphany. It *was* hot, and I had nothing to hide. The next thing I knew, I was topless, flexing a little, and pondering the idea of skin-on-skin contact.

The sensation faded a second later, and I felt a little stupid, like I'd poured coffee on my morning cereal in a half-awake daze.

Jocelyn looked on with a grin. "See? You don't know *where* that came from."

"Pavlov's dogs," I said. "But I can't do sexy."

She hooked one leg over the other. "I dunno. A bit pale, but you work out."

I tugged my shirt back on, conscious of the heat in my cheeks. It didn't escape my mind that she had been pointing a gun at me seven minutes ago. But there we were, trading banter like a coffee date.

"I think that's enough wizard flirting for today, Hermione."

Her smile flattened out. "Sorry. I don't meet many Versed casually. My mentor was all business. It's kind of nice to talk shop and not feel I'm being talked down to."

"Yeah." It *was* nice. Most of my life, I'd lived two identities, presenting myself as normal to others and hiding the truth for their sake and my own. It made life kind of lonely.

Jocelyn sipped her coffee. "Please, Alex, tell me what you know. I've been chasing echoes for months. I talked to the Sheriff, but he doesn't believe my brother is here. I *know* he is. I think he's involved in the boy's death."

I sat up. "He's the necromancer?"

She nodded. "Growing up, we only had each other. It wasn't easy, but I, well, my magic helped. At first it was petty stuff, you know? Talk a guy into handing over a few bucks here and there. As I got stronger, I moved on to bigger things. Had a little flock of well-to-do gents, back home."

82

My left eyebrow crooked. "A magic sugarbaby?"

She winced. "I'd like to think I didn't stoop that low. Nothing physical. But if I sang them a lullaby, they'd wake the next morning convinced they've had the best sex of their lives. I was making a few grand off each of them a month, and I never had to take off my shirt."

"So how does Jesse come into this?"

"He's my twin, older by a few minutes. He always wanted to be the one taking care of us, even when I had a good thing going. I think he resented my abilities, or what I did with them, but his only ever gave us trouble. Every Versed we met treated him like he was diseased."

I sighed. "Yeah, I know how that feels."

"When the Society refused him a mentor, he went looking for one outside of their reach. Do you know what a hedge witch is?"

"Yeah. I traveled with a clan for almost five years, but he isn't likely to find a mentor among them, either. Most don't like necromancers any more than the Society does."

Jocelyn nodded. "I haven't heard from him in two years. No letters, no phone calls. Then some contacts said they had seen him in Haiti almost a year ago. The mages there are independent of the Society, ingrained in the Vodou faith, something that skirts the Edicts. But they've been losing influence, I hear some have been making overtures to join the Society. Others broke with the faith and went looking for other ways to gain power."

I saw the connection. "Stig?"

She nodded. "They practice alchemy forbidden by the Edicts, pretty dangerous stuff in the wrong hands."

"I don't imagine it made them very popular with the Vodou community?"

"No. Our contact in Port-au-Prince is a houngan priest named Papa Williams. He and his associates rejected getting into the drug trade. But some of their Versed went rogue. A man named Samuel Kincaid founded a group called the Brothers Midnight, and they're operating in the States."

"Here in the city."

"Yes, and they were seen with someone matching Jesse's description."

"You believe this 'Papa Williams'?"

"I want to say 'no', but when we were teens, we did some unsavory things to survive." She sighed and put her head in her hands. "I thought you were with *them*. You were my first lead in months."

The Brothers Midnight. I had a name for the group fighting the Lincoln Street Mambas. I had no reason to disbelieve Jocelyn's story. She'd admitted a lot, and her concern for her brother seemed genuine. Flirting aside, I didn't see an ulterior motive. Instead, she just looked tired. On the verge of despair. If she could be honest, I could be honest.

"I do some work for a black marketeer, he pays me to clean crime scenes."

Her brow twitched into a frown.

"Yeah. Unsavory things, like you said. But two nights ago, I helped a few members of the Lincoln Street Mambas dispose of a body. One of them said the dead guy was Haitian."

Jocelyn sat up. "Go on."

"Then last night, they called again. The Mambas wanted me to dispose of one of their own. The Haitians—these Brothers Midnight—had overdosed him on Stig. I was smuggling him out of the area when the police got me."

She hugged her arms. "Would the Mambas know where the Brothers Midnight are hiding?"

I shook my head. "If they did, they wouldn't be on the defensive. And if they've found the body I was trying to smuggle, the Mambas will be out for blood."

Like mine, I thought.

Jocelyn nodded. "They'd stretch their lines thin. Between the Brothers and the cops, they'll be exposed."

"They already are. And now the Brothers have that body. They could leave it wherever they wanted."

Jocelyn stood. "Thank you."

"Where are you going?"

"To talk to the Mambas. See if they can point me to the Brothers."

"Whoa, whoa," I jumped to my feet. "You can't do that."

She glared at me. "I don't have a choice. If my brother had a part in murdering an Untold…"

"I know. But if the Brothers have the body, Lincoln Street could already be a warzone."

"I can handle myself. I'm very persuasive."

"It's not that easy. Yeah, you could get a few boys talking, but if they see you coming onto their turf while they're busy fighting a street war? They'll shoot first, ask questions later."

Jocelyn folded her arms under her chest. "Assuming you're right, what do you suggest I do?"

"Let me talk to some people I know. Maybe they can point us to the Brothers without getting shot at."

"What's your stake in this? What are you getting out of it?"

I sighed. "I've already got a bullseye on me thanks to your bro- thanks to the Brothers. I have to point Sheriff Agni at the real culprit, or this hex in my chest goes off."

Her gray eyes darkened. "I'm going to find my brother. I won't hand him over to the Society if it means they'll kill him."

"We don't know he killed Josh."

She chewed on her lip. "I don't know."

"Please. Let me help, like you asked."

She stared at me for a moment, then a business card appeared in her hand with a flick of her wrist. It only had a phone number etched on it in glossy black numbers. "Okay, Alex. Call me the minute you find something."

"Tomorrow afternoon, no later."

"Tomorrow then." She offered an apologetic smile. "Thank you. I'm sorry I drew a gun on you."

"I'm glad you didn't pull the trigger."

The sway of her hips drew my eye as she walked to a spotless, yellow European speedster. It was as fast as it was expensive-looking, departing Sutcliffe with the hum of a high-performance engine.

With her looks and talents, I had a pretty good idea how she could afford it. By day she dressed to the nines, hanging off the arms of billionaires at public events. By night, she whispered sweet magical nothings in their ears, and turned them into melted butter with loose wallets.

And I hacked up *corpses* to pay my bills.

My gut told me she was sincere. She wanted to find Jesse, but that meant going through the Brothers Midnight. They had to have at least one or two power-hitters, if they could shield themselves from the Society. And they were using magic to make drugs. Anyone could cook meth or grow pot, so there had to be more to Stig than just getting customers hooked.

I thought about Josh's body, saturated with necromancy. But for what reason?

Shutting my door, I tucked the card into my pocket, and went to call Piotr. One way or the other, I'd get my answer.

NINE

I grabbed my burner phone off the kitchen counter and dialed Piotr's number. His voicemail answered.

"I'm out of office. Leave a message."

Piotr wasn't the type to ignore calls, and he seemed to live out of his box truck. So either he was lying low, or he was dead.

"It's me," I said. "Call when you can."

I considered a nap, but I didn't want to miss his call, so I cleaned the house, did my laundry, had an early dinner of eggs and salad, and a dozen other chores I'd neglected over the past few days.

It wasn't productive for my problem, but I needed a taste of routine to clear my head. When you feel overwhelmed, it can take the edge off to perform some mundane tasks. It restored that feeling of control over my life I had lost.

I think of myself as a boring person, ominous criminal activities aside. Also the necromancy. But I was a *boring* necromancer. I didn't make my lair in a mausoleum, or shun human contact, or murder people in the night to join my undead army. I didn't cavort with vampires or stitch body parts together to craft Frankenstein's monster.

Yeah, I had my macabre side, a familiarity with death that most people didn't want to imagine. But cleaning up a few crime scenes and feeding corpses to some hard-luck ghouls beat the alternative of becoming an active menace to people. Right? Sure.

I had my feet in three different worlds: civilian, criminal, and mage. It wasn't a life anyone else wanted, but I had found a balance and I was content. Sometimes you don't need to shake foundations or build eternal monuments to yourself. Living a life you're comfortable with is nothing to sneeze at. Even for a mage.

Besides, I would have worked a groove into the floor if I just paced back and forth. I needed Piotr to call me, otherwise I had nothing to offer Jocelyn.

While I pondered my next step, the landline rang. I grabbed it. "Yeah?"

"Hey Alex," Donnie replied. "We talked to those cops. That chick was fine, man. I mean, personality aside-"

"You *met* them?" I interrupted.

"Yeah, they wanted to meet, so we went to that pizza joint on the Riverfront, about three blocks from here? Thirty dollars for a pizza with *chicken* on it, can you believe that crap? 'Gourmet' my ass."

I gritted my teeth. "You took Max *outside?*"

"Relax, he was cool. Weren't you?" I heard an annoyed grunt. "He's leveled off."

"What did you tell them?" I growled.

"Oh you know, we dropped out of college, met you at a bar, you got us a job with the Kellers, told 'em you were a stand-up guy. Never keep us on too short a leash, know what I mean?"

I rubbed my eyes. "Fine, I get it."

"No worries, man. Deb, Bill, Ichiro and a few others are coming with us tomorrow night. We're gonna hit the mall and a steakhouse. Then us guys are gonna see Skullfucker!"

"Skull-*what?*"

"This underground band," he said. "Warehouse concerts, packed to the gills, totally illegal. One time the lead guitarist got head on stage from a groupie. He never missed a chord, man, it was intense."

"I'll bet." Whatever happened to good pyrotechnics?

"How about you? You wanna come? I mean, you don't live in the dumps with us, but you don't get out much, either."

"I've got shit to deal with. Remember, the cops?"

"Your loss, I guess. Anyway, just letting you know, bro. Later!" He hung up.

I stared at my phone, then put it on its cradle.

"This was a bad idea," I told the empty house.

I thought about making more coffee, but dusk had fallen. Almost three days had passed, and I was on six hours of sleep, total. I sat on the couch, one eye glued to my phone, and tried to work out all the details I'd learned so far. The players on the board.

The Brothers Midnight. Jesse. Jocelyn. Josh. Stig. Runner. Lorensdottr, Walter, Agni...

At some point, my mind succumbed to exhaustion. My dreams were a jumbled mess of thoughts and sensations. Detective Loresndottr and those intense blue eyes, Jocelyn and her better-than-Hollywood good looks, Josh Wilkes drowning in a sea of Stig...

A cold full moon one chilly April night.

Fire and howls, screams that turned into digital shrieks-

The sound jolted me from sleep. My burner phone rang for about the tenth time.

I grabbed it. "Yeah?"

Piotr's voice, angry and tired, rumbled over the line. "What happened?"

I glanced at my clock. 7 AM. I didn't know how much sleep I'd gotten, but it hadn't been enough. "How much have you heard?"

"Friend on the force says they arrested you, but let you go. What happened?"

"I have no idea. I was heading home when the cops snared me. I thought they had me, but then the body vanished from the morgue, and they had to release me."

He cursed. "Where is it?"

"Don't know."

Another, longer curse. "This is bad. This is very bad."

"What's the word on the street?" I asked.

Piotr grumbled. "So far? Nothing. I have not spoken to the Mambas yet. But I must tell them something, before they find the body."

"So, tell Philip," I said.

"The big one will gut me!"

"He'll gut you if you don't warn him. It's that or run."

He sighed. "Dammit. Why do you do this to me?"

"Me? You dragged me into this. Those cops were *waiting* for me. They got a tip saying my truck was shipping Stig out of Lincoln. So you tell me, who's fucking who?"

"Inside job?" Piotr asked. "Someone knew!"

"My guess is it's the same group that killed Josh. The gang the Mambas are fighting. Who are they?"

"Hm? Eh, no idea," Piotr said. "New players in the city. No one I have heard of."

"You're lying."

"I am not!"

"Bullshit," I snapped. "An operation like that doesn't walk into his city without you noticing. Tell me you aren't playing both sides in this."

Piotr hesitated. When he spoke, his voice was clear and cold. "You are a man I respect Alex, so I say this only once. *I do not play both sides.*"

"Okay, okay, but you know about these guys. And I need to know, because I'm the one under their scope."

He grunted. "I didn't learn their names. They showed up late last year, sent a man to meet me. Looking for materials for a grow op. But other things; aquariums, chickens, booze, crates and crates of each. I tell them I cannot get all these things. They buy what I have and never return."

"Any idea where they're holed up?"

"Not really..." He mumbled.

"C'mon man. I know you pride yourself on confidentiality, but they're not going after a customer, they're going after me, and by extension, you."

"I don't know where their operation is. But they are the only ones who sell Stig. One of their customers came to me a month ago, looking for a fix. He says, 'they threw me out of Arlington for not paying'. My guess is the Arlington."

"The Arlington? Where's that?" I asked.

"Downtown," Piotr sighed. "Old hotel. It is a drug den now. Police stay away."

"Okay. Thanks."

"You didn't hear it from me. Whatever you intend on doing, leave me out of it. I left home to get away from this. Violence is one thing, but war is hell. Don't start a war, Alex."

"I don't want to start anything, but if they want one, it'll happen. No matter what we say."

He sighed. "Be careful out there."

"You too," I said.

I plugged the burner in to charge, then I dug out Jocelyn's card and dialed her number on my landline.

"Yes?" She asked. I heard something in the background. Toddler noises. "Sorry, hello? Who's this?"

91

"It's Alex."

"Hold on." The baby's voice faded. "What did you find out?"

"Not much, but it's a lead. Think we can meet somewhere?"

A piercing wail interrupted us. "I've got a dental checkup for the little guy this morning. Do you know the Northstar Mall? It's on the northeast side. Twilight and Forty-Second."

"Uh, sure," I said.

"Let's meet there, okay? After lunch, one o'clock?" The crying got louder. "I have to go. See you then."

"Yeah," I said, hanging up.

Northeast. Where all the rich people lived. Color me shocked.

I dug out a pair of clean khakis and a purple polo shirt, so I wouldn't look so poverty-line chic. I put on a dash of body spray, and the nice watch my mom had given me when I'd graduated from high school.

This is what rich people think is casual, right? I thought.

I looked like an extra in a college dorm comedy, the type who wrapped sweaters around their shoulders and mocked the cool, disheveled dorm for being disheveled. Kappa Lambda Lame. Perfect.

Then I got into my oh-so-discreet Funeral Home van and headed north.

☠

The Northstar Mall tried to be a market, a park, and an art exhibit all at the same time. The architecture boasted angled glass and stone-tile walkways, decorated with hanging gardens and open galleries that displayed sculptures and portraits.

In my khakis and polo shirt, I could pass for a janitor. I walked to the food court, where unheard of franchises sold organic yogurt and soy-rich salad and other crap people thought was a step above the usual swill. I refused to spend five bucks on a 'pequena'-sized coffee, from a cafe that specialized in decorative frothing, so I sat at a table and waited.

Ten minutes later I saw Jocelyn, dressed in sensible slacks and a knee-length Autumn jacket. She carried a toddler in her arms, a pudgy little guy with big gray eyes and thin, dark brown hair. He brandished a toothbrush like he was ready to shiv someone. When I waved, she veered towards me.

She'd brought friends, too. Keepers. They'd traded in their monastic uniforms for cargo pants and light jackets, but they still had their sunglasses, earbuds, and humorless glower. Men in Beige. They did a poor job of pretending they weren't creating a perimeter, but they kept a respectable distance from us.

"Hey," Jocelyn said. She set down a sports bag of baby gear that would make a soldier blanch and sat the toddler on her knee. "Thanks for waiting."

"Yours?" I asked.

Jocelyn beamed. "Mine. Say hello, Eddie."

"Hogger!" The kid said, more to his mother than to me, and pointed at the ceiling.

"Eddie?"

"Edwin. After his dad's grandfather," she said with a shrug.

"Hello, Eddie." I offered my hand. A bodyguard took a step towards me, so I withdrew it. "He's well protected."

Jocelyn nodded. "The father's idea."

"I didn't notice a wedding ring yesterday."

Her smile withered. "Yeah. It's an arrangement. Can we talk about my brother?"

"Sure. I talked to some people I trust, who know other people they may or may not trust. They pointed me to a condemned building Downtown. A place called the Arlington."

She frowned. "What does-"

"It's condemned, but not abandoned. Some drug dealers—if you have a lot of customers—find it more economical to set up shop somewhere the police can't find them, or won't risk going near. Let the customers come to you, where you can dope 'em, drain their wallets, let them accumulate a debt so you can make them pay it off. Muling, labor, prostitution..."

"I get it." She wiped the drool from Eddie's face with a napkin. "So what can we expect to find?"

"It's not a grocery store," I said. "They'll have guards inside and out, watching the streets and the doors."

"Okay, then what can *I* expect to find?" She asked.

"That's not- No, *you* can't go in there. Places like that eat good-looking women alive."

"Cute choice of words, chauvinist." She smirked. "I'll be fine. Fonourge, remember?"

I shook my head. "You're serious?"

"I am."

"You'd risk yourself over your brother? Why not get them to do it?" I gestured at the Not-So-Secret Service, who pretended not to watch.

"They're not here for me. They're here for him." She patted Eddie's head. "Anywhere he goes, his bodyguards go."

I frowned. "Who is the kid's father?"

Her silver eyes darkened. "He's on the Council."

Oh. "Oh," I said.

Jocelyn sighed. "Before you ask, no, I don't want to talk about it." She drew Eddie close. Protective, like a mother. Eddie found the disruption to his playtime bothersome and wiggled until she loosened her grip.

"Okay," I said. "Then how about you take Eddie home and I'll go check out the Arlington?"

"How about I take Eddie home, and *we* go check out the Arlington?"

I chewed my lip. "You really want to do this? Will they let you?"

"If they cared enough to stop me, do you think they could?" She smirked and kissed Eddie's forehead, making him giggle. "Yes, momma doesn't think so, momma doesn't think so."

"Well, if we're gonna sneak into a drug den, you'll need a change of clothes," I said.

"Sure." She smirked. "You can lend me some of your factory seconds."

"Eddie likes it, don't you, buddy?"

He looked at me and started crying.

"You've made an enemy for life, kid."

☠

I watched Jocelyn speed off with a black SUV escort and got into my van. She—and Eddie—were VIP's in a very exclusive club. As I headed for home, I mulled over what I knew about babies and weddings in mage culture.

The way the Visatori explained it, mages don't come from any specific part of the world. If you've got it you've got it, and your gender, race, culture and geographical location have no say. It's not genetic, it's not in the blood. It's in the soul.

Some people just have 'bigger' souls, a font of life-force to tap into that allows them to bend reality's rules. Most of the theories about what makes a mage are steeped in myth, everything from being descendants of the ancient nephilim to random spiritual mutations.

Point is, it's difficult to predict when a mage will be born, *unless* they're the child of two mages. Something about all that excess spiritual energy makes it a guarantee.

There were entire bloodlines of mages who hadn't bred with ordinary people for centuries. That included the Visatori, who are all mage-born. Being nomadic made attachments very difficult, and there was a taboo against intermingling with normal people. The clan kept meticulous records on their geneal-

95

ogy, and 'reproductive contracts' were always a topic whenever clans discussed important business. Having kids for them wasn't a matter of personal desire, it was their duty to keep the clan healthy.

Archaic, but it made sense. Hedge clans relied on one another to avoid the likes of the Society and the things out in the wilderness that would love to prey on them. They couldn't afford to raise a non-magical child, or risk an inbreeding mishap that resulted in some less-than-ideal offspring. I had lived with the Visatori for four years, but a contract had never been in the cards for me. I don't know my ancestry on my father's side. It wasn't worth the risk of diluting the gene pool.

And I was a necromancer. Even among hedge witches, I was a pariah.

It seemed the Society had similar views on marriage and childbearing; archaic but practical. Formalizing alliances and bumping people further up the totem pole. Seniority had to be a factor in their hierarchy, since mages grow in power as they age, but like the Visatori, the Society must have kept opportunities open for mages of rare talent.

I suspected Jocelyn's 'arrangement' with Eddie's father fell into that category. A voice-mage would be very handy in a clique of advisors.

And I was about to walk her into a drug den full of gangsters.

Yeah, that'd look good for me.

TEN

Jocelyn beat me back to my place. She sat on the hood of her yellow speeder, spinning her keyring on her finger. "Do you drive everywhere in that sexual-predator POS?"

"No, I usually drive a rusted pickup POS."

I led her inside, and she went into my room. "Kind of cramped, isn't it?"

"Yeah, but it's mine."

"Any roaches?"

I sighed. "This place is clean. I know a spell to break down organic matter. You could eat off the floor here."

"No, thanks." She smirked. "Isn't magic like that dangerous?"

"Only works on dead stuff," I said.

"Ah. How much dead stuff?"

I shrugged. "Don't know. I've never tested it on anything more than a few pounds at once."

She shrugged and went through my dresser drawer. "I'll say this much, you have a consistent look, Alex." She held up a threadbare T-shirt and gave me a suffering look.

"Just for that, you can't take any superhero shirts," I told her.

She gathered an armload of clothing and entered my bathroom. "No peeking, and if I find mushrooms in the bathtub, I'm burning this place to the ground."

I shook my head. Jocelyn said she hadn't been born rich, but you wouldn't know it from the attitude. "We can't take your car, you'll never see it again if you park it Downtown."

"No worries," she said through the door. "I've got a private spot, Uptown. You don't mind a bit of walking from there, do you?"

"Better if we show up after dark."

She stepped into my living room dressed in a pair of my jeans cuffed at the ankles, and a black T-shirt she had tied to show off her midriff. The fabric strained against her assets. The clothes—meant for someone almost twice her size—gave her an impish sexuality.

"Do I look like a junkie?"

"Are you saying I do?" I asked. "You definitely don't have a mom-bod."

She smiled and slipped on one of my spare hoodies. "That's the flirtiest thing you've said to me."

We climbed into her car, and I breathed in the smell of fine leather and her honey-heather perfume. "Feel like I'm staining this car just sitting in it."

She started it up, and heavy metal blasted through her stereo.

"Okay, the music wins you a few cool points."

"Hold on," she said.

The vehicle surged forward, hitting sixty by the time I'd inhaled, and left my house in the distance. Jocelyn worked the car like a stunt racer. We hit the highway and rocketed towards the city center, weaving in and out of early evening traffic.

"You're looking a little green," she said.

"I don't like speed." I hissed as she nearly clipped a sluggish box truck. My mind conjured some very recent memories of falling out of the sky.

She laughed. "I can imagine you hangin' on for dear life in a British compact."

"You'd have to drug me first," I grunted. "I like *car* around me. Lots of *car*."

Jocelyn shrugged, shifted gears, and we slowed from 'suicidal' speeds to a mere 'thrill-seeking'.

I let my hands unclench a bit. "Did your baby-daddy buy you this?"

"No, paid for it myself."

"Ah, the sugar-daddies," I grunted. "That's skirting your Society Edicts, isn't it?"

She rolled her eyes. "It's not like they don't give it up willingly. Edict of Consent, yeah? They have to agree to what I'm telling them, if only subconsciously, or it won't work properly. Their brains fight back. Nature of free will and whatnot."

I grunted an acknowledgement. "Can you make them do something they don't want to?"

"You mean if I didn't care about breaking the Edicts? Sure, with enough juice I could make them obey me. But that can damage the psyche, and it would wear me out fast." She was quiet for a moment, her eyes distant, but she shook whatever thoughts she had aside. "Anyway, I don't have to use it like that. If you're smart and subtle, you can make them think it was their idea. Then they'll go for anything you say."

I frowned. It wasn't fair. Jocelyn had the magic, looks, and skills that made her life infinitely easier than mine. Even if she weren't a mage, it wouldn't be hard for her to make most men—and some women—do what she asked.

A necromancer couldn't dream of having a car like hers, and while I wouldn't trade my rusty pickup or my magic for anything in the world, it still felt like the universe was playing a cruel joke on me.

"You're quiet," she said.

"I'm wondering how we're going to handle getting into a drug den."

"Leave the talking to me, sweetness." She winked.

Yeah, wasn't fair.

☠

Jocelyn parked in a well-lit, high-rise parking garage about six stories up. An armed guard approached, and Jocelyn flashed him a badge he had to scan with a digital tool. He glared at me like I was not part of the system, and thus a problem.

"Go easy, Burt," she said. "He's a friend."

Burt grunted. His eyebrow twitched in a dismissive gesture. *Kiss off*, he told me in American Thug Language.

We rode an elevator to street level, then started hiking towards Downtown. Uptown's nightclubs were alive with light and the steady, muffled heartbeat of techno or dubstep or whatever people liked these days. It followed us until we hit the Center Street Bridge. Then the only sound was the sloshing river some fifty feet below.

"What I wouldn't give for a nice steakhouse on the way," I said. My breath came in a plume from the November chill.

"Getting cold feet?" Jocelyn asked.

"What's to be nervous about? Walking alone with a beautiful woman?"

She smirked. "Hand-in-hand into a crackhouse."

I smiled back and shrugged. "She picked the venue."

My eyes wandered over the water below, to the marinas that lined the south side of the river. Amidst crowds of smaller craft I saw a small cruise ship, or a large 'rich-person boat', sitting in dry dock and bathed in spotlights. A repair job, I guessed. There was no reason to bring a big boat so far upriver, otherwise.

Jocelyn turned and walked backwards to meet my gaze. "Would you date me?"

I was taken aback by that. "That's rhetorical, I'm guessing?"

She shrugged. "A little. Jesse didn't like me hangin' 'round boys. And by the time I knew what romance was all about, I could already make a man strip and beg me to talk dirty to him."

"How old were you?" I asked.

"Seventeen." The shadows around her face deepened. "Never thought much about it after that. Dating. Romance. Even after I met Edwin's father, and especially *after* Eddie. If I had to pick between a date or a nap, I'd choose the nap."

"You must have had a few dates that weren't business?"

"They never went very well. You tell a guy what they want to hear, and he'll do backflips for you. But the moment you want to be honest, to be real…"

To be real, like she was now? I wondered what to say that wouldn't make me sound like an idiot.

"I know a little how that feels," I told her.

She looked up. "Necrourges get treated like criminals, yeah?"

I nodded. "Those hedge witches I ran with, I met a girl there. We got close."

"What happened?"

"The truth," I said. "Her mom had a bad run-in with a necromancer, and it left scars. So I told them I was a fearcrafter, er, a Fovourge? Whatever you Society-types call a fear mage. A long lie. For years."

"But she found out."

"Yeah. Woke up one morning, and they were gone. The entire clan. That was almost a year ago."

"I'm sorry," Jocelyn said. "You'd think, being Versed and living these double lives, she would be more forgiving."

I shook my head. "I used to think so. But if she had stayed, she would wonder what else I lied about for the rest of her life. And I'd be walking on eggshells for the rest of mine."

She flinched. "I guess so."

We walked in silence for a time. The confession had roused my sense of loneliness. But even in arm's reach of Jocelyn, we may as well have been miles apart. I wondered why she had opened up about the skeletons in her closet to me. Was she as lonely as I was? She wasn't exactly single, as far as relationships went.

But I got the impression that the father cared more about Eddie than Jocelyn. Maybe she loved Eddie's father. Or thought she did. Between that, and the sugar-daddies? The hopeful first dates that withered on the vine? I was lonely because I was a creepy bastard. But I could imagine being in Jocelyn's shoes. Being seen as a commodity. A beautiful prize for the shelf. Or something to play with and then discard.

No wonder she was so desperate to find her brother. He was the only person in her world who might still give a damn about her.

You do, too, I thought to myself. *You don't have to embarrass yourself by trying to woo her, but you can at least be her friend. Maybe that's all she really needs?*

Yeah. I could do that. But for the moment, I needed to keep my head in the right place.

"So what's the game plan?"

Jocelyn shook her head. "We go in, split up. Cover more ground."

"Not a great plan."

"Nope. But we need to move quick and quiet. If you see someone who fits my brother's description, follow him until I get there." She patted her pockets. "I hate not having my gun."

102

"If they see a piece, it'll send up red flags," I said. "We'll have to be smart."

We stepped into Downtown, with its old goth-deco architecture and archaic ideas of power, where the slum lords and syndicates ran the streets under the shadow of old money dynasties.

I steeled myself for what I was about to face. I'd have to lie, and hurt people, to get what I needed. I wasn't comfortable using magic on the living, but would I have a choice? Would doing so breach the Edicts? And would the hex kill me where I stood if I did?

The whole idea suddenly felt stupid. I wasn't a cop, and I was barely a mage. Now I was about to toss myself into the meat grinder, and for what? The blind hope of catching the guy who framed me? To find Jocelyn's brother?

"You alright?" She asked.

"Those cold feet are catching up to me," I admitted.

She nodded, but didn't stop. "Look. This'll be dangerous. You don't owe me anything, but if my brother is in there, I'm gonna get him, with or without you. I'd rather have someone watching my back, you know?"

"You barely know me."

"That's true," she said. "And you don't know me. It's your choice. Stay outside if you don't have the balls for it. It isn't your blood on the line, right?"

"I didn't mean it like that."

She snorted. "Yeah, I've heard that before."

Hey, remember friends? My mind scolded. "You wanna start fighting on the doorstep to this place?"

"No. Do you?"

"No."

"Good. Tuck your balls in your purse and let's do this."

☠

103

Once upon a time, the Arlington Hotel had been a fancy establishment. An ancestor to the modern nightclub, full of old-school glamor and class. But in the present day, it was a corpse, dead almost a century. A fire had gutted its top floors. Boarded windows, condemned signs, and graffiti only added to the decayed look. The surrounding neighborhood didn't look any safer. The city had abandoned it. No one cared.

"What do you think?" Jocelyn asked.

"I think if I look too hard, this place will collapse."

She grinned at me. "Balls, purse, tuck."

"Yeah, yeah," I said. "I see two sets of street watchers. Three men outside, at least one inside near the front door. Don't stare. We're supposed to look like customers, not casing the joint."

"How do we get in?"

"The alley. It's out of sight. A fire exit or kitchen entrance. There'll be more guards, and someone to check us at the door. C'mon. Let's get this over with."

She hooked her arm around mine and leaned against me. Through her borrowed clothes, she smelled of heather and honey. The warmth of her arm and the curve of her breast in the crook of my elbow were distracting.

Jocelyn giggled, then gave me a slap on the chest. "Don't be such a sourpuss, babe! You'll love it!"

It took me a second, but I caught on that she was putting on an act. "I dunno. 'D' said he knew the guy to talk to."

"D sells regular shit," Jocelyn said. "This isn't about getting high, it's about religiosity. Like opening the door to the spirit world and shit!"

We turned the corner into the alley. It was dark, but dim lights glowed over a steel door further in. A skinny man in a fancy blue suit stepped into the light. He had dark skin, a shaved head, and eyes hidden behind a pair of round sunglasses.

"What do we have here?" He rubbed his hands, his attention on Jocelyn alone.

Jocelyn untangled from me and put her hands on her hips. "My buddy says you've got some candy to sell."

"That we do. Sorry, gotta check you for a piece." The doorman got so close he was almost in her ribcage. His hands snaked around to her backside, not shy about checking for ripeness.

I fought the sudden urge to slug him and did a slow turn to scan the alley. I spotted the glint of a cigarette nearby. It illuminated the face of a bigger, meaner-looking thug who looked on in silence. I pretended not to see him.

"*Handy.*" Jocelyn didn't flinch as the doorman ran his hands over her curves.

He grinned. "I guess you're clean. What's yer pleasure?"

"Stig," she said. "Heard you got it."

"Mmhmm. Seventy-five each to get biblical. Unless you wanna pay some other way?" His eyes roamed her body.

Jocelyn looked my way. "What do you think, babe?"

I didn't like it, but I dug out my wallet. I wouldn't let Mr. Handy try to settle the bill with Jocelyn.

"You wanna search me, too?" I asked, handing over a handful of twenties.

"Watch your mouth, or you'll be taking a different flight." He knocked on the door. "Enjoy your trip."

"Thanks," Jocelyn drawled.

The door opened, and a third guard waved us into an old kitchen. "Damn, girl. Where have you been all my life?"

She laughed until I closed the door, isolating him from the men outside. In a pleasant voice she said, "Go fuck yourself."

The man's eyes bugged out. "Uh, yeah. There's uh, there's stuff upstairs. Excuse me." He hurried off, out of the kitchen into the hallway beyond.

I chuckled. "Is that breaking the Edicts?"

"It was just a suggestion. He's already in the mood. Sorry you had to lose your cash."

"You can pay me back later," I said. "What now?"

"He said the Stig was upstairs. You check there, I'll scope the main floor."

"Okay, thirty minutes. Then we meet here."

Jocelyn grabbed my hand. "Hey, if things go sour, don't wait on me. Get out of here, as soon as you can. I'll call you."

"I never gave you my number," I said.

She smiled. "This was my idea. I'll feel like shit if you get hurt. Be safe, okay?"

"That's my line."

She gave me a gentle push, then followed the guy she'd sent away.

Here we go, I thought, and headed for the stairs.

ELEVEN

I headed upstairs, unimpeded by any guards. Either security was lax, or they only cared about who got in. After that, the junkies could find whatever corner they wanted and shoot up. My plan was simple; ascend as many floors as I could, then take a quick look on each floor as I descended. If I were a magic drug lord, I wouldn't want to stick to the ground floor. I'd want a view of the city, a place to feel above it all.

I made it as high as the fourth floor before I realized going further wasn't safe. Fire damage and years of exposure to the elements had weakened the structure. I turned back to the third floor, where the gang had reinforced the floors with slabs of scavenged particleboard and plywood. It bent under my weight, but if the floor hadn't given way before then, I told myself I would be fine, probably.

Hotel rooms lined the hallway, their doors destroyed or pulled off their hinges and used to reinforce the floor. I thought the Brothers would hold court there, but I saw no guards or pushers. Each room had a filthy mattress or mat, where people could seek escape in a syringe.

A few haggard junkies occupied the beds, sprawled out and lost in their high. Most looked like they hadn't bathed in months. Instead, they had traded every penny they earned or stole to feed the monster that was addiction. They were so weathered by life on the streets that I couldn't tell what their ages were.

Curious, I stood by one door and watched a man with a wrinkled pug face prepare to shoot up, so intent on his task that he didn't notice me. On the mattress in front of him were two plastic capsules I realized were syrettes, like the army used for battlefield first aid. A dose of chemicals in a plastic bag, with a syringe on the end. Inject, pinch, and done.

The two capsules had different colors, one blue, the other red. He steadied his hands long enough to inject them both into either wrist. It didn't take long. He gasped, his back arched, and he relaxed onto the mattress with a wheeze. After a moment his rapid breath became steady, and he smiled. Tears stained his craggy face.

I had no idea what a magical narcotic could do. An illusion of a happy life? A visit to the Layered, or the Far Lands? Or Stig could just be an ultra-powerful hallucinogen, a madhouse of dreamlike visions that was a welcome escape from the harshness of the actual world.

I continued my search. When I reached the end of the hallway, I had nothing but junkies or empty rooms to show for it. Disappointed, and more than a little frustrated, I started back.

How much time left, I wondered. Twenty-five minutes? Twenty?

I descended to the second floor. It was in better shape, but the air smelled damp and moldy. The hotel rooms here were closed, and I could hear music and muffled voices within. From the sound and smell, I could tell some junkies had traded themselves for their fix.

Anger bubbled in me. However they got themselves hooked, the Brothers had exploited it. They fed on desperation and pain, offering nothing but a toxic placebo in exchange. The dead rotted cleaner than the poor dregs in the Arlington.

A door at the end of the hallway opened, and two big men in expensive clothes lumbered into view. More thugs, like Mr. Handy and his boys downstairs.

I didn't have time to hide. Thinking fast, I shuffled my step, rubbed my wrists, and leaned against the wall. "Hey, hey," I croaked, trying to sound half-awake. "Hey man, where's it? Where's it at?"

One thug made a disgusted sound and pushed me out of the way. I let myself hit the wall. "Outta the way, shithead."

"Just wanna find some more," I slurred.

The other thug grunted. "You want more, you can either sit n' wait for Bettany to get 'round to you, or you go join the prayer circle at the end of the hall."

Prayer circle? That sounded ominous and helpful.

"Hey, thanks, man," I said, drawing the words out.

"Whatever." They kept going and didn't look back.

I lurched my way towards the door they'd come from, then dropped the junkie act when they vanished downstairs. I hoped they didn't run into Jocelyn.

At the end of the hall I heard low, rhythmic, guttural chanting. Hand drums joined them. I twisted the doorknob and spied a private banquet hall or conference room through the narrow crack. There were no tables or chairs, but a squat stage stood at the far end. About two dozen men and women sat cross-legged on the floor in front of it, with simple hide drums on their laps. They swayed and chanted in a constant, disharmonious rhythm.

A contingent of men, stripped to the waist, surrounded the drummers. Their faces were pointed downward and their lips quivered in mumbled prayer. Like the Haitian I'd dismembered days ago, they had sun-weathered faces and an assortment of tattoos depicting dancing, leering skeletons.

The Brothers Midnight, I thought.

Three of their number stood on the stage. The first, tall and dark-skinned, had to be the one Jocelyn called Samuel Kincaid. His face was painted white like a skull, and his intense eyes watched his flock like an angry god demanding worship. He held a gnarled cane in one hand, and a chicken in the other. The poor creature flailed in a hopeless struggle for freedom.

To his right was an old woman, by centuries if she were a mage. She wore a sarong made from sackcloth and carried a basket of white and purple flowers like it was a newborn baby.

Dread knotted in my stomach as I spied the third. Scorpions and skeletal snakes tattooed his tanned skin, but the resemblance to his sister was clear. Jesse Kendall. He had the same good looks as Jocelyn, but he scowled at everyone around him with naked contempt. His eyes were an ashen gray, almost white. An automatic sat in a leather holster on his belt, next to a coiled whip.

Samuel spoke in Haitian over the drums. Jesse dug into the pouch-like pockets of his cargo pants and produced a lighter and flask. He and Kincaid doused the chicken with the flask's contents. The old woman spoke in a creaky, dry voice.

The drums dropped to almost nothing. The worshipers watched with rapt attention. Her voice rose to a cackling pitch, and Jesse ignited the chicken. The room filled with a hellish, fiery glow.

The audience went into a frenzy of chants and drums. The animal shrieked and thrashed in Kincaid's grip. He held the bird aloft, shouted a series of curses, and hurled it into the crowd. The worshipers scurried out of the way as the poor animal thrashed for a few tortured moments.

They held their arms—their wrists—towards the stage. Some spoke in English, their voices full of desperate tears. "Let us walk with you! Let us walk with you!"

Jesse uncoiled his whip. If a worshiper drew too close, he lashed out at them. Skin split and blood flowed, but addiction and misguided fanaticism drove them forward. I could feel the magic being drawn from the ritual, and it made me queasy. It wasn't Vodou. Even an uneducated white boy like me could tell you that. It was cruelty and mockery. A deception, to convince the worshipers what they saw was something spiritual.

Over the centuries, I knew mages had invented or usurped existing religions, depicting themselves as gods. The goal was to harness spiritual energy. Faith. The trust humans show in others. It was spiritual parasitism. That so many fake gods turned their worshipers to blood rituals and sacrifice to harness said power proved as much. It breached the Society's Edict of Sanctity, and the Visatori said it was one of the 'big five' crimes, along with murder and dominating the mind.

The old woman tossed flowers to the crowd and revealed the syrettes of Stig in her basket. The audience turned to her, arms raised, like starving children begging for food. She seemed to call on each to offer an oath, and they gave it. I couldn't tell if they were honest in their conviction, or paying lip-service to get their fix. It didn't matter. The old woman took their word with a nod and offered a gift of Stig, which the worshipers injected into scabby wrists.

Kincaid watched over his 'flock', seeking some sign among them. He pointed at one, and two of the Haitians hauled the target to his feet. Jesse produced a glass bottle wrapped in a leather cord, decorated with coins and slips of paper.

I felt the hot sting of Jesse's necromancy filling the room. My magic felt comfortable to me, the cool dampness of a fresh grave. Jesse's was vile, like a vulture that feasts on an animal before it has succumbed to the desert heat, or the sting of a scorpion. It was the same magic I'd felt in Josh Wilkes' body.

The junkie let out a wheeze, and Jesse held the bottle to his lips. Not to drink. I felt an uncoiling, the release of some crucial component to life, and a luminescent mist poured from his throat into the bottle, which Jesse corked shut. The junkie's face went slack. Kincaid gestured, and the entranced worshiper fell into line behind him.

Not death, I realized. But something so close as to seem that way.

Jesse produced a beeping phone from his bottomless pocket. He tapped Kincaid's shoulder, and they filed the worshipers out through an exit behind the stage. Even riding their high, the junkies rose and followed like puppets.

My gut nagged me to get back to Jocelyn and get out of there, Jesse or not. But I couldn't leave yet. Their magic had a purpose. It wouldn't hurt to learn a little more about it.

I entered the room and knelt over the dead chicken. The poor thing had not died fast. Jesse's magic lingered all around me. The malice, the desire to inflict pain, convinced me that the brother Jocelyn was seeking was not the man she would find.

They were making Zombies. The old Haitian version, not the cannibal corpses of modern movies. A human being, entranced and robbed of his will, to serve whoever had stolen it. Held in a state of near-death, mindless and obedient.

That's what Stig was. Some kind of modern, narcotic take on traditional zombie powders. Turning addicts into slaves.

That meant Josh wasn't dead. Just being controlled.

Okay, you've learned all you can! Now get out! My brain shouted.

I turned to leave and ran right into a Haitian. Without a word, he grabbed hold of my neck, slammed me into the floor, and closed his fists around my throat.

I tried to claw my fingers under his, but it was like peeling wood. I kicked, kneed him in the crotch, slapped his face, and punched at his nose until the cartilage crunched. He didn't so much as flinch.

112

Not a priest. Another zombie. For whatever reason, the Brothers had converted one of their own.

I could feel the pressure in my lungs as they struggled to inflate. My limbs were heavy, and spots appeared in my fading vision. I only had one option. Dangerous for him, sure, but also for me.

But when I'd touched Jesse's power in Josh, it had caught me off guard. He was strong, but it was raw force with no finesse. If I was smart, I could push that force aside, target the flaws, and free him from it.

Or I fail, and he kills me, I thought. Or I succeeded too well, killing him, and guaranteeing my execution from Walter's hex.

I closed my eyes and focused on my magic. Fear and pain screamed for my attention, but they couldn't save me. I rose above my animal reflexes, held onto the discipline that made me a mage, and planted my thumb on his forehead. Then I shoved my magic into his brain like a tack.

The sizzle of feedback hit me, the strain of my power against Jesse's. Pain lanced through my arm, but I saw patterns in the energies at work. The drugs and magic bombarded the zombie with mental noise, an overdose of chaos. His mind was a hurricane, and the only safe place for his sanity was in the storm's eye, far from consciousness. I could feel the storm's course, and guided my power into it, like a boat crashing through waves.

Each tiny push gave me confidence. Jesse's necromancy relied too much on raw power, on simple force. It could weather the worst and keep coming, but it had a weak spot, an Achilles' heel, a cluster of metaphysical nerves further down the spell's body. I struck that point with my will, as hard as I could.

Basically, I kicked the spell square in the balls.

As the magic recoiled, I filled the void where the zombie's consciousness hid. The moment I made a connection, I could feel his awareness reach out. He was a mage, like me. His power surged in recognition of my intent. We turned it against the storm together and raced back towards the surface.

I landed back in the real world with a jolt. The Haitian released me and stumbled onto his back. My neck felt like a limp sponge, and my heart hammered in my ears as I sucked air into my lungs. I sounded like an angry sea lion.

Each ragged breath was a balm, but I couldn't remain on the floor if more zombies were about, and forced myself onto wobbly feet. The Haitian shivered on the floor, his clothes soaked with sweat. Who knew how long he'd been under their control?

"Hey." I waved my arms. "Hey! You speak English?"

He stared at his own hands, mumbled under his breath in his native tongue, and made a gesture to the ceiling that I guessed was some kind of prayer. Not like the mockery I had witnessed in the Brothers, something sincere. Something remorseful.

I snapped my fingers, and he met my gaze with bloodshot eyes. I braced myself for a renewed attack, but instead he wrapped me in a too-familiar hug and wept.

"English?" I asked.

"Bad. Bad."

"That's okay," I said. "I only speak Bad English, too."

He shook his head. "Bad. Sick."

"Drugs," I said. He looked at me, so I pointed at my wrist, making an injection gesture. His face paled, and he shoved himself away from me. "Yeah, no more drugs, I know."

I had a million questions to ask him, but no time or way to communicate. I gestured for him to stand. "Leave. Go."

"Home?"

"Home, yes!" I nodded, and my neck bones popped. "Home. Go home."

He looked relieved, but then doubled over in pain. He groaned, and his face smoothed over into an expressionless mask before he grabbed at me. I slapped his face, and the shock startled him back to reality. He clenched his head and sobbed.

The Stig in his system was like a battery. I'd bought him a moment of freedom, but he wouldn't be able to resist for long.

"Kill," he said, and gestured at himself. "Kill, kill me."

"I can't." I shook my head to convey the message. I didn't want to admit that I needed him, an eyewitness who could clear my name for me.

Then I smelled smoke.

I had missed it back when I couldn't breathe. Now it was strong enough to permeate my survival instincts. Smoke. Fire.

Oh hell, I thought. The Brothers had set the Arlington on *fire*.

The Haitian sobbed and clutched his temples. He was losing the fight for his own body. He spoke in his native tongue, but I could only make out a single word of it.

"Baron?" I asked. My mind flickered with recognition from a lifetime of pop culture, the only source I had for Haitian Vodou. "Samedi?"

Hope lit his face. "Please. Please." He grabbed one of the discarded flowers off the floor and pushed it into my hand.

"What are these?" I asked.

"Go. Go home." He produced a handful of the syrettes from his pockets, all blue. I thought he was going to hand them to me, but he jabbed them into his neck instead. His body tensed, and I could see the pain in his eyes, but he smiled with relief.

"No, no!" I yanked the syrettes away and got my arms around him, trying to lift him. "Come on! We gotta get you out of here. Hospital, yeah? Hospital!"

He smiled and pushed me back. Tears still ran down his face, but he didn't seem in pain anymore. He spoke a farewell in Haitian.

A sound drew my attention. Distant, but clear through the thin walls of the crackhouse. Police sirens. I offered the man a frustrated farewell gesture. He nodded and closed his eyes. He had been a mage, a member of the Brothers. So why had they done that to him?

The sirens closed in. No more time for answers. I retreated downstairs, and each step made my neck ache. I shouted warnings to the junkies, but every room was empty. Like the worshipers, they'd filed out to their master's command.

The kitchen was on fire as I entered, and spreading quickly. "Jocelyn?"

No one answered. I held a sleeve to my mouth as I pushed through black smoke and kicked open the exit door. Police cars blockaded the alley. I let out a yelp and leapt back inside, before the spotlights could zero in on me. Gunfire, honest gunfire, zipped over my head and smacked against the ceiling.

"Hold your fire!" Someone snarled through a bullhorn. "This is the police! Throw your weapons and step out with your hands over your head!"

Not likely, I thought. If I got arrested, they'd only find my ashes by morning.

"Alex!" Jocelyn appeared beside me and pulled me away from the back door. "Where the hell have you been?'

"Upstairs," I said. "Where have you been?"

"Trying to get info out of that guard. But he just got up and ran out of the building. Then this fire started. What happened to you?"

"I'll tell you later. Right now we've got a lot of cops outside, and this place is about to become a fireball."

"This way," she said. We ran to the front of the hotel, into a lobby that was repurposed as a squatter's camp, full of garbage and broken furniture. The front entrance was boarded up, and I could see police lights on the other side.

"Dead end," I said. "What now? Maybe there's a sewer exit? A maintenance-"

Jocelyn threw arms around my neck, and we fell into sudden darkness.

TWELVE

The teleportation was a shock, but after a moment of weight-lessness, we appeared in a small gray room. I kept my knees steady and took a breath.

"I'll never get used to that. How did you-?"

Jocelyn showed me a bracelet she hadn't been wearing earlier. "A gift from Eddie's father, made by the Sheriff. For emergency use."

"Hey, smart. Nothing like a quick-" The words died in my throat. A wave of lethargy cut my legs out from under me, and I hit the floor.

I heard Jocelyn curse and run out of the room, calling for help.

This is it, I thought. *You took more damage than you thought, and you're tapping out.*

But aside from being motionless, I remained conscious and alert. I rolled my eyes and took some controlled breaths, felt the cool tile under me, and the discomfort of my position on the floor.

I could see my arm beside me, and black-blue tendrils, like smoke, leaked from my skin into the floor. It was the weirdest damn thing I had ever seen, like worms being pulled from my flesh. My mind recoiled in disgust, but I couldn't compel myself to move.

Footsteps approached. Someone grabbed my ankles and dragged me through an open doorway.

"Easy with him," Jocelyn said, out of my line of sight.

I left the threshold of whatever field had drained me. The darkness stopped oozing out of my body, and my limbs responded. "I'm okay," I said with a groan. "I'm alright, now."

A Society Keeper hefted me to my feet and dumped me in a high-backed chair.

Jocelyn put her face in front of mine. "Alex, can you hear me?"

My head wobbled in a limp nod. "Ow."

"Easy." She touched my neck. "Who did this to you?"

"A zombie," I said. "Any water around here?"

"Zombie?" She looked behind me. "Go get him a glass."

I turned to see her Keeper bodyguard exit the room. No doubt he would report me to Sheriff Agni. Great.

I tried to catch my breath, making sure all my digits still worked, and rubbed my arm where I'd seen my strength being leached out. It didn't feel like anything was missing.

We were in a small study. Shelves filled with leather-bound books lined the walls. Some were ancient, the leather cracked and brittle, others looked fresh and oiled. I sat next to a polished table in the center of the room.

A portrait hung over a small fireplace. It depicted a clean-shaven young man with hazel-brown hair and eyes, dressed in a blue officer's coat. He looked familiar, but I couldn't place who it was.

Jocelyn closed the safe room behind a sliding shelf. Maybe 'safe' was the wrong word for it. I saw a bare white cot next to a metal desk and chair. No other furnishings, no stores of food or water, no bug-out bag for an escape or even a phone. It looked more like a patient's room in a psychiatric hospital. Or a prison cell. The door snapped shut with a metallic click and sealed the paralyzing magic in.

"That felt weird," I grunted. "Wrong."

Jocelyn gave me an apologetic smile. "It's- yeah. The bracelet is for escapes. The room is for anyone who tags along uninvited."

"Catch them inside and lock them in?"

"That's the idea."

"Smart."

The Keeper returned with a tall glass of water. It hurt, and the water was lukewarm, but I drank it. She nodded to him, and he closed the door as he left.

"Where are we? Your place?"

"No. Yes. It's Eddie's father's home."

"Think he'll mind us being here?"

She smiled. "Focus, Alex. We barely got out of there with our lives, and criminal records, intact."

"Speak for yourself. Okay, you first. What did you get out of Spanky?"

"Who? How hard did you hit your head?"

"The guy you told to go self-fornicate."

"Oh. Nothing. He babbled for a few minutes, then ran off. Wasn't even finished his 'task'. Craziest thing I ever saw."

"Explains how the building cleared out," I said.

"Why?"

"I saw a congregation of junkies, and a ritual. The Stig was affecting them, making them obedient. Some were getting turned into zombies. Maybe a lot of them. That's how they got everyone out before starting the fire."

"Who was in charge?" Jocelyn asked.

"A scary-looking guy, my guess is he's Samuel Kincaid. There was an old woman with him, passing out Stig like communion wafers." I sighed. "And I saw your brother."

"You saw him? When? Why didn't you tell me? What happened?"

"Jocelyn, he wasn't there for the show. He was part of it. He got a call on his phone and the group bugged out. When I followed, a zombie jumped me. I broke him out of his trance, but I could get much out of him. He chose death rather than lose control again."

"Damnit," Jocelyn snapped. "Damnit!"

"I'm sorry, Joce."

"We have to go back. Find out where he went-"

"That place will be an inferno by now, and swarming with cops."

"Damnit!" She hugged her arms. Tears welled up in her eyes.

"Joce, I know he means a lot to you. But this isn't a question about bringing him home anymore. The things I saw him doing in there-"

She jabbed a finger into my chest. "You *don't* know that. You said they were zombies. He might not have a choice! He could be under their control, too!"

"Zombies don't answer phones and they don't..." I hesitated to tell her about what I'd seen in Jesse, the cruelty in his eyes.

"I'll call you a cab," Jocelyn said. "It will take you home."

I grabbed her arm before she could dart out of reach. "Joce, wait. He's breaking the Edicts. You know what will happen when he's caught."

She yanked her hand away. "You, you only care because your neck is on the line!"

"And he put it there!"

We glared at each other for a moment, then she swept open the door. The Keeper was waiting on the other side. "Make sure Mr. Fossor leaves."

"Jocelyn!"

The Keeper blocked me at the door and touched his earbud. "Have a cab come to the front." He waved for me to move. "This way."

No 'sir' for me, but I was too weary to be petulant. The mansion's interior was a labyrinth. We never passed a single window, and the hallways were erratic and decentralized. With all the closed doors and no landmarks to go by, I didn't know what part of the house I was in, until he shoved me through a door that descended into a garage. A fleet of vehicles—some dating back to the 1930s—sat in pristine condition.

"Touch them and lose a hand," the Keeper warned.

I scowled at him. I'd take my rusted-out shitheap over that collection of expensive *useless* any day. The garage door opened ahead of us, and we stepped onto the front driveway. Tall trees and stone fences topped with razor wire surrounded the yard. There were cameras everywhere. Security was definitely the owner's priority.

A cab rumbled up the driveway, a bulky yellow number that I recognized. Agni gave me a smug smile from the driver's seat. "Hop in, Alex."

I hesitated. "If you try teleporting me anywhere, I'm going to puke in your cab."

☠

Agni drove south. The splendor and wealth of the neighborhoods, gated and secure against the vulgar, unwashed commoners like myself, dwindled away until he exited onto the highway.

"You've had a long day, Alex. What brought you to this part of town?"

"Wasn't my choice. Jocelyn had that bracelet of yours."

"Yes. The question is, why did she need to use it?"

"We were at the Arlington. A drug den Downtown."

"Curious place for a date."

I flinched. "It wasn't a- we were trying to find her brother."

"Hm. Jesse Kendall. Did you?"

I glanced out the window towards Downtown. I thought I could see traces of hazy smoke in the night air.

I told Agni everything. I didn't like him, or the situation, but keeping secrets and acting petty wouldn't save my bacon.

"They're using drugs and magic to make zombies," I concluded. "Violating that one Edict. Sanctity. And a bunch of others. Who knows how many they've changed? How many are hooked?"

"And where did they go?"

"They bolted. Summoned all their junkies away and burned the place down. I bet they called the cops to pin us there."

"Did Jocelyn witness this ritual?"

"No."

"So you have no evidence or witnesses to corroborate your story? This doesn't inspire confidence, Alex."

"It's what happened. What reason do I have to lie?"

A sudden sharp pain formed in my chest. Walter Breckenridge's hex glowed through the fabric of my shirt.

"That's a pretty compelling reason, isn't it?" Agni asked, after the pain had faded.

"You want evidence?" I dug into my pocket and produced the flower the Haitian had given me. "How's this?"

"A flower?"

"The man who gave it to me thought it was important, before he died."

"And what do you intend to do with this flower? Present it to the Council and say 'case closed'?"

The jerk had a point. "I don't know. I need to talk to someone. Someone familiar with Vodou, or the potions they use to make zombies."

"The mages of Haiti keep many secrets from the Society. Possibly because their traditions violate the Edicts."

When we arrived on Sutcliffe Street, Agni parked in front of my house. "What's your next step, Alex?"

I shrugged and got out of the car. "Hit the internet. Look for some answers."

He shook his head. "Are you familiar with the Westbank Art Gallery?"

"No."

"Take a visit tomorrow morning. Ask the receptionist about Vodou. You may find better answers there than on the internet."

His ancient taxi roared off and disappeared.

Westbank? Ask the receptionist? I didn't know what game Agni was playing, but it almost sounded helpful.

My answering machine was beeping when I got through the door.

"Alex, it's Dietrich. I just had an interview with two detectives who wanted to know about you. They wouldn't tell me much, but they don't have to, do they? I want to talk to you the moment you hear this, I don't care what the hour is, understand?"

I deleted it and stripped out of my street clothes. I caught a hint of Jocelyn's perfume on my jacket. Heather and honey. It was hard to get her off my mind. She had been the most helpful person involved in my dilemma so far, she needed *my* help, and she was beautiful.

But our motives didn't sync. I didn't care about rescuing her brother. His actions convinced me he was trouble. When the Society came calling, and I had to give them Jesse, would she back me up? Or would she run with him and leave me to burn, only for him to turn on her later? I thought about how tight she held onto Eddie. Her family, twisted as it was, meant more to her than anything.

I shook my head. All I had was a flower and a few ideas about what the Brothers Midnight wanted. Vodou and zombies. I'd see where that took me and get evidence on my own.

I downed some Aspirin from my bathroom cupboard and sat at my computer to do some research. You'd think you can't research magical lore online. That's not true. Basic information is prevalent across the web, often shared by ordinary people with an interest in the occult and supernatural. They could never, in a thousand years, guess that they were toes-deep in the real deal. That's the beauty of being a mage, you know it when you see it. Most ordinary people don't, so they pass over it like it's fantastical nonsense.

Still, that doesn't mean all information is easy to find. Mages covet their secrets, and even those born before electricity recognized the power the internet represented. So they did what they always do with forbidden knowledge, they destroyed it or hid it.

So what I found was mostly bullshit. Hollywood, and racism, had done a number on both topics, presenting Vodou as a savage faith practiced by 'primitive' African immigrants and evil wizards. As for zombies, well. Everyone knows how modern perspectives on zombies turned out.

I had even less luck with the flower. 'White and purple' was a description that applied to a lot of different plants, and after a few hours of browsing, I pushed away from the PC in frustration. My eyes ached, and I was torn between brewing a fresh pot of coffee, or trying to get some sleep.

Maybe a few hours will help, I thought. For all I knew, I could have been staring at the answer the whole time and not realized.

I jumped as my burner phone rang.

"Alex, I heard about the Arlington." Piotr's voice was icy. "You told me you did not want war. This looks like war. I wipe my hands of it. Don't call me again until I call you."

He hung up before I could utter a response. "Sorry, Pete."

Agni's tip started to sound more appealing, so I looked up the address for the Westbank Art Gallery. The clock read past midnight, so I crawled into bed, hoping to visit the Gallery first thing in the morning.

☠

The squeal of tires on asphalt outside woke me up. Frantic voices approached my home, and fists pounded on my front door. It felt like my head had just hit the pillow, but the clock by my bed said it was two in the morning.

What now? I thought. Jocelyn, Jesse, the Mambas? An army of zombies, come to finish me?

I lurched to the door and swung it open. Donnie was on the other side. He was pale and shaking.

"Alex!" He cried. "Y'gotta help! Help her!"

Max hovered outside. Blood stained his face and shirt. He babbled to himself, eyes vacant. Frankie and Jeb pushed by him, and carried a body into my home. It was a girl, in her late teens or early twenties. She gurgled through a tear in her neck that pumped blood onto my floor with every dying heartbeat.

THIRTEEN

I never expected to discover the Gallows. When the Visatori had abandoned me, they'd destroyed my sense of belonging, of family. Rudderless and numb, I'd ventured into the city, somewhere I knew the Visatori wouldn't go, and tried to make sense of the empty world I found myself in.

I was riding the subway when I felt the tinge of undeath. Norton Mwela was on one of his rare trips to gather 'food', medical waste from a local hospital. He tried to evade me, but I blundered into the Gallows, struck by suicidal curiosity.

As Deb had explained it, the sanctuary's founder, one Artemis Lindquist, had gathered them together over the decades, and taught them as best he could on how to survive, before he vanished. They had survived, but they lived in darkness and squalor like rats. It was heartbreaking, and I felt compelled to help them, to show them some compassion, some dignity, so they didn't have to feel like monsters. Because they weren't.

And I thought I'd be part of something again.

I got a job, found a place. Every penny I could spare, I invested in the Gallows. Beds, electricity, the internet. Weeks turned into months, and then a year. It became a home, not a miserable hole to hide in. To see them take joy and pride in that was a balm for the soul.

But as proud as I was, I couldn't help but feel responsible for them. That meant being the authority. I set limits. Hounded them to be sure they ate and kept underground. Because the hunger was always there, and one moment of weakness would break the cardinal rule of the Gallows. Lindquist had carved the words into the brickwork of their refuge. A daily affirmation.

We do not eat the living.

☠

A year of being the caretaker of the Gallows flashed through my mind as I watched Jeb and Frankie put the bleeding girl on my bed. They shouted, pleaded for me to act. To have some sort of answer.

"No." Panic shattered my last ounce of calm. "No, no, no!"

I yanked them off the girl. The wound had opened her jugular and windpipe. That she was still alive seemed impossible.

"The kit in my bathroom!" I snarled at them.

It doesn't matter. It can't save her.

I told that part of my mind to shut the fuck up.

Jeb ransacked the bathroom to find the First-Aid kit under the sink, and I swept my nightstand clean to spill the contents out and rummage through it.

Don't kid yourself, you're no EMT.

I had dismembered bodies. I'd never had to fix them.

You can't fix her.

Jeb and I pressed the wound with some cotton, and then one of my own discarded shirts. Tried to get pressure on the wound so it would stop bleeding. The tall, studious wight looked beside himself with grief. Donnie and Frankie stood behind us, arguing over what to do.

128

"What the hell happened?" I asked, loud enough to silence everyone.

Frankie grimaced. "We were at a concert, they were talking-"

"Who?"

"Max," Jeb said. "She's his girlfriend, Maddie. They were talking, then arguing-"

"He bit her?" I sounded hysterical, despite how calm I felt inside. It was like I wasn't in my body, but away from it, apart from the chaos. "Call Nine-One-One!"

Donnie blinked at me from the doorway. "But-"

"You should have taken her to a hospital, you fucking moron!" I snarled. He retreated, his footfalls thumped down the front steps. "Get out! All of you!"

They retreated to my yard to pace and curse at each other. I didn't care if the cops showed up. Everything had gone south in the worst way possible.

There's no way to help her.

The bitter truth of it settled onto my shoulders. A doctor would know how to help her.

If they could get here...

But there was no time. Her blood was a puddle on my sheets, and her skin was so pale it was almost blue. Haggard gurgles came through the hole in her neck. Her eyes—sharp green like fresh leaves in Spring, or a river stream—locked on mine.

Oh God, I thought. *She's dying on my bed, she knows it.*

They had attacked her, then carted her off to a stranger's house to die on his bed. I took her hand. Her grip was weak, and her heart-rate had slowed. Air bubbled from her wound.

"I-I'm sorry," I whispered. "This is all my fault. If I hadn't let them-"

I paused. Her wrists had scabbed puncture marks, maybe a dozen each. And more near trailing up to the inside of her elbow.

Was she a Stig user? She hadn't been at the Arlington.

Flesh and blood, bone and breath. Could she know something? Something that would help? A grim choice formed in my mind. I had seconds to go over the morality of what I was about to do.

"Hey." Her eyes met mine again. "I… can help you. You won't like it. It will hurt. It will leave you *different*. It's not a choice you should have to make, but I can let you die, or I can do something that may feel worse than dying. You won't understand, you'll never understand, even if we had time. You won't be alive, but you won't be dead. That's- that's the best I can do, kid."

I took a long, shaky breath. "One blink for yes, two blinks and I… I let you go."

One blink. She squeezed my hand with all the strength she had left.

I nodded and got to my feet. I needed things. Symbols. Items. I went into the living room and grabbed Lindquist' book. When I had introduced myself to the wights, Deb had given me a journal written by its founder, left behind when he vanished. Artemis had been two centuries old, and devoted his existence to understanding the undead condition, buried under millennia of mythology and conjecture.

It was as scientific as he could make it, for someone born in the 19th century. From his journal, I knew why wights feel a hunger for human flesh. Why they needed to stay close to their burial soil, and more.

Unavoidably, his observations had insights into necromancy, though Lindquist wasn't a mage himself. The journal didn't have spells to memorize—magic doesn't work that way—but it gave me ideas on how to create them. A burst of necrotic energy that stunned the undead like a taser. A spell that scoured dead organic material from an area, and one that decayed it into ash. I could preserve a corpse for months without refrigeration.

And I knew how to make someone into a wight.

I had never considered it before. I didn't have any friends, or enemies, I'd want to inflict such an existence on. But there I was, about to perform it on a complete stranger.

I went into the living room and grabbed the terracotta herb pot by my door. The girl's eyes followed me as I returned.

"Yeah, you're not gonna like this one bit."

I dumped the soil over her legs and torso. It was enough to count as a burial. Then I ran into the kitchen and grabbed a knife. Her eyes widened as I cut my palm.

"Sorry about this," I said.

I grabbed a clump of earth and pressed the bloody muck against the hole in her neck. She let out a gargled scream. I grimaced, then took a long breath and cast my magic on her, as much as I could muster.

Her soul rocked in its moorings and tried to pry free as death overtook her. I saw her divided, one body and one soul. Her scream turned into a shriek that battered at my ears and made the windows rattle. I didn't know how she could scream so loud, even if her lungs weren't full of blood.

But her body hadn't made a sound. It was her *soul* that screamed. Her spectral eyes met mine. I stared back, uncertain of my course but determined to see it through.

Her body went limp, but ensnared by my magic, her essence returned to it. I held the mud against her neck until I was sure it would stay put. Then I pushed the remaining soil around, so her body was more or less covered, and pulled my blood-stained blanket over her like a shroud.

I sent a steady current of magic into her makeshift grave. The pulse of necromancy chilled the room and fog gathered at my feet. When I sensed the fractured bonds between her body and soul, I bound them together again. That magic was a part of her now. It would be what held her together for the rest of her existence.

The process was slow. Whenever I felt a 'leak' of soulstuff, I gathered it back into her body and sealed it with my power. After a while, I could feel the broken bonds begin to 'clot'. She was whole again, more or less. But not in any way that was natural.

I heard the rattle of her last breath. Her heart went still in her chest.

But in death, her soul did not depart.

Finally, I collapsed against the nearby wall. Every bruise ached, my throat was sore, and I hadn't moved from her side in almost an hour. I limped into the bathroom to wash off, bandaged my cut, and got dressed.

My reflection stared back at me from the mirror. I knew what I had to do next. Part of me resisted, but I knew that if I let it go, I'd never get a handle on it again. I took the box down from the fridge and tucked its contents into my belt behind my back.

Outside, the frat boys loitered on my lawn. They'd ended their shouting match to wait, confused and scared, like family members in a hospital waiting room. Only Jeb had the guts to meet my gaze, but the hope he had drained away into a quiet despair. Frankie watched his shoes. Donnie looked past me, into my house.

Max sat on the front step. He rocked back and forth, holding temples. I could see the blood on his hands, but I couldn't see his face.

"Why didn't you take her to a hospital?" My voice was cold and steady.

Donnie didn't have it in him to answer, so Jeb did. "We thought you could stop the bleeding. Donnie said maybe you could save her."

Donnie gawked at his friend, and then to me. "I didn't- I don't-"

I stared him down, and he shut up. Then I turned my gaze to the wight on my porch.

"Max."

"I didn't mean it." He repeated it several times. "I-I didn't. She wouldn't listen, wouldn't let me explain. So stupid-"

He muttered to himself, over and over, a broken record of half-completed thoughts. He didn't mean to. She wouldn't listen. He just got so mad.

"It won't happen again," he promised. "It won't. I swear to God. It won't happen again."

I exhaled. "Yeah."

Then I drew the old revolver from my belt and shot him through the skull.

FOURTEEN

Max's body flopped into my long-neglected flower bed.

"What- *what did you do?*" Donnie shouted.

I met his gaze and stepped onto the lawn towards him. He stumbled over his feet and landed on his ass. The surrounding air darkened into an icy fog.

"You were supposed to watch him," I said. "You said he was *fine*. Was he fine, Donnie?"

He didn't have an excuse left in him. He stared at Max's body and started sobbing. Black tears streaked his face.

My gaze fell on Jeb, who withered at my stare. "Get back to your tomb."

He nodded. "W-what about Max?"

I snarled and lashed my arm at Max's corpse. His flesh and clothing blackened and crumbled. In moments, there was nothing left but ashen dust. I went inside and slammed the door behind me. A few moments later, I heard Donnie's old town car leave my yard.

Fury compelled me to hate Donnie. He'd nagged, pleaded, and blackmailed until I'd given in. But deep under my anger, I hated myself. I let Donnie and his friends run free. Four wights who had been sneaking out for months, letting the hunger build, until one of them had gone over the edge.

But *I'd* let them go, because I had a thousand things on my shoulders, and I decided it was easier to give in than force the issue. I'd let them out, gotten them jobs, let them worm their way into a position where they could abuse my friendship and sympathy.

I let the monsters out, I thought.

A moan came from the bedroom. The bloody, dirty grave stirred.

And now I've made another.

I regarded my revolver. It wasn't some fancy automatic, or a monster of a hand cannon that could floor a moose. Just an old army pistol from a century ago. Time and use had worn its ornamental markings to almost nothing, and there were notches carved in the ivory handle. A dealer had laughed when I'd tried to have it appraised. You could buy a better looking piece at a pawnshop for the cost of a burger and fries.

But it was an heirloom. It had protected three generations of my mother's family. When I'd moved out, she had given it to me. I know she had meant well, but given its grim history, especially between her and I, there was an underlying symbolism to it.

Giving someone the gun that should have prevented them from being born is… it says *something.* I don't know what.

I put the revolver back on top of the fridge, took a deep breath and went into the bedroom. The body under the sheet pushed with unwieldy limbs, tossing aside earth and cloth. I helped her free herself. The girl groaned, bleary-eyed. Black tears stained her face.

"Wh-where?" She croaked. Her hands went to her neck. It was undamaged, albeit discolored, in the vague shape of a bite. She tried to stand, so I put a hand on her shoulder.

"Easy. Take a minute to collect yourself."

She stared at me like I had two heads, then shoved me aside and stumbled into the bathroom to throw up in my toilet. A hacking session followed as she cleared her lungs of blood.

"Oh, God." She stared at the bowl. "What is this?"

I sat on the corner of the bed. "You died."

Piercings—loops, studs and little spikes—decorated her face. She kept her hair shaved on the left side of her head, and the rest fashioned into shiny black locks. A little tattoo of a raven in flight sat behind her left ear. Cute, in a naive 'anarchy-as-fashion' kind of way.

But it didn't hide how young she was, maybe younger than Donnie and his friends. She was gaunt and pale to the point of being unhealthy, and her green eyes had a haunted distance in them. Trembling hands clung to her neck.

"What did you do to me?" She asked.

"What do you remember?"

"I was at the concert. I saw Max he- we-" Her eyes widened. "What did you do to me?"

"I brought you back. Do you remember coming here?"

She stumbled, but caught herself on the bathroom doorway. "You- you brought me back?"

I nodded. "You were dying. I couldn't save you. So I did what I could."

"What you could-?" She scratched at her neck. "Why don't I feel it?"

"Because it's gone. I filled it in with a little of you, a little of your grave, and a little of me."

"A little of my- a little of y-you? Who are you? *What* are you?"

"My name is Alex. Alex Fossor," I said. "I'm a necromancer."

She sank to her knees, her eyes going flat.

I pulled her to her feet. "Don't go into shock. A catatonic undead can't learn what she has to learn, you hear me?" She let me herd her into the living room and I sat her on the couch. "Look at me, kid."

"Am I… dead?"

I grunted. "Technically, yes."

"How?" She drew the word out in a sob.

I sat beside her. "You've got a million questions, I know. I'll try to answer them all. But first, what's your name?"

"Maddie. M-Madelyn MacLaith."

"Madelyn," I said. "Take your time, Madelyn."

She let her hands fall limp at her sides. "Where am I?"

"My place. On Sutcliffe Street. Do you know it?"

"That shitty college neighborhood?"

"Yes," I said with a smirk.

"The men who brought me-"

"Gone. I sent them away."

She closed her eyes. "What happened to Max?"

I stared at my front door. "He's gone."

"Good." She wiped her eyes, and her expression hardened. "Why did they bring me here?"

I ground my teeth. "Because they're idiots. They thought a hospital couldn't help, or the cops would get involved, or because they thought I could make you what you are now."

"You did this?" She rubbed her throat. "You did this to me?"

"Yes, I- my magic let me do it. I wish I had the power to have preserved your life. This was all I had."

"What am I?"

"The most accurate term I know is *haugbui*, from old Norse. It means 'barrow-wight' or 'grave man'."

She frowned. "From Tolkien?"

I smiled. "Yeah."

"What does that mean?"

I shrugged. "You don't have a pulse, you don't need to breathe, but your brain will keep trying. Autonomic systems, and all that. You won't get sick, but you can still poison yourself if you eat something you can't digest. And you have to stay in or near your grave-soil-" I pointed at the bed. "Or you'll get hungry and eventually decay."

"Hungry? You mean, like-?" Her hand went to her throat again.

I nodded. "Max and his friends are wights, too. They've been straying from their graves. The longer you're away, the hungrier you get. And there's only one thing that will satisfy it."

Fresh tears formed in Madelyn's eyes. "You mean I have to, to eat-"

I held her shoulders. "It's management, kid. Like any disease. Some wights, if they're smart, can go months or years before they feel hunger pangs. Wights guarded the tombs of kings. The magic that binds them to their grave sustains them indefinitely. When you leave the magic fades, and your body tries to keep itself going using the life force of others. You'll get hungrier and hungrier until you get what you need. And if you can't get that, your body will decay into nothing. Then it's dead for good."

She wiped her face, then grimaced at the sight of her tears. "What the fuck? What the *fuck?*"

"All undead have them, if they can cry at all. I don't know why. But it doesn't stain."

She snorted. "Are you like them? Like, like me?"

I shook my head. "No. I'm worse. Like I said, I'm a necromancer."

"That's a little geeky, isn't it?" She snorted.

"It's old Greek. For oracles who spoke to the dead. It's the most apt title for what I do."

"Like a wizard?" She couldn't keep the incredulity out of her voice.

"I prefer 'mage', but whatever the term, they almost always come from a word for 'wise man'. Pretentious bullshit." I tried to chuckle. "Magic is real, kid. Surprise."

She shuddered. "Fuck, this is too heavy. If you'd told me an hour ago? Fuck. I was- I was *alive* an hour ago..."

"You'd have laughed in my face. We don't go sharing the news. Most people don't believe in us, and it would scare others shitless. We have rules about keeping things secret. Most mages consider it pointless to mess with ordinary people. Normal people."

"Normal," she croaked. "God. I'm... some zombie thing!"

"Zombies are worse. Speaking of, where did you get those punctures on your wrist?"

She frowned. "I'm not suicidal."

"They're familiar to me. Stig, right?"

"I didn't, I'm not..." Madelyn held her wrists close to her. There were more than a few marks on both.

"An addict?" I asked. "I'm not here to accuse you of anything, Madelyn. But Stig? That stuff is necromancy too. I've seen what it does to people. It's bad stuff."

She blinked. "How?"

"It's meant to weaken your mind and leave it vulnerable to a necromancer's influence. Like the Haitian zombies of old."

She rubbed her wrist. "You mean you-?"

"No. I thought I was the only necromancer in the city. But there's a new group in town. They call themselves the Brothers Midnight. Heard of them?"

"Uh, Tyler, my um, dealer. He mentioned a 'Brotherhood'."

"They're trying to spread the drug as far as they can. I need to know where you got it. I'm running short on leads."

"Leads?" She asked. "What are you, a cop?"

I smirked. "No. I'm a man with a bomb in his chest. If I don't clear my name and prove I'm not the necromancer behind all of it, I'll be dead. I try to take care of the wights in this city, undead like yourself. If I go, they won't have…"

What are you about to confess to her? I asked myself.

Everything. She was already stuck in it, for good or ill.

"One thing I do as a necromancer is provide them with food. I don't kill people, but I do work for criminals. I make bodies disappear. And those bodies go to feed the wights. When they need it. Otherwise they could go out and-"

"Do what they did to me?" She asked, disgusted.

I nodded.

Madelyn stood. "You fucking suck at your job!"

"Yeah," I admitted.

"So now what? You bury me? Or do I have to spend the rest of my life hanging around near your fucking bed? Like that's some fucking coincidence!"

I tried to keep myself calm. "The gravesoil is what matters. We'll collect it and take you to the Gallows. It's where the other wights live. Under the city. We can get you a room, we can get you the things you need. TV, clothes, they even have Wi-Fi."

"Oh, great!" She said. "It sounds like a fucking party! I can't wait to hang out with the dead people that killed me, sitting on a pile of fucking dirt and waiting for some asshole to feed me a corpse like hamburger! No. I won't let you lock me away! I won't be your fucking pet zombie! I want out! I want to go home!"

She went for the door. I shot to my feet and pulled her away. "Hey! Hey!"

"Get the fuck off me!" She shoved me. "Don't touch me!"

"You can't go running off! You're my responsibility now, like it or not."

"Fuck you!"

I slammed my palm on the door, and she jumped. "You don't get to decide! I told you you wouldn't like it, but it was this or death! If you go running around, away from your grave, you'll get hungry."

Fear flickered in her eyes, but her lips curled into a snarl. "You fucking bastard! You did this to me! I wish you'd fucking killed me!"

She slammed her elbow into my jaw. The blow was clumsy, but she had a wight's strength now, and while it wasn't super-human, it was enough to knock me on my ass.

When the room stopped spinning, my door was open, and Madelyn was gone. I pushed to my feet with a curse and grabbed my revolver from the fridge, but stopped myself at the door.

I'd done it again. Let a monster out into the streets. What-ever happened, whatever havoc she caused, it would be on my shoulders. And I'd know when the Society found out, when I *exploded*. I sat on my porch, heedless of the cold, where Max had been when I'd blown his brains out. There was no trace of him. The ashes had scattered.

I hadn't even shot him face to face. I'd put him down like a rabid dog.

Walter was right. Necromancers couldn't make it to their first century without breaking the Edicts. Destruction came so easily. How many had faltered under the weight of their grotesqueries, and the macabre choices they made? I dismem-bered corpses to feed to the undead, I wiped away crime scenes for the benefit of murderers, and I had the balls to consider myself one of the *decent* ones.

"Come on, you old bastard," I whispered. "Put me down."

Nothing.

Sutcliffe Street stirred. I saw lights in windows, silhouettes peeking out to see what had caused all the racket. I forced my-self to go inside and dumped the soil from my bed into the planter pot.

Maybe a new Madelyn will sprout, I thought in my daze.

I didn't know what else to do with it, so I left the planter by the front door. The blood had soaked into my mattress. I conjured my decay magic—weakened from all the juice I'd poured out that night—and scoured the blood without fraying the fabric. I dumped the pillows and blankets into my washing machine, and took a cold shower to torture myself some more.

Then I laid down on my couch and closed my eyes.

☠

When I awoke, the sun shone through my kitchen window. The clock on the microwave said it was a little past ten. How much sleep was that? Four hours? Three?

I let the minutes tick by with agonizing slowness, each one punctuated by every mistake I'd made. It always came back to Max and Madelyn.

Rubbing my eyes, I grabbed the landline and dialed.

"Keller Funeral Home," said a crisp, morning-ready voice.

"Dietrich." I didn't bother to keep the weariness out of my tone.

"Alex." He tapped on a keyboard. "Finally."

"Yeah," I said. "Had a bit of trouble last night."

"Police trouble?" He asked, a little too fast.

"No. Max got into a fight at a bar last night. I stopped him, but someone got hurt. I fired him."

"Fired him?" He asked. "Just like that?"

I sighed. "Yeah. Just like that."

He paused. "Very well. I'd suggest you take a day or two off as well, Alex. This business with the police has me concerned as your employer. I think you should take some time to consider where you stand in all of this and-"

"I'll do that," I interrupted, and hung up. I didn't need a lecture from someone who couldn't fathom the shit I was dealing with.

But what next? A trip to the art gallery, like Agni said? An insightful yet dead-end bit of research? How would that help?

There was a knock at the door. Detective Runner was on the other side, and Lorensdottr lurked behind him.

"What?" I asked. "Oh, you. Now what?"

Lorensdottr's scowled but said nothing. Runner flashed his million-dollar smile. "Good morning, Mr. Fossor. Can we come in?"

"You got a warrant?"

"No."

"Then right here is fine."

The smile vanished. "We had a few questions about your location last night."

"Here," I said. "Took a long walk for a few hours. Why?"

"Anyone who can corroborate your whereabouts?" Lorensdottr asked.

"No. I don't have friends."

Runner shook his head. "We had a complaint last night of a gunshot in the neighborhood, and a vehicle leaving the area at speed shortly after. Know anything about it?"

I looked at the street. "Punk kids with an engine backfire?"

"The report was adamant that it was a gunshot. Are you sure you heard nothing?"

"If something happened I either wasn't here or I was asleep," I said.

"On your walk that no one else saw," Lorensdottr said.

I scowled. "Homicide detectives don't answer domestic disturbance calls, so how about you tell me what you want, or get the fuck off my property? It's too early in the morning for this bait-and-hook bullshit."

"Careful," she warned.

"Or what?" I asked. "You'll arrest me for being grumpy?"

Runner sighed. "Sorry to disturb you." They returned to their car, speaking in hushed tones.

They didn't deserve the guff, but I was sick of people pissing in my face and daring me to do something about it.

Fuck it, I thought. If I was going to be angry, I'd at least be productive. I shut the door, put on some clothes, and headed for the Westbank Art Gallery.

FIFTEEN

Downtown was a mess of traffic on the best of days, but the Arlington fire had turned it into a slog. I cranked the music and nursed a lukewarm coffee as we inched forward for most of the morning.

Every few meters I glanced back at the unmarked gray cruiser in my rearview, about ten cars back. Lorensdottr was in the driver's seat, wearing a pair of shielded sunglasses and a baseball cap that made her look like the world's coldest, sexiest soccer mom. I couldn't see him, but I suspected Runner was in the passenger's seat, his ostentatious duster replaced with something less obvious, like a tricorne hat and foam football jersey.

The Westbank Art Gallery sat on the edge of Riverside Park, the beachhead of the city's efforts to gentrify the area with outdoor cafes, gazebos and pavilions along the water. The Gallery itself was like a castle, surrounded by high walls and stringent security. I parked at the far end of the lot, and when I tossed my coffee in a waste bin, I saw the detectives drift by.

A pair of enormous stone wolves flanked the front doors to the Gallery, and the interior was spacious, with padded carpets and arching ceilings. People kept their voices muted as they drifted from one gallery to the next. The artwork and historical items sat in glass cases, or were cordoned off by velvet rope.

A doorman with a tweed jacket and an upturned nose greeted me at the door. He reminded me of a capybara, those big South American rodents, calm and unimpressed with everything around them.

"May I help you find something?" He asked, in a low, nasal voice.

"Yeah, a friend recommended a gallery here on Vodou."

He looked me over. "Membership, please?"

"I don't have a gallery membership, I was-"

He glanced around him, then drew a dull gray eye that hovered in the air. "*Versed* membership?"

"Oh." I gave my finger a shake and drew my anchor magemark, but the magic fizzled halfway through. "Uh, sorry. I had a long night."

"Hm."

I took a long breath, relaxed, and tried again. This time my mark hovered in the air for a few seconds before it faded out.

That worried me. Maybe I had burned more 'mana' reanimating Madelyn than I'd thought. Everyone has their limits, of course. Like any exertion, spell fatigue was a real possibility, especially for young mages. I should have recognized it sooner, but I was mentally and physically on the verge of burnout already.

"Very good," the doorman said. "Second floor. Take the stairs to your left."

I nodded my thanks and continued inside. Following his directions, I found cultural exhibits from Africa. From centuries-old clothing to masks, tools, weapons, and elaborate headdresses, progressing to works from modern, African-descended artists. There was a strong North American influence over the recent paintings, which depicted slave auctions and the cramped conditions on prison ships.

I paused in front of a painting where black slaves toiled in a field while a white man cracked his whip over their heads. The slaver's clothing and sadistic expression reminded me of Jesse, almost too similar to be a coincidence. The more I thought about the guy, the less I liked him. Did Jocelyn truly not recognize that part of her brother? Had he been that way before going underground?

I walked to the end of the exhibit, but found nothing about Haitians, Vodou, or the answers I sought. Had Agni played me? Sent me on a wild goose chase to give himself more time to prove my guilt.

A woman cleared their throat behind me. She looked like a museum employee, with a frumpy brown turtleneck, ankle-length dress, and shiny black hair bound in a plain tail. It did nothing to hide how attractive she was, and I suspected if she chose to, she could dazzle a room with her caramel skin and unusually dark eyes, such a dark brown as to be almost black. It gave her a naturally smoldering look.

"Alex Fossor. You are early." Her voice had a dry, matter-of-fact tone to it.

"Uh, excuse me?"

"This way." She guided me to a door at the back of the exhibit, warded with an 'Employees Only' sign. Hands stained with blue and black ink produced a long, brass key and touched it to the door handle. I heard a shiver of magic, like a neon sign had been switched on. She opened the door and stood aside.

Beyond was a hollow tower, one so tall I couldn't see the ceiling. A carpeted staircase spiraled upward, connecting to floor after floor of books arranged on shelves that extended as far as my eye could see. As I crossed the threshold into the tower, I knew I wasn't in the Westbank Gallery anymore.

My breath caught just to see it. For the second time, I felt like something small in the face of the Rimbault Society, an ignorant witness to a global power that had reigned unopposed since before the United States.

But am I still in the city? My rational mind wondered. I didn't combust, so I assumed I was still within the limits of Walter's hex.

The woman strode to the center of the room, and her presence changed. She *became* the place, the way the perfect piece of art completes the space it occupies. I couldn't imagine the tower without her. "You may wait here until your appointment, Alex Fossor."

"You know my name?" I asked.

"I am Luciana Del Lago, Pillar of Knowledge, and this is the Library. If your name is written here, I know it. I know every word, on every page."

I must have been staring too hard, because Luciana cleared her throat again.

"Sorry," I breathed. "Just comprehending. So I have a file, huh? Don't suppose you could show me?"

Her eyebrow curled. "No."

I expected as much, but her candor made me smile. "So what's the story of this place?"

"Construction of the Library began January First, in the year Eighteen Hundred, at the approval of the First Council. The project was completed on August Ninth, Eighteen Forty-Seven. I have served as its caretaker for seventeen years, after the previous caretaker passed. Since its inception in Seventeen Sixty-Four, the Society has strived to archive a near complete record of factual human accomplishment, both magical and mundane. The earliest of these records date to the seventh millennium before Christ."

I blinked at the limitless stairwell spiraling into the distance above. "Not just *a* library. *The* Library."

"Yes." She allowed a hint of a smile to touch her face.

I cast my eyes heavenward again, considering the sheer scope of what I was seeing. I would have given my left leg to spend a few months browsing its contents. But I was on a literal deadline.

"So, you know about Haitian Vodou?" I asked.

The smile vanished. "Less than is satisfactory. General information is prevalent, Vodou has roots in African spiritualism, but the upheavals of European colonialism changed it on a fundamental level. The Versed of Haiti integrated themselves into the faith and are unwilling to share information on their more esoteric practices."

"I came for answers, and now you're telling me you don't have them?"

She narrowed her eyes. "I do not. I was instructed to receive and escort you to the Lounge when it is time."

"How long am I waiting?" I asked. "I don't have a lot of time on my hands, if you've heard."

"I have," she said. "Council meetings are a matter of record. I must inform you that, in the event of your death, I must eject you from the Library to ensure no damage comes to the books."

I burst out laughing. It was almost alien to my ears after the week I'd been having.

"Why are you laughing?" Luciana asked.

"*'In the event of my death'*? Do you grab a broom and dustpan the ashes, or just toss my burning body out the door?"

"I am- I did not-" Color touched her cheeks. "That is not funny at all."

I took a breath. "Sure it is. A macabre sense of humor came with the magic."

She huffed and regained her composure.

"I don't suppose you've got anything on necromancy? I'm not well-versed in my particular brand."

"The Society's policy is to deny mentorship or study to any Versed who wields inherently dangerous forms of the Art," she said.

"Dangerous because it's necromancy, or dangerous because it's me?" I asked with a smirk.

"Yes." Her expression didn't change. I couldn't tell if she was joking or not.

Assume she's way too clever for you, I thought.

"What makes necromancy 'inherently' dangerous?" I asked. "The Archmage can turn me to ash with a thought, and he doesn't have to be in the same room. How is that more dangerous than me puppeting a corpse about?"

Luciana hesitated. "Aside from the ethical and moral concerns of defiling the physical form of a deceased individual, and the potential coercion, entrapment, and wrongful harm of an individual's soul?"

"Yes," I said.

She blinked. "It is a matter of statistical record. If you will forgive the archaic nomenclature, the Society has classified six-hundred and sixty-six of the known forms of magic as the 'Black Arts'. Records show that, without fail, their practitioners inevitably pursue actions that breach the Edicts, often in grievous ways. The risk increases exponentially with age. Versed are therefore forbidden from receiving mentorship from the Society, to dampen their development."

I scratched my chin as I thought it over. "That's a lot of mages being stepped on."

"The Edicts exist to protect the Untold from magical abuse."

"Spoken like the words are branded to your brain." A scowl came to my face. "And guys like me are your scapegoats. Told to bend the knee for your enlightened Society, just so you can put your boot on our necks."

Luciana's eyes darted to my arms. Wisps of fog snaked off my fingers. I gave them an absent shake.

"So the Archmage is a pyromancer," I said. "Or a *Pyrourge*, since you Society types name your magic like it's a science doctorate. Sheriff Chakrabarti says he's a *Tilemetaforurge*, like that isn't two mouthfuls, but I have the air miles to believe it. What are you?"

Luciana took a breath. "I am a Grafiurge."

"A what?"

She clasped her ink-stained hands in front of her. "Grafiurgy is a branch of Skafosurgy—the Art of enchanting man-made objects—that specializes in the written word."

"Could you demonstrate?"

She tilted her head. "I know the driver's license in your wallet is a forgery."

"You can read it without even seeing it?"

"Every word on every page," she restated. "My art allows me to be very efficient in cataloging, translating, and referencing our records. As the Library's caretaker, I also have access to its distinct properties that improve my talents further. In many respects, I am the Library."

It was a simple statement of fact, but I detected a hint of pride in it. And why not? If knowledge was power, then Luciana Del Lago stood several steps above everyone on the planet, including the Archmage. A woman of her position should be advising the Council. Or running it. Not playing receptionist to a nobody like me.

Still, I wasn't sure what to make of her. She was the first Society member who didn't immediately treat me like a potential threat, or a bug only worth stepping on. It was a refreshing change of pace.

"Then, if necromancy is off limits, is there anything I may read?"

Her eyes darted to a level above us. She opened her hand, revealing a ball of green light that expanded into the shape of a book. It solidified, hovering in the air before me as if resting on an invisible table.

"I will prepare the Lounge for you. Damage or theft of Library property comes with severe consequences. Do not explore the Library without an escort."

"Will I get lost?" I joked.

"You will be *found*."

She left the statement hanging between us and walked to the door. With a flick of her wrist, a pattern of glowing runes appeared on its surface. She touched one, and the door opened into an unfamiliar white room. Luciana closed it behind her as she left.

Found by what? I wondered. I didn't see or hear anything. I didn't feel any presence in the vast Library, but the absence of it only made me more suspicious. I put it out of my mind and opened the book.

Its author named himself Theodore of the Red Mantle, which I had to assume was a prestigious—or pretentious—title. Ted's grammar and spelling were typical of 19th century English, but despite its age, it read like a basic history textbook for children, an overview of the Society's founding, the fundamentals of its goals, and how it grew to be a global organization.

I frowned. Was Luciana trying to wag her finger at me for poking at forbidden knowledge? But I fought the urge to close it. I needed to know more about the Society, free of Visatori prejudice.

According to Ted the Red, the Society and the Edicts were a response to centuries of magical abuse, irreparable damage to human culture, and a self-destructive trend among the Versed. In-fighting and games of influence had been rampant, often involving human proxies who had no idea the wars they were fighting or the monsters they encountered in the darkness were the machinations of wizards trying to prove their superiority to one another. They brought entire kingdoms and nations to ruin, all to besmirch one mage's reputation in the eyes of his contemporaries.

It didn't surprise me. Men like Walter and the Council were as close to godhood as you could get this side of mortality. It wasn't a tremendous leap to imagine them using humans like toys because they got bored.

But from that realization, the largest cabals and covens had convened in the late 17th century, in what many of its members considered the center of the world, London. Back then, humanity was taking its first steps towards becoming a global community, and its mages sought that same connection. The gathering debated, discussed, and decided the course of their kind for centuries to come. The Rimbault Society was founded, a new nation of spellcasters named for the salon in which it was born.

From the Society came five Edicts, the laws that bound them together. Five would later become thirteen, and then seventeen as the knowledge of the Society grew, and they reinterpreted old traditions or norms to suit modern perspectives. With the Edicts to rally around, the Rimbault Society set about enforcing it on others. First in the nations its members considered home, and later to less 'civilized' parts of the world. That included any who refused to attend the convention, or were considered 'too primitive' to be invited.

I frowned. Ted's recounting of an 'enlightened magocracy' sounded more and more like arcane colonialism. Enforcing their will and power over others, with their justification being 'they don't know better and we do'.

As sensible as the Edicts sounded on paper, the Society had been well aware of their imperialistic intent from how fast they turned the Edicts against their rivals. Who knew how much knowledge the Society had destroyed, or stolen and se-

153

creted away? What truths were lost, because they were 'improper'?

As I flipped pages, the hair on my neck stood up. It felt like I was being watched. I looked around me, trying to pinpoint the source. The darkened rows of books offered plenty of places to hide.

Luciana cleared her throat behind me, and I jumped. She stood at the open doorway, stoic as ever. "Your appointment is waiting."

The unknown presence in the Library vanished, quick as it had come. I backed away from the floating book and moved to her side. "I felt something, it was-"

"That is the Librarian."

"I thought *you* were the librarian."

"As the Pillar of Knowledge, I am the Library's caretaker. But the Librarian is its protector."

"I must have pissed it off, somehow."

"You didn't dog-ear a page, did you?"

I stared at her for a moment. "Is that- what?"

"Your appointment is waiting." I saw a glint of amusement in Luciana's eye as she led me through the door and closed it behind me.

SIXTEEN

The lounge was clean, inviting, and quiet. No infinite staircases or unseen observers, just plush chairs with low tables between them. I could hear rain washing against the opaque windows, further relaxing the atmosphere.

My 'appointment' had yet to arrive, so I sank into a chair, glad to be off my feet. The comfortable ambience threatened to pull me into an impromptu nap, but I reminded myself I was there for a reason.

When the door opened I rose to greet my guest, but felt a chill run through me. He had the same piercing gaze and dark complexion as Samuel Kincaid. They could have been brothers. Twins. But the newcomer had a head of wiry black hair, a trimmed beard, and his tattoos—while also depicting cigar-smoking skeletons in top-hats—looked more jovial than sinister.

Like the mages I'd seen at my trial, he dressed in a way that both spoke of pride in his traditions and a lack of concern for modern norms. He wore trousers frayed off below the knees, a top hat rested on his head, a tattered black dress coat with tails hung over his otherwise bare torso. He carried a cane with him, capped with an ivory skull.

"They tell me you need my guidance, gravedigger. I am Papa Williams." He had a heavy Creole accent, unaccustomed to English, but confident and forthright.

I recognized the name. "You're the mage Jocelyn spoke of. The representative from Port-au-Prince."

He finally blinked, and his eyes swept the room in thought. "The one seeking her brother? I fear she will not find the man she seeks."

"Yeah, I had the same impression. I'm Alex Fossor."

"You have questions about my former companions."

"Yeah, like why Haitian mages went into the drug trade, and what they hope to get from it."

He shook his head. "Not simple mages. Bokor."

"What's the difference?"

"That depends on how much you know about Vodou, Mr. Fossor."

"Very little. But I try to keep an open mind."

"We shall see. The mages of my faith enjoy a rare tutelage under the *Iwa*, or Loa. Passed down by the very spirits we serve. But mortal men—even we mages—must choose how to use that knowledge. The bokor are those who abuse that bond. To use their knowledge to harm others. You know of the Loa?"

"Spirits who serve God?" I asked.

He offered a slight smile. "In Haiti, they are the servants of Bondye, the Creator. So yes, and no. Our beliefs stem from traditions older than the Christian God. Or perhaps they are the same God? There are many nachons, many families of Loa. They are Immortals, from what you Society types call the 'Outer Layered'. Once mortal, but Ascended. Do you know what this means?"

I had to puzzle over what I knew for a moment. "The Visatori explained that mages accumulate magical power over the course of their lives. Sometimes, a mage becomes so powerful that they transcend mortality. Ascend into the Layered as a kind of lesser god."

"Or a devil," he added. "Or a prisoner. Ascension is not necessarily a reward. The mage has become so powerful that the world abhors them. Nature—or perhaps Bondye—does not permit them to stay. So they must Ascend into the Layered, where their power can no longer threaten lesser beings."

"So the Loa are prisoners?"

His smile deepened. "If they are, they are at least dutiful ones, serving Bondye. And we serve them in turn. They offer us great wisdom."

"What about the Brothers Midnight?"

"The Brothers are bokor. They broke their bonds to the Loa and used their knowledge for selfish gain. They are an affront to those like me, the houngan and the mambo, the priests and priestesses who serve the Loa."

"I saw them performing a ritual last night."

"Tell me what you witnessed."

I recounted the events in the Arlington, as I had for Agni. Papa Williams's face slowly twisted into a grimace of anger and disgust.

"These things you tell me, they sound familiar and yet very wrong." He made a gesture to the open air above him. "They go against the ways of the Loa, and of Vodou. I cannot stress enough how much of a defilement this is to our beliefs, and the Loa themselves. These are not our ways."

"And the zombies?" I asked.

Papa Williams shook his head. "That is not Vodou. That is Necrourgy. The bokor use poisons to separate the *ti bon ange*, the 'little soul'. You may think of it as one's personality and will. The poison drives the little soul from the body, while the big soul, *gros bon ange*, remains. The body still lives, susceptible to the bokor's control, and a special bottle contains the little soul. We know them as zombie astrals. Bokor use them as fonts for power. Dark magic."

I sat up. "That's how they're powering their spells. Making zombies to make more zombies? Is that what he was trying to tell me?"

"He?"

"One of their zombies attacked me. It seemed he was one of the bokor. I brought him out of his trance, but I couldn't understand what he was trying to tell me. He chose death over losing control again, and he gave me this." I produced the flower from my pocket.

Papa Williams nodded. "That is datura, the Devil's Trumpets. They are very poisonous."

And I've been keeping it in my pocket all day? Yikes. I set it aside. "This is an ingredient in their drugs, then?"

"It is, but they would need more. The flesh of a pufferfish is another ingredient."

"Someone who was in contact with them said they had tried to purchase aquariums."

"Very dark magic," he said.

I nodded. "I've told you what I know of the Brothers. What do you know?"

Williams sighed. "The bokor of Haiti have always been insular, by necessity. But their power has been growing over the past decades. More and more of our mages turn away from the Loa every year. Do you know about the earthquake some years ago? One of many disasters to affect my homeland, and one that left many dead. Many of the priesthood argued Haiti was suffering. That we were not doing enough to protect its people and our faith."

"Mages can't be expected to protect a nation. We're barely a part of normal society."

He looked me in the eye. "Live in a country as poor as mine, and tell me you would ignore its plights, white man."

I held up my hands. "Fair enough. Go on."

"We debated what to do for a time, whether it was better to maintain our traditions, or take a more active role in providing for the people. Some considered ending our isolation and joining the Rimbault Society. That abandoning our ways and living was preferable to slowly dying with them. Even if it meant forsaking our bond to the Loa." He shook his head. "It is a debate we are still having. A debate that has made us more useless than ever. Then one of our own—Samuel Kincaid—said that if we could not provide for Haiti, then it was time for the rest of the world to make its restitution to the nation. For the generations of slavery and exploitation."

"Drugs?"

He nodded. "How many poor nations have found cruel prosperity exploiting the vices of wealthier ones? He saw it as poetic justice, but it would make Haiti an enemy of the Society. When we refused his plan, he gathered many bokor to his side and fled."

"Why do the Loa allow them to act this way? Why not strike them down?"

Williams frowned. "The Loa are not weapons for you to wield against your enemies. They offer knowledge. They do not choose how you will use what they give you. That is the balance of things."

"Can't you talk to them?" I asked. "The Brothers are here, right now, making an army of zombies from the city's addicts."

He shook his head. "Maintaining an army would be impossible. The poison is difficult to make, and the zombie must receive it constantly. Eventually their supplies will dwindle, or they will have too many zombies to drug. Then the people would be free, little souls and all."

"So he's not making an army. But he wants them for *something*."

"An answer I cannot provide," Williams said.

159

I tried again. "Can the Loa? I'm looking for wisdom, Papa Williams. I need to know how to find them, to stop them."

"The Loa are not at the beck and call of the living."

"Not even to stop the bokor?"

"No," he said. "I can offer you this advice, Mr. Fossor. The Brothers will need specific equipment to create their drug. Gardens for their flowers, aquariums and seawater for the pufferfish. Find these things, and you will find the Brothers. Bring the Society proof of their deeds, and no force on this planet will protect them from justice."

I sighed. "Assuming they don't kill me first."

Papa Williams shrugged. "I will give your concerns to the Loa. If they deem you worthy, perhaps they will offer an answer. For my part-" He dug into his pockets and produced a metal flask. "All I can offer is something to take the edge off."

I hesitated, but took the flask. The contents smelled like rum, but when I took a sip, the sweetness turned to fire on my tongue. "Shit," I coughed. "That has a kick."

He smiled. "Goat peppers. I would put some milk on that tongue if I were you, white man. You look ready to cry."

"I'm man enough to cry." I sealed the flask and offered it back to him.

He shook his head. "Keep it. May it bring you luck."

He turned and left. I panted through the pain on my tongue, and studied the flask which was decorated with cigar-smoking, top-hatted skulls. As I did, the beginning of an idea brewed.

After a few minutes alone, I heard Luciana clear her throat. She stood in the doorway, which now opened into the Westbank Art Gallery. "I trust your visit was educational?"

"Very." I tucked the flask and the Devil's trumpet into my pocket. "Thank you, Luciana."

"You are welcome. This way, please."

Aquariums, I thought. *That's all I have to go on? No.*

160

I'd talk to the Loa myself and get my answers.

SEVENTEEN

I returned to the Gallery and breathed the cool, dusty air of the real world. Luciana remained in the Lounge, and when the 'Employees Only' door shut, I felt the magic connecting it to the Library wink out. She may as well have been on the moon, in terms of the metaphysical distance between us. Too bad, too. She was the first Society member I didn't immediately feel on edge about.

The rain from the Lounge had been prophetic, because a cold, coastal deluge was washing over the city as I exited the gallery. I didn't see the detectives, but I wasn't dumb enough to think Lorensdottr had given up. I headed home and hopped on my computer, my web search savvy revitalized, now that I had a better sense of direction.

After an hour of compiling traditional Vodou practices and the various Loa they worshiped, I'd pieced together enough ideas to make a summoning work. It wasn't a legit religious ceremony, but I was confident my magic could get the intended result. I took a walk to Kent's, a grocery and liquor store a few blocks north of Sutcliffe, and found everything I needed there. Score one for me.

My last stop there was the butcher's section in the rear. You should have seen his reaction when I asked for a pint of chicken blood.

"You serious?" He asked. "Is this some kind of hipster thing you got off the internet?"

"Blood sausage," I lied. "But its gotta be chicken."

He chewed his lip. "You want beef or pork for blood sausage."

"Chicken. Can you make it happen?"

"Gimme a minute," He said, and went into the back.

Some other customers gave me odd looks, but no one questioned the canned peas or bacon-flavored mayo they had in their baskets. A few minutes later, the butcher came out with an opaque plastic tub used to sell pickled sausages. I could see the reddish substance clinging to the inside.

"This stuff is already congealing, so you'd better use it fast. And ah, this ain't regulation, so if you get sick, you didn't get it from me."

By the time I left Kent's, the afternoon rain was coming down in sheets and I cursed my decision to walk to the grocery store. I was half-way home and soaked through when a blue compact car pulled up alongside me.

"Enjoying the weather?" Detective Runner asked.

"Still tailing me, huh?" I asked.

He grinned. "Nah. Lorensdottr left hours ago."

"What do you want?"

"Need a lift? I'm offering."

I frowned. "Isn't this a conflict of interest?"

"A ride home won't make us friends, Fossor."

"You're a weird cop, Runner."

"You're a weird suspect," he said. "So you gonna jump in, or do I reconsider getting my upholstery wet?"

"Fine." He unlocked the passenger door, and I climbed in.

"So what's in the bag?"

Already with the interrogating, I thought. *These guys don't quit.*

"Dinner." I set the bag on the floor, under my legs.

He chuckled. "So, when did you realize we were tailing you?"

"Morning traffic," I said. "Tell your partner she's too cute to be inconspicuous."

He snorted. "She'd pull my nose off. Figured you'd spot us. Loren is a good cop, and she doesn't miss many details, but she's a little too-"

"Hostile?"

"Assertive," he corrected. "And maybe a little stubborn."

"What about you?"

He shrugged. "I like to think I'm good at this, but hey, I'm still learning."

"And the coat?"

He chuckled like he got asked about it daily. "After my promotion, some of my friends in the beat squad gave it to me. It was a joke, but hey, I look good in it."

"You are a bit young for a detective."

Runner shrugged. "Long story. Short version is I caught a triple homicide suspect while I was a beat cop. A little under a year ago, three dead on the Northeast end?"

"I don't read the papers."

"It looked like a murder-suicide. Husband, wife, and her lover. Husband comes home, finds them in bed, he takes them out and then eats a bullet, right? But my gut started bugging me. Not like a stomach problem. The house smelled like hot pastrami."

"Weird detail to pick out."

"I was hungry. Or I wanted something to distract me from the bodies on the floor. But I couldn't find a trace of it in the house. No one else seemed to notice. I went to keep the crowds back. But then I smell it again, and zero in on a man who smells like the house. When he sees me watching him, he runs."

I grunted a laugh. "Did his head melt into a sandwich, too?"

Runner smiled. "I must have chased him three blocks before I tackled him. The guy was so spooked I'd sniffed him out that he confessed to everything. He was Man Number Three in the woman's life, and when he found out, jealousy took its course."

"Some people, huh?"

"Yeah," he said with a sigh. "Anyway, it was a field day for the press, 'cause they were there when I made the arrest. I've got the newspaper clippings at home. *'Cop Sniffs Out Suspect.'* I guess Captain Wright decided it would be good PR to give me an early promotion. They stuck me with Lorensdottr, 'cause she needed a partner after her last one transferred. 'Creative differences'."

"No good deed goes unpunished."

"Well, it ain't so bad," he said. "She's a good cop. Knows more than anyone at the station. She'd make captain if she was more cooperative with... well, *everybody*. But I've learned a lot."

"But she gets stuck with a rookie."

"Like I said, she's assertive. Honestly, the only reason she doesn't come at you swinging is because she's got no evidence, yet."

"So why am I here, Runner? Getting a ride home from her partner?"

He shrugged. "Don't get me wrong, Fossor. No body means no official investigation. But everything about you? It stinks of a double life, and anyone who knows what they're doing can see it. Your employer thinks you're decent, but your buddies, those college guys? They spoke a little *too* highly, know what I mean?"

I frowned but said nothing.

"All that said, my gut tells me you're not the bad guy."

I noticed we had passed my house, and he started circling the block. "Then this isn't about a non-existent murder investigation then, is it?" I asked. "If your gut tells you I'm not a bad guy, why not just ask me? People have been giving me the sideways approach all week, it'd be refreshing to talk straight for once."

Runner shrugged. "You mind if I run something by you? You don't have to answer but…"

"Please."

"Okay. So you didn't hear this from me, but right now Homicide and Narcotics are at each other's throats. Specifically, Loren and her ex- er, *Detective* Jefferson, who is working the Stig case."

"And?"

"And, after four months of investigating, he has zero leads. The junkies he talks to disappear. The pushers they pointed to don't exist. We know they're using some kind of disposable injector, but we haven't been able to get our hands on one. Statistically, we should have *something* by now, but we don't have enough Stig to do a proper chemical analysis."

He drifted by my house again, without slowing.

"So for weeks now, Jefferson has been circling the drain," Runner continued. "Then he gets an anonymous tip, a truck smuggling out of Lincoln. He jumps at it, the first lead in forever. And we find you with a body in your truck, allegedly dead from a Stig overdose. But then the body walks out of the morgue."

"Walked?" I asked, to keep up appearances.

"Walked. Station security cameras spotted him getting into a white van outside," Runner said. "Any chance it was yours?"

"I was with you when it happened, Detective."

"Right. Well, after we arrested you, Loren wanted you for murder, and the Captain agreed. Narcotics has to deal with that shit a lot. But the body vanishes, and the Captain makes us let you go."

"Seems a little odd," I said.

"There's more. Did you hear about the Arlington Hotel fire?"

I blinked. "The where now?"

"Downtown," he said. "It was a drug den, we thought it was owned by the Russians. Jefferson got another tip that Stig was being sold there. Everyone was sort of on-edge after what happened with you, so it was easy for him to get everyone to head out in force. But it was burning down when they arrived."

"Sounds heavy."

Runner finally stopped the car in front of my house. "So with all this shit happening, my gut tells me you're another carrot on a stick leading us in a direction we shouldn't be looking."

"I don't suppose you'll stop, then?"

He smirked. "No. Even if you're a distraction, my gut tells me you know more than you're letting on."

I let the statement hover between us for a moment. "Is that so?"

He leaned towards me. "C'mon, man. I'm not looking to arrest you over smuggling or whatever it is you do. I'm after big fish here. I want Jefferson to find something substantial, before it becomes *Homicide's* problem, know what I mean? I want to find these Stig-sellers. The Lincoln Street Mambas won't talk. I'm guessing you know something."

"And?"

"Anything," Runner said. "A name, a place, a breadcrumb. Give me a direction that leads to something substantial, and maybe you won't have to worry about us following you around anymore."

I weighed my options. On one hand, Runner could be baiting me. If I implicated myself any further, he would have an excuse to slap the cuffs on me. It was also possible he was struggling for something to show his superiors, desperate to prove himself beyond a single well-publicized but incidental arrest.

On the other hand, he had come to me alone and gave me everything the cops had on the Stig case, which wasn't much. It convinced me he cared more about preventing deaths than making arrests. It was easy for me to dismiss cops, being so much of a crook myself, and see the police as just crooks with badges.

I wanted to believe it was rare to meet one who gave a damn, but that wasn't true. There are plenty of good cops. An overwhelming number of them. My mother's husband was one. And James Runner, however young, however naive, was one, too.

"Okay, Jimmy. You didn't hear this from me, alright?"

He held up a hand. "Scout's honor."

"I *knew* you were a scout," I muttered. "Some people are saying the guys fighting the Lincoln Street Mambas call themselves the Brothers Midnight. They're Haitians, or at least their leadership is. And whatever is in Stig, they need two things, gardens and saltwater aquariums."

"Gardens, so grow op. What are the aquariums for?"

"No idea," I lied. "But I know they're important. Look for aquarium purchases. Big ones, and lots of them."

"That's not much to work with," he said.

"No, but it's more than you had." I stepped out into the rain with my bag.

"Hey, if this pans out, it could take the pressure off you, but no guarantees. If you think of anything else-" He dug into his coat and produced an embossed white card. It wasn't as fancy as Jocelyn's, but it was official. "Call me. The more you give me, the better for everyone. Keep your head low in the meantime, Alex."

"You're all heart, Detective."

I went into the house and started to unpack my groceries.

Someone knocked on my door. Nothing but trouble had come through it in the past few days, so I grabbed my revolver before I answered it.

Madelyn MacLaith was on the other side. She hugged her skinny arms, drenched from the rain.

"I need help."

EIGHTEEN

I stepped aside to let Madelyn in, sticking the pistol in my pocket before she could see it. "Lemme grab you a towel."

She dropped to her knees and leaned over the terracotta planter in which I'd dumped her gravesoil. She looked like a sad little goth-rock puppy as she dried herself with the towel I offered from my bathroom.

"I didn't- I'm sorry." Tears streaked her face as she stared at something in the middle-distance. She looked even more gaunt and haunted than the night before.

Dread crawled through my guts as I sat on my couch. "What happened?"

"I went home. Christ, I-I haven't been home in months. Not since I-" She frowned and shook her head. "I went home."

"And?"

"Mom was so happy to see me. It was like we never fought. I-I..." She put her head in her hands.

"You got hungry."

Her head snapped up. "I ran. I didn't know where I was going until I realized I was coming back this way. It didn't hurt so much, the closer I got to your place. I don't feel it now."

"The gravesoil will suppress your hunger," I said. "But it won't diminish. If you get too hungry, you won't be able to walk more than a few steps from it."

Madelyn shuddered and gave me a pleading look. For the first time, I saw a young woman buried under the confusion, shock, and painful addiction. She was struggling to come out of that miasma.

I nodded. "Give me a minute. Then we'll go visit the Gallows."

She watched me put my groceries away from the living room. "What is all that?"

"I'm preparing a ritual to talk to one of the Loa. It's Vodou."

"Vodou?" She asked. "Serious? That stuff is real?"

"Among other faiths. I'm not a priest, but I can use symbols the Loa are familiar with to create a beacon for them. Compel one of them to come forward for a discussion. Come on. Bring your pot."

Madelyn didn't look like she could lift two bags of groceries, but she hefted the pot with ease. "What's the Gallows?"

☠

When we arrived at the pump station, Bill Weber answered the door for us.

"Oh, hey, Alex," he wheezed.

"Bill," I said. "Heard you had trouble last night."

He backed away as we entered. "It wasn't like that. Everything was fine for us. We got what we needed and came home. Then Donnie and his friends took the car and went to a concert. When they came home, and Max wasn't with them... " He sighed. "Jeb told us what happened. Look, was it necess-"

"Yes." I let the word linger in the air, then turned aside. "This is Madelyn."

Bill blinked as he noticed her. "Oh, uh, hello."

171

"Hey," she said.

"She's Max's- she's why he didn't come home."

"Oh," Bill saw the pot in her hands. "Oh, damn. Listen, Madelyn. I'm sorry about all of this. But Alex, are you sure it's a good idea to bring her here now? We're all still a little shaken over what's happened."

"I need to grab some things for her."

"Oh, well, alright," Bill said.

We descended through the station and took the lift to the Gallows. Deb opened the door for us. She glanced between Madelyn and I, then shuffled out of the way.

"This is the Gallows," I said.

"People live here?" Madelyn asked.

"They do. Gloomy as it is, it used to be worse. Like a medieval monastery, all candles and bleak silence."

"At least it feels like a crypt," she said. "Better than a sewer?"

"Silver linings."

I guided her to the kitchen portion of the cistern and flicked a few switches. Neon beer logos and an 'Open' sign flickered to life.

"Homey," Madelyn said. Her tone was flat, hesitant. She knew what was coming.

I opened a freezer and picked a piece of plastic-wrapped flesh from inside. "Pull up a chair."

She sat at the bar, her eyes locked on the package in my hands. "Is this- who *was* that?"

"Drug dealer."

She grimaced. "Anyone I knew?"

"Maybe. This guy sold Stig. The Lincoln Street Mambas killed him for selling on their turf. Or just being on their turf. I don't ask a lot of questions." I unwrapped the meat and set it in front of her.

She grimaced. "This doesn't feel right."

"Madelyn, look at me."

172

She took her time doing it.

"Nothing about this is 'right'. It shouldn't feel normal. It should be something that makes you feel a little sick, even hate yourself. Because otherwise, if you get a taste for it? That's not the wight saying it, or the magic making you do it. It's you. This condition is monstrous, but only you can decide to *be* a monster."

"But if I don't, I go nuts? Or rot away to nothing?"

"Slowly but surely," I said. "Either from hunger, or because you sit on your grave day after day, unable to move."

"What kind of life is that?"

"A terribly unfair one." I leaned against the counter. "Selfish, rich kings created wights to guard their treasures forever. They said it was an honor, but they never thought about what eternity meant for the guardian. It's why people don't find wights in tombs anymore. They went mad and died, or ended themselves."

Black tears welled in Madelyn's eyes. "That doesn't sound like a life at all."

"Not back then. It's a little easier these days."

"How?"

"The only tomb you have to protect is your own. Cell phone reception is shit, but the Wi-Fi is pretty good down here."

She snorted. "Are you going to cook it?"

"I can, but that kind of normalizes this, doesn't it?"

"And it can't be normal, huh?"

I took a breath. "Max thought it was normal. To bite. Even the people he cared about."

Madelyn glared at me. "You're an asshole."

"Yeah, I am," I said. "I'm the only necromancer, the only mage in this city who gives a damn. Anyone else would burn this crypt to the ground, because they don't think you're worth the effort. They think what you are makes you evil, they don't care that someone stole your life from you, that you didn't want this, that you aren't a psychopath, or that you haven't lost your mind to hunger. They'll destroy you because they decided you're a threat."

"So, what, you're allowed to kill us?" Madelyn snapped.

"In terms mages use, you're 'created'. Something built from magic. It doesn't matter what your component parts were. As far as they're concerned, you're not human, and they'll destroy you if you threaten those human beings."

She stared at the flesh in front of her like she wanted to throw up. "You're some kind of zookeeper. A prison guard!"

I pursed my lips. "You're not wrong."

"It's not fair. I'm not even twenty yet. Will... I mean, will I age? Can I have k-kids?"

"No," I told her. "I can't fix that. Nothing can."

Madelyn hugged her arms. "I want to die. I don't want to live like this!"

I sighed. "You can't think like that."

She screamed. *"Just kill me!"*

The sound battered my eardrums, but worse than the sound, I felt a sudden sense of grief and pity for Madelyn. She hung her head in her hands and sobbed.

I heard doors open in the access tunnels. The other wights emerged, drawn to the noise, but they kept a respectable distance. It was the Gallows, after all. Crowds gather when the hangman has a neck for his noose. Even Donnie, haggard and heartbroken, had arrived, with Jeb and Frankie standing between him and me.

While Madelyn cried, I drew my revolver and cocked the hammer. The metallic click made everyone freeze.

"If that's what you want. I can do that, too." I met each wight's gaze, and they looked away. "Max was turning over. It wasn't hunger. It was his attitude. His anger. He didn't like living here, feeling caged."

I looked at Madelyn. "He wanted out. He wanted freedom. It made him meaner and meaner until he lost sight of where his anger and hunger were separate."

Donnie looked like he wanted to say something, to protest, but I continued on.

"And Max killed Madelyn for it. She wouldn't give him the time of day, and his solution was to tear out her throat. And Donnie's solution? Bring her to me. Not a doctor, or a hospital. To a *necromancer*. What was your logic, Donnie? That I'd make her a wight? That she could live with Max like a pet?"

Donnie's face twisted into a mix of rage, hate, and grief. Madelyn looked disgusted.

I shook my head. "Did you think that if he had her around, Max wouldn't be so preoccupied, and watching everyone like a shark? You lied to me. You were out without permission, treating this condition like it's a leash. Not a disease you have to manage. A curse you keep in check or else some poor bastard dies!" I punched the counter. "How many times did you go out? How long did Max go hungry? Or were there more people? Like Madelyn? Did Max indulge himself, and you kept quiet?"

"No!" Jeb said. "No, we never let him go alone and we never-this never happened before!"

I glared at him. "So when he got hungry, did you tell me? Or did you tell him to sit on it? You dragged him out for more fun times, knowing he was starving. All the while he was getting more desperate, getting meaner?"

Jeb stammered but couldn't articulate a sentence. He folded his arms and shut his teeth.

"This is how it is," I said. "If you want to act like prisoners, I'll be the warden. I don't want to. I shouldn't have to. You're adults, for fuck's sake. You don't think it's fair, well it *isn't!* It's cold, it's cruel, and it will never be fair!"

The Gallows averted their gaze, but Madelyn's eyes had a sharper focus.

I met her gaze. "So you've got two choices. Same one I gave you last night. You decide to live, and you treat this terrible, rotten existence as serious as it deserves. Or I put a bullet in you. Because I would rather kill each of you than let you run free, and risk innocent people having their lives torn from them, too!"

"Because you're protecting them?" Madelyn asked. "Or yourself?"

"Myself," I snapped. "The Society will kill me if I let this shit get out of hand, because I made myself responsible for you. That's all the excuse they need now. I'm a lonely, miserable bastard, but I want my life, no matter how much it fucking sucks. You should, too."

She took a breath. "If someone gave you the choice, would you pick to be like me? Like them? Us?"

I leaned closer. "Only if I knew someone would end me if I went rotten. What about you?"

She had steel in her eyes. It told me everything before she spoke. "Deal."

My lip twitched in a grim smile. I eased the hammer on the revolver. "Good."

Nineteen

Madelyn stared at the flesh for a moment. It was frozen, but she was a wight. Humans already have greater jaw strength than we realize, but we have a mental limiter that protects us from injuring ourselves using it. Undeath had dampened that failsafe. She could chew through a two-by-four to get what she needed.

The first bite was hesitant, but she put on the pressure until it broke off in her mouth. She winced as she chewed, eyes shut tight. It sounded like she was munching on wet gravel. She finished the entire thing in minutes, wiped her lips, and looked like she wanted to puke it all over the counter.

"How do you feel?" I asked.

"Gross. Worse than-" She started to dry-heave.

I opened the fridge. There was a fresh pack of beer there. I cracked open a can, and she guzzled it.

"Okay?"

She wiped her lips and nodded.

"Okay. Everyone, come meet Madelyn."

The wights approached. Donnie retreated to his room, and Ximena also withdrew. Miguel watched her go before he fixed me with an angry stare. I gave him an apologetic shrug, but he turned to follow his sister.

"Hey, Maddie. I'm... so sorry," Jeb said.

"We both are," Frankie added. "We never- we didn't want this to happen to you. Or anyone."

Madelyn frowned at them. "You should have told me. Or stayed away from me."

"Yeah," Jeb said.

"Did Alex make you, too?" Madelyn asked.

Jeb met my gaze. "No, no. Donnie met this girl, said she was big into the occult, a real pagan. Had this book full of rituals involving getting wasted on absinthe and group sex during a full moon..." He scratched his head, embarrassed.

Frankie piped in. "We woke up in the morgue. The park ranger figured we'd OD'ed on something. When we returned to the campsite, she was long gone. We spent weeks trying to figure out what happened to us. Jeb finally figured it out."

"I was in medical school," Jeb said. "There were cadavers..."

Frankie nodded. "Norton is the one who found and brought us here."

Norton puffed out his chest a bit. "We have police and EMT scanners thanks to Ichiro, and I keep an ear out for crimes that relate to our condition. Stolen bodies, grave-robbing, bite attacks-" He grimaced, and gave Jeb and Frankie a dark look. "When they tried to steal a cadaver from the school, I heard about it, and went to find them. Alex found this place a few months later."

Frankie sighed. "Worst hangover ever."

Madelyn was quiet so long I thought she had stopped talking to them. "It's like having a boot so far up your ass it's kicking your brain."

"Yeah, a little." He offered a shy smile. "But it doesn't ache all the time, you know?"

"Get something solid for your dirt," Jeb told her. "Something you can seal tight. Alex got us urns. Keep it under your bed. You'll never have a bad night's sleep in your own grave."

"What about the rest of you?" Madelyn asked. "Were you all cursed by something or someone?"

"My husband brought a trinket back from the Korean War," Deb said. "It made us both sick but… I was the only one who came back."

"Refused to pay the toll at the River of Three Crossings," Ichiro said. He dangled the string of Japanese coins that hung from his wrist. He glared at the open air beside him. "Yeah, I'm telling her. She's dead, too."

"An associate sent me a strange doll from South America," Henry said. "I put it off as a cheap souvenir until I woke up the next morning without a heartbeat."

"Don't know what brought me back," Bill wheezed. "Lung cancer did me in, though."

"As you can tell from his heavenly singing voice," Frankie piped in. Jeb gave him a smack on the arm.

"I had an unfortunate run in with a gang in Jersey," Norton said. "I believe one of their number may have been a necromancer, like Alex."

"Cheated some Libyans out of their plutonium," Roger said with a smirk.

I retreated to the far end of the bar and left the wights to talk awhile. It was cheesy, like an alcoholic's support meeting, but maybe seeing them as people meant Madelyn wouldn't see herself as a monster.

While she talked, Jeb approached me, dropped his voice to a murmur. "She can't stay here."

"First Bill, now you? Why not?"

"Donnie has been out of it since what happened."

I leaned against the freezer. "And-?"

"And he—*we*—need time to process," Jeb said. "Whether or not it was necessary, you can't expect us to let go, just like that. Especially Donnie. He and Max were close."

"You think he's gonna blame Madelyn?"

"He could think that if he hadn't brought her to you, if he'd let her die, or if he'd taken her to the hospital… Max would still be here."

I closed my eyes. "Jeb, if he's going to think that way, if he's only seeing this in terms of what he can get away with-"

"He's not. But he lost his *best friend*, Alex. They knew each other from diapers. Max was there when Donnie lost his dad. I know you don't expect him to just shut those feelings off. He needs time to grieve. Please."

I mulled it over a bit. What little patience I had for Donnie had been lost. It was hard enough to deal with him when I was in a good mood. He was a brash alpha-bro douchebag that, in high school, was a bane to socially awkward loners like me. He wanted to be out partying, drinking hard, getting laid and showing off how invulnerable he was. The petty glories of the typical college jock.

It wasn't Madelyn that deserved to have a gun in her face. Donnie needed to understand that he wasn't some boy-prince anymore. He was just another dreg, like the rest of us, and he could either get with the program or start chewing lead.

But I saw the concern in Jeb's eyes. Undeath had torn apart their lives, forced them into an existence that no one should have to experience. All they had was each other. They'd tried to protect one of their own, and failed.

To me, Max was a petulant kid who went rotten. But to Donnie, Jeb and Frankie? He was a brother, someone who had gotten sick and wasn't himself. Like someone with dementia, or Alzheimer's, or a drug addiction. You watch their personality change, and you want to help them, you try to, but they can't or won't help themselves. And then they're gone.

I pinched the bridge of my nose. "Fine. For a few weeks. In the meantime, I expect you to keep everyone here. Donnie can piss and whine all he wants, but I'm zero tolerance on the dickish behavior."

"Thank you." Jeb thumped Frankie on the shoulder, and two departed.

I didn't give Jeb enough credit. The kid had a solid head on his shoulders, and he had to tolerate bullshit from both me and Donnie.

The rest of the wights withdrew after that, returning to their routines. Only Deb remained, speaking in hushed tones to Madelyn in a way I hoped was reassuring. The oldest wight, passing some advice onto the newborn. I felt a stab of guilt, but I kept my distance.

When Deb departed, she flashed a glare my way, a reminder that she and I would be having a talk about my actions later. I wasn't looking forward to it, but at least she was smart enough not to swing her own authority around, like a cudgel, as I had.

When only Madelyn and I remained, she approached, looking pensive. "So. Home sweet home, huh? It's not the worst place I've slept."

"In a few weeks. But this place doesn't have spare beds. We'll need to grab a few things so you can at least be comfortable."

She nodded. "If it's okay with you, I don't want to go home again. Not yet."

"You can stay at my place for now. Assuming I'm not arrested."

"Arrested?" She asked. "Ah."

"Or explode," I reminded her.

"Or that." She offered a weak smile. "I guess I'm not the only one with a gun to my head."

I sighed. "Who doesn't?"

☠

The ride home was quiet. Madelyn watched the icy rain sloshing over the windows, but the thousand-yard stare had faded. As weary as she was from life's hard turns, seeing that little ember of inner-strength was reassuring. She didn't seem so frail or nervous.

As we pulled up in my driveway, I wondered about the etiquette of summoning a Loa. I had what I needed for an attempt, but not the where or when. Outdoors at night? I couldn't leave the city with the hex on me. Riverside Park? Not worth the risk. The summoning looked to be a noisy affair, and it would draw attention, even at night, in the pouring rain.

We entered through the back door, and I flicked on the kitchen light. "You can stay in my room."

"The bed I bled out in. Kinky."

"I, uh-"

Madelyn smirked. "I've crashed on worse couches. But don't get any ideas, or I might get peckish."

I rolled my eyes. "You want some coffee?"

"Coffee would be nice. I wanted to ask if it's okay for me to drink beer?"

"Well, inebriation and lowered inhibitions aside, you can eat any regular food you want. It won't satisfy your hunger, but it's something."

"No, I meant, I'm still not old enough to drink," she said. "Shit, I'm gonna be getting ID'd for the rest of my life, aren't I?"

"It didn't *look* like your first drink."

A guilty smile crept over her. "What about these?" She lifted her arms, showing the Stig-marks on her wrists.

"I'm not sure. Stuff injected into your bloodstream doesn't work, because your circulatory system doesn't function anymore. But Stig is also magic, so if you feel any weird compulsions, let me know."

"Like wanting to eat people?" She winced. "Sorry. Bad joke. It's been awhile since I took a hit. I keep waiting to crash."

"Count your blessings." I went to make her some coffee.

Madelyn sat on my couch. "So… I don't have a pulse. I don't need to breathe. What do I have?"

"Your digestive system still works. And it's a good idea to eat and drink regularly."

"Why?"

"Your body doesn't need food energy, but it'll still lose or gain mass. And if you don't keep moving things through your stomach, corpse gasses can build up. It's uncomfortable, for all concerned."

"Great," Madelyn said. "Will I sweat?"

"Yes, and spit, and cry. Dehydration won't kill you, but keep drinking fluids to avoid turning into a mummy."

She chewed her lip. "Can we, I mean, can wights still have, y'know-?"

"You can still have sex. But you won't be having any more periods." I puzzled over the idea. "I don't know how male wights get a hard-on without a heartbeat, but they do. Muscle action, I guess. But none of them have functioning swimmers. We can go to a doctor, see if you still have viable eggs. Could be a good idea to freeze some, if you still want kids, but you'll have to find a surrogate..."

I snorted when I saw the way she was looking at me. "Sorry. I'm not pushing the idea. Professional curiosity. Just want you to know that you have options."

"Hm. How do I regulate body temperature?"

"You don't. Near as I can tell, you can't freeze, either. Did you meet Ichiro?"

"The one who kept talking to air?"

"Yeah. His Yakuza buddies dropped him in the river. Spent most of the winter there, unable to move. Luckily, the spot counted as his grave."

Madelyn smirked. "Is that why he talks to himself? Poor guy." I handed her a cup of coffee and she sipped it with her eyes closed. "Shit. That's good."

"So, you want to tell me what happened at home, or do you want me to demonstrate my keen powers of deduction?"

"Go ahead, Holmes. Wow me."

I sank into my seat. "So you haven't been home in a while. You were in college, but I'm guessing you haven't been there in a while, either. You like music. Not the safe stuff. You went hardcore. Underground. Bands I'll never hear of, playing music no record company would sign. Wasn't long before someone put a needle in your hand, and you were willing to go deeper."

She stared at her reflection in the coffee.

"My guess is that's how you met Max, before all this. Someone who shared your love of music. But he didn't go down the rabbit hole you did. Max didn't have any kind of drug problem before he died, so I'm guessing you pulled away from him before he vanished. And it didn't matter anymore, because the drugs were doing the thinking for you. Then he reappears. He wants to see you, you think he's trying to drag you away from the life you were hooked on. You don't realize he's got his own addiction now. You fight. And you have the worst night of your life."

"Last night of my life," Madelyn said. "You're not bad at that, but you're a bit of an asshole about it."

"Yeah. You want to take over for me?"

Madelyn stared at her coffee. "Weed first, then Ecstasy, then Stig. It was all experimental, but Stig blacks you out, and I wanted to be blacked out. I told mom I was still going to school so she would keep sending me checks, but I... hated everything. Me. Max. Lying. Eliza- I-" She shook her head and wiped her eyes. "My *life*. I don't know why. The things I liked hurt me. I couldn't deal with it. I wanted to stop feeling anything."

Eliza? I filed the name away for later.

Madelyn shuffled in her seat to face me. "And then all of *this* happens. It's like, even when I'm dead, I'm not free of it. I wanted to be anywhere but here, so I went home. I forgot how much time had passed since I'd talked to them. I wasn't at school. They thought I was *dead*." She snorted. "I expected mom to yell and scream and threaten me. But she cried. And I cried. I had to tell her my mascara was running."

I imagined the scenario and smiled.

Madelyn pulled her knees to her chest. "I didn't care about anything at that moment. I was home, you know? My mind was clear again after so long. I thought it was a second chance. That everything had been a bad dream. I could tell mom I was a user. Go to a clinic, get clean, walk away from the bad shit in my life."

Her face darkened. "My sister Katie is thirteen. She was angry, because I never- I promised I'd write to her every week, and I didn't. Do you have any idea what it's like to be giving your sister a hug and then, suddenly all you can think about is *biting?* It would be so... so soft..."

Madelyn gagged and was on her feet in a flash, spilling coffee across the table. She made it to my kitchen and vomited into the sink. After retching a few times, she sank to the floor and hugged her arms.

I washed the vomit down my garbage disposal and let it run for a minute.

"Do I have to eat m-more?" She asked.

The pain in her eyes made me want to hug her, but I couldn't bring myself to. I had been ready to kill her an hour ago. Instead, I sat beside her on the floor.

"It's not the meat you need," I explained. "From what I've read, you either absorb lingering life-force from the flesh, or the act itself is purely symbolic, a ritual to keep the magic working. Digestion isn't necessary."

185

She shuddered. "Isn't there any way to do this without eating?"

I wanted to do something, *anything,* so she wouldn't have to suffer like she did. But I'd done everything in my power. It wasn't enough, it never would be, but her life wouldn't be any easier if I treated her like a broken bird with a clipped wing.

"If there were, I wouldn't make you do it," I said. "So after you got hungry, you ran?"

She nodded. "Found my way back here. Shit, I should call them. I should let them know I'm okay."

"What will you tell them?" I asked.

She wiped her face and rested her chin on her knees. "I don't know. I feel like I should tell them… I mean, all this magic shit? How come no one's ever heard of it before?"

"Chances are you have," I said. "On TV or the internet. But you never question it, because you know there's no such thing, right? It has to be special effects. Computer editing. Hell, a lot of the fake stuff out there looks *better* than the real thing. And I recently learned the Illuminati is real, sort of, and keeping magic a secret for centuries."

Madelyn thought it over. "And anyone who knows is probably happy to be in on the secret, huh?"

I smirked. "Even before I met the Society, I was careful about hiding my talent. I knew it would scare people, and it did feel kind of good to know something they didn't. To have a deeper understanding of things."

"Sounds like a wizard to me." Madelyn laughed.

I did, too. We sat together for a while, the idiot necromancer and his unwitting creation, trying to come to terms with the events that had brought us together.

"You said you wanted to summon a Loa?" Madelyn asked.

"That's right. It isn't my first choice, but I need a fresh lead and I don't have a lot of options. What about you? I don't suppose you know anything about Stig that would crack this case open?"

Madelyn frowned. "Sorry, you kept me alive for nothing."

"I didn't mean it like that."

"Yeah, you did. You operate on an 'Alex first' mindset, you know that?"

"I like to think I'm pragmatic," I said. "With a healthy case of self-preservation considering the world I live in."

"Was it pragmatic to let Max run free?" She asked.

I winced. "You got me there. I'm sorry, Madelyn. You're right. I've got all this shit on me right now, and I'm not giving you the time you need to deal with yours. I wish I could."

"I don't mean to be a bitch," she said.

"It's fine. I deserve it."

We both chuckled again.

"Well, we both have one thing in common," she said. "Self-depreciation."

"In spades," I agreed. "You don't have to like me, Madelyn. You can hate me. But don't ignore what I tell you. And if we get through this, if we find some moment of calm, I'll do everything I can to help you deal with this."

She offered a weak smile. "You can call me Maddie. Everyone else does."

"Sure, but I'm not everyone else," I said. "I like Madelyn."

Her smile grew. We sat for another moment.

"So, anything you *can* tell me?" I asked.

She huffed out a laugh. "I was on Stig for about three months. The pushers show up to all the raves, and a few underground concerts. They have other drugs too, but the Stig is so cheap it's like they want to get rid of it."

"Yeah, they're not after money. Who's your dealer?"

"His name's Tyler. I don't know where he operates or anything like that. Whenever there's a rave or a concert, the kind that the cops don't know about, he's usually there. Him and a few others."

"Anything distinct about them, appearance-wise?"

Madelyn shook her head. "He's kind of short, black, shaved head. Acts like a player, but he's a dick. Likes to feel up girls. Made me cringe."

I remembered Mr. Handy from the Arlington. "Small world. When's the last time you saw him?"

"Dunno. A week? He wasn't at the concert when this happened." She touched her neck.

"No, he was elsewhere. What about his buddies?"

"Big guys. But quiet. They weren't so bad. For drug dealers, anyway."

"Haitian?" I asked.

"Uh, they were black. Is it racist if I say I don't know?"

I shrugged. "Until they hear me say 'about' most people don't know I'm from Canada."

"*Aboot?*" She grinned. "Oh my God, you're Canadian?"

"I don't hear 'boot'," I said. "I say 'about' like everyone else."

Madelyn laughed. "I hear it. *Aboot.* And you said *'eh'* earlier! I heard it!"

"Uh-huh," I grunted. "Do you know where these guys will show up next?"

She thought it over. "You got a computer around here?"

I led her to the PC in my room.

"Shit, this thing looks more expensive than your house *and* your van."

"I like video games."

"Nerd." She rolled her eyes and started logging herself onto social media sites and chat rooms. Not the usual hangouts grandmas post pictures of their cats.

"This crap won't dump viruses and spyware on my PC, will it?"

"You only get that from super-weird porn sites," she said. "If I look up your browser history, what'll I find?"

"What are you, a cop? Plus-sized gingers with big booties. Focus on your dark web nonsense."

She snorted. "This is gonna take a while. You don't walk into these chatrooms and ask where the next illegal venue is going to be, you know? Maybe go make me some more coffee?"

I gave her a cockeyed stare, then left her to do her thing. "I'm serious, don't go looking at my porn."

"Perv."

"You were gonna look."

"No doot aboot it." She giggled.

I let her. Tender egos about my proud Northern heritage aside, she'd had a rough couple of days. No reason to sour a rare moment of levity. I cleaned the spilled coffee and made her another cup. She hugged it close, with her knees pulled up to her chest.

It wasn't right that I had trapped her in my shitty world. I was glad she had something to distract her, because the weeks and months to come would be hard. How would she handle it, I wondered, when she already had an addictive personality? Would she seek relief from her hunger the way she had sought escape in drugs? What would she be willing to do to get it, if I wasn't around to provide?

I turned my mind back to my summoning project. I wondered if it was possible to find some place in the city that had a connection to the Loa, one untainted by the Brothers Midnight. It might make the ritual less offensive.

Summoning is always a tricky business. Imagine a cockroach putting a bullhorn to your ear and demanding your attention. The Loa were old entities, regardless of their origins as Ascended mages, and worshiped in some form or another back to ancient Africa. They couldn't manifest on Earth without help, but the ritual would create a link between them and myself. They'd be well within their means to punish me if they decided I was being discourteous.

Then again, if you sit here on your hands doing nothing, you'll still die, I thought. *Better to apologize later than ask permission now. At least you'll have died doing something about it.*

"Give me a hand here, kid," I said to Madelyn. "We're gonna perform some authentic necromancy."

TWENTY

I gathered the ritual materials I needed and carried them into my basement. Madelyn kept her distance, but craned her neck to watch from the kitchen.

"You're gonna do it now?" She asked.

"You bet. No time like the present. There's a sound file on my desktop. Turn it on and turn the volume up. It'll play on repeat."

She did as instructed. A blaring mix of drums and wordless chants came from the speakers. "What is this?"

"It's called banda. Vodou practitioners use it as part of their rituals."

She followed me into my basement, and her eyes lingered on the mortuary slab. "Um, I don't want to say this is a red flag, but..."

"I don't carve cadavers in the Gallows."

She grimaced. "Um-"

"Relax, I keep it spotless. And we're not dismembering anything today."

"Okay, but if you do anything like that, tell me first? So I don't have to be here for it." She looked like she could vomit again.

"I promise. That's why I work here. You guys have it hard enough without having to see that part."

She nodded and closed her eyes. "Okay. What do you need me to do?"

I showed her a printout. "This is a veve. It's a religious symbol that identifies one of the Loa. This one belongs to Baron Samedi. Heard of him?"

"From a few movies, sure." Curiosity won over, and she approached the slab.

"Yeah, he's among the most well-known in pop-culture. He's the Loa of gravediggers, like me. And he hates necromancers. Also like me."

"Oh. Good." She hugged her arms.

"Yeah. But we're hunting another necromancer, one who's worse than me, and I'm hoping Samedi will hear me out." I produced the other items for the ritual. "Some witches I hung out with on the road once called forth Sarah the Black for guidance and knowledge. I didn't get to watch the event, but they explained the basics of the process to me."

"Witches, like, Satanism?" Madelyn asked.

"No," I said. "*Saint* Sarah is Romani. Point is, most of the old gods and pagan spirits were just mages like me, who got real strong and Ascended into the Layered."

"Which is?"

I thought it over. "The Layered is… eh, think of it like an onion made up of different dimensions. There are dozens of sub-realities that overlap our own, flowing through and around ours, shaping and shaped by our very minds. Space and time are arguably infinite, but they're part of the *triangle*. The Layered is the third infinite: Thought, or Soul. Whichever you prefer."

Madelyn made a face. "I don't get it."

"Technically, you can't. Ordinary humans aren't able to perceive the Layered. For magic, intention and symbolism are what's important. It's about the willpower of the mage and the potency of his magic that makes spells work, not an understanding of formulas and principles. Belief, for lack of a better word. Mages just have souls strong enough to make those beliefs real."

Madelyn looked over the ritual implements. "So what is all this, then?"

"To call Samedi, we need a beacon. Each of these items is something that symbolizes him. By attuning my magic to them, I can get his attention. The veve is important. It's his magemark, like this-" I drew my simple anchor mark in the air, and Madelyn's eyes lit up.

"Wow."

I smirked. "The chicken blood is because chickens are important to the Guede, the Baron's extended family of Loa who represent fertility and death."

"A family of Loa?"

I nodded. "Each family represents basic aspects like fire and water, life, death, dreams and such. The Guede—as far as I can tell—are all associated with death in some way. Baron Samedi is the head of the family. He has brothers, like Nibo and Kriminel, and a wife named Brigitte. The Guede don't fear death, and so live pretty audacious, hedonistic lives. That's what these are for."

I set items on the slab, one by one. "Spicy rum, cigars, apples. When Samedi arrives he's gonna want a drink and a smoke, to savor the taste of these things, and he won't answer my questions until he's appeased."

"Okay," Madelyn said. "So what do I do?"

"That's the tricky part," I said. "The Ascended are spirits. They don't show up in a body of their own. He'll need a mount."

Madelyn's eyes widened, but I held up a hand.

"Not you," I said. "Samedi doesn't like possessing women, or so I read. It'll be me."

"You? This doesn't sound-"

"Safe? No. But it's my best chance for answers. Anyway, I'm going to be unconscious. Or distracted. He's gonna jump in my body, ride it around a bit, smoke cigars, drink rum, and eat the apples. Samedi is a wild sort, but he's not a bad guy. He's not gonna run off and kill people or attack you... even if you are undead, and he hates that."

Madelyn grimaced. "You're not selling me on this, Alex."

"I know. Keep your distance, let him do his thing, and then he'll address you, ask for more rum or cigars. Tell him I can get them for him, so long as he answers me a simple question. Just one."

"Which is?"

"Where can I find Samuel Kincaid?"

"Where can Alex find Samuel Kincaid," Madelyn repeated. "What if he asks 'why'?"

"He'll know why," I said. "Tell him Alex will pay his price once he has the answer."

Madelyn nodded. "Okay. I think I'm ready."

"Good, because I need a minute," I said.

I didn't fancy the idea of a god-like spirit using my body like a puppet. My research said Baron Samedi was friendly, a guide and protector of souls. But necromancers denied the dead their rest. Everything I'd learned about him suggested he'd find me despicable.

But Kincaid, Jesse and the Brothers were doing worse, they were making zombies, *enslaving souls*, which was something Samedi hated more than graverobbers like me. I had to hope Kincaid was higher on his shit list.

I put my fears from my mind, made room on my slab and opened the tub of chicken blood. It smelled thick and coppery in my nostrils, but not as strong as human blood. I breathed in and let it fill my senses. It was thick and slippery on my finger. Using the printed image as a guide, I drew Samedi's veve on the slab in blood.

The music upstairs thrummed in my ears. I opened the spicy rum and swirled some in my mouth, letting the heat sear my tongue. It wasn't as strong as Papa Williams' brew, but it made me wince. I lit a cigar, puffed it into my lungs and blew a thick plume into the air. I set the lit cigar aside and bit into an apple. It was sour, crunchy, and left a dry feeling in my throat.

I gathered each of these sensations into my mind, then cast my magic in no particular direction, with no particular spell in mind. Magic is attuned to the Layered. Or it's a part *of* the Layered. Every time I cast a spell, I sent a little ripple of it echoing through the expanse, and somewhere in that tangled mess of sub-realities were beings that felt those ripples like a breeze. That rarely warranted notice, but I had laced my magic with the symbols I had gathered. The idea was to catch Samedi's attention the way the smell of fresh bread or coffee draws the hungry or tired. A very human reaction, even for Immortals.

It was an invitation, with everything Samedi coveted on the menu. I hoped he'd be polite to Madelyn. She didn't sign on for any more trouble than-

The pressure in the air changed. One minute I was alone in a makeshift butcher shop with a newborn wight. The next, I felt watched. It was more intense than at the Library. I took a breath to relax myself.

You're opening your body up to an outside force, I reminded myself. *Being paranoid is warranted.*

I didn't know what was in the Layered, what entities might have been waiting for someone like me to open a doorway into my world. I fought my fear down and tried to concentrate on the music, the smoke, the taste of spiced rum.

Something *big* brushed against my consciousness, like a whale shark swimming past a minnow. It made me dizzy just

to feel it, but then it turned its head and noticed me *back*. It rushed at me, taking in my spiritual view, my whole world, eclipsing my very soul as it *reached out-*

I yanked myself away from the table and fell on my ass.

"A-Alex?" Madelyn asked nearby.

I answered with a string of pained profanities through clenched teeth.

"Samedi?" Her voice was timid.

I sighed, breathing in and out until the pain subsided. "Damnit. Sorry, kid. It's me. What happened?"

"Nothing." She hovered near the ladder. "You were standing over the table, and then you fell over."

I got to my feet and looked at my shrine. It hadn't changed. The cigar was still smoldering. It couldn't have been burning for more than a minute. Did Samedi make me blink first? Or had I attracted something else to my beacon? Maybe I just freaked out over nothing.

"It didn't work?" Madelyn asked.

"I don't think so," I said. "I think I did something wrong. Samedi isn't answering."

"Are you going to try again?"

"No. Not tonight." I gathered the ritual materials, fast-decayed the bloody veve mark, and followed Madelyn upstairs. She jumped back on my computer, but with nothing better to do, I laid down on the couch to brood.

Someone knocked on my door a few minutes later. I answered it, and found Jocelyn in the doorway, dressed in black pants and a padded jacket, with an umbrella to protect her thick brunette curls.

"Alex."

"Oh. Come to walk amongst the common folk?" I asked.

She accepted the barb with a nod. "Sorry I didn't call but, um, can we talk? I brought these."

She offered me the clothes she'd borrowed. I tossed them onto the couch.

"Sure. What about?"

Madelyn poked her head out of my room. "Who's here?"

"Who's that?" They asked at the same time.

"This is Madelyn," I said. "She's a friend."

Jocelyn looked her over. "Really? What kind of 'friend'?"

"Gross." Madelyn wrinkled her nose and retreated out of sight.

"She's helping me do some research," I said.

"Ah-huh," Jocelyn said. "Could we talk somewhere more private? Over dinner?"

I wanted to laugh. Everything was turning to shit around me, and Jocelyn wanted to go have *dinner*.

She tilted her head. "Alex?"

I folded my arms. "I don't know. Last time we went out, it ended with your goon showing me the door."

"That's part of what I wanted to talk about. Put on a nice shirt, and we'll talk."

I didn't want to. What I *wanted* was to close the door and get back to that important work of saving my ass from the fire. But Jocelyn reached out and put her hand on my chest, then traced it down my arm to curl our fingers together. After a week of cold, pain, and feeling lost, it was like a little shiver of electricity. Warm, tingling.

"Please?" She asked.

"Okay. One sec." I went into my bedroom.

"Hey," Madelyn said. "Where are you going?"

"Out. Keep at it. If something comes up, call me." I pocketed the burner phone and scribbled the number on a notepad. "Otherwise stay put, eh?"

"But-"

"Coming, Alex?" Jocelyn asked.

I put on my denim jacket. "Later, kid."

197

"Hey wait-"

I joined Jocelyn, and we walked to her car. Madelyn watched us go, then shook her head and shut the door.

"She's a little clingy," Jocelyn said as we climbed into her car.

"She'll be fine. Where are we going?"

"Someplace fancy. My treat."

☠

I endured another white-knuckle ride in Jocelyn's car, made worse by the sheer amount of rain that hit the windshield. But we arrived in Uptown none the worse for wear. I thought her goal was one of the fancy nightclubs, but she pulled into the parking lot of a quiet, featureless brown rectangle of a building. The place almost dared me to find something noteworthy about it.

And yet, a *valet* waited for us outside. The falling slush hit an invisible barrier over his head and flowed away from his body.

I chuckled. "A Society club?"

"Aubergine's." Her eyes fluttered in a smile. "My favorite place on the continent. I thought you'd like a taste of the high life. Just to try it."

The valet took her hand and guided her to the awning above the entrance. "Welcome back, ma'am."

"Thank you, Patrick." She dropped her keys in his hand. "Is Yolinda here?"

"Not tonight, ma'am."

"Good."

Patrick didn't look like he wanted to hold my hand, so I got myself out of the car. He sank into the driver's seat and showed far more consideration for the speed limit than Jocelyn as he drove away.

I gave Aubergine's a closer look. My eyes passed over beige spackle siding and tinted windows, but there was more. My mind tried to dismiss what I saw, and every time I made out a detail, it seemed to melt out of my awareness.

"A ward," I said.

"A deterrent field for the Untold," Jocelyn said. "Think about eggplants while you look."

I gave her a funny look, but did as she said, imagining a fat purple vegetable, and all at once the details blossomed into crystal clarity.

Aubergine's was *beautiful*. The walls looked to be polished glass that shimmered like moving water. Bioluminescent plants in hues of blue and violet hung from floating pots. It was like a garden made of starlight. Ordinary humans would walk by the building every day and not realize—or care—what was inside.

I whistled. "This place is above my pay grade."

"Yes, and no. But there is a dress code."

Jocelyn handed me her umbrella and jacket. I caught her honey-heather perfume again, and felt her warmth like a sunny breeze.

She produced a slender gold bracelet from her purse. When it locked around her wrist, her clothing blurred and stretched into a form-fitting, forest green dress. Hundreds of tiny emeralds sparkled in the fabric. Larger gems woven into gold earrings sprang from her lobes, and her lips turned a glossy shade of scarlet. Even her hair took on a more lustrous sheen, the kind women paid hundreds of dollars to imitate.

Aubergine's was a distant afterthought, compared to Jocelyn.

"What do you think?" She asked.

My jaw worked, but my brain needed a moment. "I, um… sorry, what?"

Her cheeks tinted as she smiled. "That's the reaction I was hoping for. And for my next trick..."

She took my hand, and I let her strap a polished silver watch to my wrist. My clothes turned into some kind of viscous liquid, like wet sand, then wove themselves anew. Faded cotton denim became a soft wool Italian suit, midnight blue in color. It fit so well that I could have break-danced in it. The smell of my life—soil and sweat, with vague hints of blood—became a mild, musky cologne. Even my bedhead took on a permed feel.

"Huh," I said. "Didn't think you had my size. Joce?"

Her eyes drifted down my body and lingered in places. "You clean up nice. But the cologne isn't you."

She twisted the watch's crown, and my clothes gave off an assortment of different smells all at once before it settled onto an earthy aftershave.

"Better," she said. Her fingers brushed over mine. "Don't you think?"

"I, ah, didn't get *you* anything."

"It's a rental. Borrowed, actually. I'll need it back when we're done."

I paused. "Whenever you want me out of these clothes, just say the word."

The ruby smile took in her ears, and she curled her arm around mine. "Behave yourself. This place is a bit posh."

TWENTY-ONE

We strode through the entrance, and I felt like the most important person in the world. The interior of Aubergine's was spacious, like a hybrid greenhouse and nightclub. A gentle humidity hung in the air that smelled like a fresh jungle grotto, or an island lagoon. The crystal clear water at my feet lapped against the edges of my transmogrified black oxfords.

Walking on water. That's not arrogant at all.

The atmosphere was comfortable, yet I couldn't shake the elitist vibe. Everyone was a mage, even the wait staff. I assumed they were the Society's 'minimum-wage' earners, men and women barely out of their teens, who worked the super-rich equivalent of a summer fry-cook job.

The diners took notice of our entrance. Some of them smiled at Jocelyn, others regarded me with curiosity or mild discomfort. The maitre d', a tall woman in a black pantsuit, approached us with a smile.

"Madam, so good to see you again," she said to Jocelyn. Her accent was a smooth, lyrical French. "Your table is waiting for you upstairs."

"Thank you, Rebecca."

She turned to regard me. "And someone new this evening?"

"My plus one," Jocelyn said. "Alex Fossor."

Rebecca's smile took on a plastic quality. She knew the name. "Of course. Your signature."

She held out a digital notepad, but not a pen or stylus. I remembered my embarrassment at the Gallery and put some extra effort into my magemark. The anchor glimmered for a few moments.

"Very good," Rebecca said. "This way."

Rebecca led us up stairs made of a gentle, gravity-defying waterfall. The VIP lounge had a more intimate atmosphere, with fewer tables and plenty of room for each. A bar stood to one side, with rows of unmarked bottles. The other three walls muted the garish lights of the city beyond into something like candlelight.

Rebecca led us to a table near the window overlooking the parking lot. I remembered enough of my chivalry to set the chair for Jocelyn, and she sat with a smile.

"Tonight we have a few overseas favorites," Rebecca said, and read off the wine selection in French.

Jocelyn gave me an expectant look.

"This is all a new experience for me," I said.

"I think Mr. Fossor would appreciate something simple," Jocelyn said. "The acerglyn. And could you open that bottle of Barossa Valley Shiraz?"

The two exchanged a few more lines in French, then Rebecca placed our order at the bar and returned downstairs. The bartender, a tall, slender man with a neatly cut mustache, delivered a thin-stemmed wine glass for Jocelyn and a thicker, almost goblet-like cup for me. He returned to the bar in the blink of an eye. It wasn't teleportation, but he moved faster than any human I'd ever seen, and in perfect silence.

"Relax, Alex," Jocelyn said. "You look cornered."

I exhaled and tried the mead. Maple and orange lingered on my tongue. "I'm not used to glitz. Or open displays of magic.

The hedge witches I rolled with were discreet about it, even away from the Untold."

"Sounds like they were afraid of being noticed," Jocelyn suggested. "But I suppose the hedge clans are fugitives, aren't they?"

"They believed that just because you can use magic, doesn't mean you should. But this place? You're walking on water, eating by the light of glowing flowers. It feels boastful."

Jocelyn smiled. "I wasn't used to it either, once upon a time. Sometimes I miss an old-fashioned English pub. I just haven't found one in the States that doesn't have a ball pit or something."

I chuckled. "I can't imagine you tossing back a pint or two."

"You talk like I haven't," Jocelyn said. She breathed her wine's aroma the way gourmets and supervillains do. "I grew up in pubs."

"Where the legal drinking age is twenty-one?"

"Eighteen in England, love." She emptied her glass with unladylike ease, then stretched her limbs within the confines of her dress. "You'd think raising a kid can't be as bad as people say. Especially if you're Versed. But now that I don't hear him making noise, or getting into the cupboards? Feels I can fall asleep here and now."

"So how'd you grow up in pubs *before* you were eighteen?"

Her silver eyes turned distant. "Jesse and I had foster parents, but it wasn't a home. Most days we had to be out of the house so Mary could watch telly in peace, and God help you if you disturbed Rueben's nap. But the Hearth and Doe? Mr. McAllister always had a door open for us. We sat at a back table, did our homework..."

"Sounds like a Victorian musical."

"Oh, shut it." She smiled. "What about you?"

"Very much the same," I admitted. "It was just my mom and me. She worked in this railcar diner, twelve to fourteen hours a day. I'd come from school and wait in a booth. Sometimes it felt like we had no one else. At least until I turned fifteen. Then she found a new family."

"What do you mean?"

"She got married. I never considered her husband to be part of my life, even though he arrested me a few times." I chuckled. "I left home after high school. She was expecting her third kid by then. Had the family she always wanted…"

I lifted my glass. "To somber childhoods."

"Somber memories." Jocelyn's silver eyes softened, but she clinked glasses with me.

A server arrived with two plates of fat-marbled wagyu beef, with a pinch of unfamiliar steamed greens and griddled root vegetables. The portions were smaller than the palm of my hand, but I was sure the meal had a hefty price tag.

She stared at her plate for a moment. "I'm sorry, Alex. You got about six degrees colder for a moment there. I'm sorry if I dredged up a bad memory."

I took up my polished utensils. "Don't worry about it. For a necromancer, every date is a funeral."

Jocelyn smiled, but looked thoughtful. "Is that what this is like? A date?"

Something about her tone, like she was asking permission, made me pause. "I guess it is. C'mon, let's eat before the food feels awkward, too."

We did so in silence. The price tag for such extravagance would have cost me a week's worth of groceries, so I tried to savor my meal. But I decided wagyu wasn't for me. It was indeed rich and tender, but it felt strange to my tongue. The cow had lived a pampered, carefree life. Weird as it sounded, I couldn't relate to what I was eating.

Is this what the Rimbault Society is? I wondered. *A place for rich mages to pamper themselves? Of course it is. What are you even do-*

ing, Alex? With your fake suit and your death magic. You smell *poor. You* reek *of rotten. A bad seed trying to take root in their garden-*

"Don't like the mead?" Jocelyn asked.

"Hm? No, of course." I took another sip. "Just thinking."

The plates had vanished while I brooded. The bartender had refilled Jocelyn's glass.

"I never took you for someone to nurse his drinks," she said. "Somehow, I had you pegged for someone who keeps a fifth of scotch or whiskey in his glove box."

"Because I keep my balls in my purse?"

She laughed. "No. I dunno. Sometimes it's like I'm not seeing the real you."

"How's that?"

"I honestly don't know, Alex. I like to think I have most guys figured out the moment I see them. But you're a bit harder to get a read on."

I finished my drink. "I don't think I'm complicated."

"Which is a lie."

"Well, maybe," I said. "But I don't like *being* complicated."

"You're good at avoiding it. I kind of envy that."

"It's come back to haunt me. I thought the Visatori taught me how to handle myself, how to deal with things. Then this week happened."

"I had a simple life once too," Jocelyn said. "The Society was just a fancy club to rub elbows with money. Then I started climbing the ladder. These past few days? They'll turn into *years* if you aren't careful. You feel like you're drowning in it sometimes. And just when you manage to come up for air, something pushes you back under. You have to use every trick you know to keep ahead. Sometimes you have to make choices you don't like."

I thought about Max. "Yeah. That lesson is becoming very clear."

We looked at each other. I tried to see what was lurking past those silver pools of hers, but I only saw my reflection.

"Joce, let's clear the air a little, eh? I know you want Jesse. But what if he doesn't want to come home? He could be dangerous, not just to others, but to you. And Eddie."

She flinched. "You don't understand, Alex. I can't just hand him over to the Keepers. He'll get no more leniency than *you've* gotten. And that's not all of it. I'm… I'm on the verge of a formal sponsorship into the North American Council. Do you know what that means?"

"You?" I asked. "You're the thirteenth Councilor Walter was talking about?"

"He's my husband," she said. "He's Eddie's father."

"You're married to the *Archmage?* But you can't be much older than me. The Archmage… how old is he?"

She shook her head. "Fonourgy is as rare as Necrourgy. The last Councilor—my mentor, Robert Lacroix—was the only one in North America before I moved here. Walter took an interest in my career early on. It's a once in a lifetime opportunity, Alex, and I took it. Jesse didn't like that."

I swallowed. "Can't say I'm surprised. The Council treats us 'black mages' like problems waiting to happen. You'd be a judge, jury and executioner to people like him. Us."

"I can do more than that. I can help people. North America's Council has been stagnant for years, they never agree on anything that doesn't profit them. With me on the Council, Walter would have the political clout to make actual changes. No more deadlocks, no more policies that only benefit high-ranking members. It means a lifetime, a Versed's lifetime, of helping people like me who had to do things they hated to get by in life."

A bitter truth materialized in my mind. "I get it. You won't go expose Jesse, because of the scandal. You're protecting your career."

206

She scowled. "I'm protecting the life I have. If the Council finds proof that my brother is behind this, Walter's rivals will use it to toss my application. I may as well go back to being an escort, because no one will ever open that door for me again."

I leaned back. "So what am I supposed to do? Let him frame me for murder?"

"No! Help me catch him. He's *my* responsibility. If I can get him away from the Brothers, stop what he's doing... I don't know if he'll ever come around, but I can keep him from hurting people. When he's contained, far away from here, the Council will never have enough evidence on you, and I'll be there to vote in your favor."

"Assuming I don't die beforehand."

She took a breath. "I'm asking a lot, but we can do this if we're smart. Please say yes."

I frowned. I didn't like it. Not one bit. But if I could stop Jesse, save my neck, get rid of the Brothers Midnight, and have a friend on the Council?

"Yes," I said, but I felt like a fool. "Assuming we can even catch him."

"Thank you." She sighed, and some tension drained from the table.

Rain pattered against the windows. Aubergine's was quiet as a grave.

"What do you think of this place?" She asked.

"I think I'd have to sell a kidney to eat here again."

Jocelyn smiled. "You know, Necrourges have ways to make money. Lots of money. Legally."

"Like what?"

"By talking to the dead? If you got the right papers, you could work in some very lucrative fields. Forensics, law enforcement, medical studies. There are women who make millions pretending to be mediums in California, and they're not even Versed. Imagine what you could charge to speak to some-one's dead nan?"

"There it is," I said with a smirk. "The bottom dollar."

She shrugged. "It's something to think about."

"I have, and I don't need it. I don't like complications, re-member? I had a good thing going. Quiet. Comfortable. I want that kind of life, at least for another decade or two."

"Sounds dreadfully boring."

"Yeah," I said. "But boring necromancers don't get harassed by every self-righteous asshat looking for a cause to fight."

"You sound like Jesse, you know that? Jesse before, I mean. Before all this."

"Ask your husband. He's convinced I won't survive a cen-tury before I turn bad."

"Mm, he has experience. And you have a certain creepiness about you. Cold spots when you're in a mood. Like the air in early Spring. Damp."

"Clammy," I said. "You think I'm clammy."

She laughed out loud. "Not clammy! It's more like fog. Without a fog. Sometimes there's fog. Did you notice?"

"Sure," I said. "First 'aboot' and now 'clammy.' I'm batting a thousand tonight."

"I'm used to fog. I'm from London, aren't I?" A phone in her bag beeped. She checked it and frowned. "Walter is looking for me."

"Got you on a short leash, huh? Should I be worried? He put a bomb in my chest."

"No," Jocelyn said. "But he prefers I focus on raising Eddie."

I shook my head. "Is this all worth it, Joce? Marriage, a kid, hunting your own brother, all for a chance to sit in a big chair? Half of those Councilors didn't care if I was innocent, the other half wanted to see more evidence before they put me to the flame. I don't see you doing a lot of good with them."

"Some days I don't know," she admitted. "But I've come too far to give it up now. And all this fucked up shit, it's temporary. I can deal with it."

I scowled. "I guess raising some asshole's kid is more dignified than being a sugarbaby."

Jocelyn glared at me. "Alex. Do I offend your sensibilities? Like as a person? Because I can flutter my eyelashes and endure grabby hands?"

"No."

"So why do you get so mean about it?"

"I don't. Call it chivalry, or something. I dunno."

"More like misogyny."

"No," I said. "Let's go with envy."

"Bollocks."

"No. You lucked out," I said. "You've got looks, brains, and magic. The world folds over itself for people like you."

"It isn't that easy, Alex."

"It looks that way."

"Easy getting ogled? Objectified? Used like a breeding mare? Yeah, I'm pretty and I know it, I know how to work it to get what I want. Doesn't mean I don't feel sick when they only see tits and ass, when all they're thinking of is what they want to do to me, and don't pretend you haven't done it yourself! Acting like they *deserve* me. I can't connect to people like that!"

Jocelyn leaned back and rubbed her arms. "That's my 'clammy'. To see what people want so I can use them, but all I ever see is *me* being *used*. So I'll tolerate it as long as I have to. And then I won't have to ever again. Then, when I tell someone to go fuck themselves, they'll do it, and I won't have to use my magic."

She put her trembling hands on the table and bowed her head. I wanted to reach out to her, to hold her hand and tell her *I* wasn't out to use her.

But I'd be lying. I tried to be as decent as life allowed, but I was fooling myself if I said altruism was my motivator. I needed her to help me catch Jesse. To save my skin from Walter's flames. I was in no position to judge her.

But I saw her in that Cinderella dress, with her distant marriage, and I saw someone isolated. As different as we were, I still knew how she felt. Deep down, under all the ambition and sacrifice, we just wanted to stop feeling so goddamn *alone*.

I reached out to touch her hand, and she intertwined her fingers with mine.

"I'll help you get him."

We held on for a long time. Finally, she took a breath and stood. "I've got to go. Can I give you a ride home?"

I considered it, but my eyes caught movement outside. A crowd of at least twenty people approached Aubergine's through the parking lot. They walked shoulder-to-shoulder, like a firing line.

"Alex?" Jocelyn asked.

I opened my mouth. "What is-"

Something hit the window and exploded. The blast threw me backward in a shower of glass. For a moment, all I heard was the ringing in my ear. Then came the gunshots.

And screams.

TWENTY-TWO

I rolled onto my stomach and crawled over glass towards Jocelyn. I found her curled into a ball near our table, holding her ears. Blood stained her face from a cut above her eyebrow. I had a flash of Madelyn bleeding out on my bed.

No, no, she's not dying. Stop freaking out! You need to move!

"Joce!" I said. "Hey, hey!"

She blinked her unfocused eyes. "Wha-?"

The bartender knelt next to us. "Please remain here, sir," he said, and sped downstairs.

I dabbed some blood away from her eyes. "Listen Joce, you gotta stay with me, okay? Stay awake!"

Staying low, I crawled towards the stairs. The windows of the restaurant had shattered, and howling wind filled the restaurant. I counted three bodies on the floor, motionless amidst overturned tables and chairs. Aubergine's diners had thinned out some over the course of our date, but there had to be at least a half-dozen patrons still present, and a handful of wait staff.

The mages fought for their lives. A man with a ponytail and beard hurled a ball of light at the attackers outside. It exploded like a firecracker and sent a few of them flying. The bartender zipped past the windows and rained blows on the men trying to force their way in. Rebecca shouted orders in French to the wait staff, who guided the remaining diners to safety.

The gunmen outside weren't mages, but they had strength in numbers. Each carried an old Soviet-era assault weapon, a cheap and reliable black market bulk buy. From the look, the attackers were vagrants, or-

Or the drug addicts from the Arlington.

They were *zombies*. The Brothers had sent their puppets to shoot up the place. The 'why' didn't matter; they were winning. Blank-faced and heedless of fear or pain, they marched on, piling through the shattered windows, firing controlled bursts at the mages who learned the hard way that thin wooden tables were useless as cover. The floor of magical water didn't accept the intruders, and they sank to their knees, but it didn't slow them in the slightest. A young woman got close enough to unleash a gout of flame on one, but the zombie shot her dead before he succumbed.

Anguish and panic hit me. The zombies weren't soulless husks. They were *people*, locked in their own minds, forced to march to their deaths, to murder as many other people as they could. I wanted to shout out a warning to the mages, to get them to see what they were doing. But the cold, logical side of my brain told me what mattered was escape.

I crawled back to Jocelyn, who was still conscious, but had not tried to move.

"Wha's happen?" She mumbled.

I lifted her in my arms and looked for an immediate exit. The door beside the bar looked like my only option, so I shouldered my way through, and entered a kitchen. My legs tangled in something just inside the door, and I twisted mid-fall to keep from landing on Jocelyn.

Turning in check on her, I met the lifeless eyes of the cook who had tripped me. Her throat was slashed so wide that her head hung lopsided. The kitchen was a madhouse of butchery. Three other cooks lay shot dead, or gutted with their own kitchen implements.

Jesse Kendall stood in the center of the kitchen with a rifle slung over his shoulder, admiring his murderous work. He turned his mad smile on me and wiped blood from his jaw. "Well, well. Look what the cat dragged in."

I rolled Jocelyn off me, and looked for something, anything to defend myself. Nothing was within reach. Jesse laughed and hurled a knife at me. It struck the door while I pulled Jocelyn and myself behind a counter.

"Where are we?" Jocelyn asked with a dizzy slur.

I heard Jesse cock his assault rifle. "Alex Fossor. Life is full of surprises. I knew ol' Joce was comin' tonight, but I didn't figure she'd bring a mutt like *you* with her."

"Are you fucking nuts?" I called out. It wasn't the sanest thing to say in that situation.

"Little bit, yeah." He laughed. "But I've got an easy out for you: walk out that door, and I let you live."

I swallowed. "Yeah?"

"Yeah."

"That's it? We walk?"

Jesse snorted. "Not 'we'. You. Jocelyn is comin' with me."

"What do you want with her?"

"That's *family* business. Figured it was time for a reunion. Me, her, and little Eddie."

"If you wanted to see her again, you could have called," I said.

"Ah now, there's the rub. I could've dangled a carrot or two in front of Joce, invited her for tea, but she and I both know that's not how this works."

I frowned. "What are you talking about? She's been trying to find you for months. Years."

213

"Don't I know it," Jesse replied. His voice dropped low and cold. "Come on out, sis. Time to get reacquainted."

Jocelyn was still groggy, but she steeled herself, and pulled the gold bracelet off her wrist. Her dress melted into her street clothes, and from her purse she produced a familiar bracelet. The one she'd used to teleport us to Walter's home.

I grabbed her arm. "Do it."

She shook her head. "Jesse! Please, just-"

Bullets tore through the stainless steel counter, punching holes in the metal. We crawled over each other to get out of the way, but Jesse stopped before he could perforate us both.

"Shut your mouth!" He snarled. "One word out of you, sis, and your boy-toy is dog food!"

I mouthed the words 'do it' and pointed at the teleportation bracelet. She gave me a strange, almost apologetic look, but shook her head again.

What the hell is her goal? To get shot? I contemplated snatching the bracelet and using it on her, but I didn't know how it worked. I peeked under the counter. Jesse paced well out of my reach, with plenty of cover between us. No way I could survive a charge. But there was an exit to the kitchen beyond him.

I needed something, a distraction. I found it, three steps from Jesse.

What I was about to do needed a fair amount of magic, and I'd been slinging new spells and rituals all week. I had never practiced what I was about to attempt. Burnout was a genuine risk. But hell, what was one more test of my limits?

"Times a'wasting, Joce," Jesse said. "Come on out."

"Any second and the law is going to be here in force, Jesse."

He chuckled. "Like I'm scared of a few Keepers."

"You haven't met the Sheriff." I reached out with my magic. "He won't need a gun to stop you."

He slapped a fresh magazine into his AK. "Gonna be long gone before they realize what's happening. Ten seconds, Joce."

"Get ready to run for the exit behind him," I told Jocelyn.

"What?"

"One, two, ten!" Jesse said. He worked the bolt on the rifle.

I brought my spell together and focused it on Jesse. As one, the bodies of the dead cooks stirred. Their movements were inhuman, uncoordinated, but I had never controlled more than one corpse at a time before. It was like steering three string puppets with one hand.

But they got Jesse's attention. The closest chef rushed him, and he opened fire on it. Bullets tore through the body, but the corpse kept coming. It tangled Jesse's limbs and pushed him off-balance. The cook with the lopsided head got between his legs and hung on like hot tar.

Jesse smashed in the chef's face with the butt of his rifle. The third corpse joined the dogpile and tried to pin him in a full nelson.

"Goddamn you, Fossor!" Jesse snarled.

"My zombies don't need their brains, *or* a pulse!" I said.

My vision blurred a bit, then doubled. I gave my head a shake. A pressure headache was forming in the back of my head.

"Go!" I said. "Now!"

Jocelyn pushed to her feet. She didn't run for the exit, though. She went for Jesse. He tried to draw his gun on her, but the bullet-riddled chef tore it from his grasp. Jocelyn grabbed for Jesse's arm and tried to get the bracelet around his wrist.

"Joce, don't!" I shouted.

The kitchen door flew open, and Jesse's horde of zombies crowded into the room. The shriveled old woman from the Arlington entered behind them.

"Get him!" Jesse ordered.

The hag glared at me and snarled in Haitian. Pain lanced into my arm, like my nerve endings were being spooled with a fork. I let out a scream and yanked the limb back.

My animated corpses went slack. Jesse slapped Jocelyn's outstretched hand aside and slammed his fist into her face. She went limp and flopped to the floor.

"Joce!" I shouted. The hag's magic slashed at my leg, and I thrashed on the ground in agony.

"I'd kill you myself, Alex," Jesse said. "But I've got a date with godhood. Kill him!"

I saw him drag Jocelyn out the exit, followed by the hag. The zombies lurched towards me as a mob. They crowded in, grabbed hold of my limbs, ready to tear me apart with their bare hands. I screamed-

-and the zombies vanished.

It took me a moment to realize I was no longer being attacked. Men rushed into the kitchen a second later. Keepers, armed and ready for battle. Agni was with them. His eyes met mine, steady and determined.

Before he could set my body on fire or teleport me to the moon, I shouted, "That way! They took her!"

☠

Agni led me into the parking lot. There were Keepers everywhere, and I observed the Society's approach to forensic analysis. Some men cast auguries, creating floating images of people replaying the moment of their death. Others cast lines of light that hung in the air, signifying bullet trajectories. A handful of Keepers moved from body to body, inspecting them. I saw Rebecca, wide-eyed and lifeless, being zipped into a body bag marked with shivering blue glyphs.

Another Keeper arrived, out of breath. "Sorry, sir. No sign."

"And Mrs. Breckenridge?" Agni asked.

216

The Keeper shook his head. "If she was here, she's gone. We don't know where, or who took her."

"What good are you then?" I asked.

Agni put a hand on my shoulder. "Steady, Alex. Don't make this worse."

I slapped his hand away. "If you had been two seconds faster! It was-"

The world winked out of existence, and I found myself in empty blackness.

"-Jesse!"

The surrounding space was almost lightless, but when my eyes adjusted, I could make out a cube-shaped room with no windows or doors. It could have been floating in deep space, or locked in some fold of the Layered.

"Goddamnit, Agni!"

He didn't respond, so I paced the room. A few minutes later, Agni materialized.

"Tell me everything, Alex."

"Every minute we waste, her life is in danger!"

"All the more reason to be thorough." He spread his arms and waited.

I growled and told him what had happened.

"An interesting story," Agni said. "But here's what the evidence tells me, Alex. You came to Aubergine's with Jocelyn, unknown parties attacked the restaurant, and you are the only survivor."

My blood chilled. "What?"

"We found you alone with a pack of zombies." He shook his head. "The staff and other patrons are dead. Fifteen in total."

"They weren't *my* zombies, and they aren't undead! They're drugged! Cleanse their systems, get them off the Stig, and they'll tell you!"

Agni sighed. "They're dead as well, Alex. I couldn't take the risk on a group that had already massacred so many Versed."

217

The chill turned to nausea. "Those people were alive! The Edicts-"

"The Edict of Defense allows lethal use of magic in matters of safeguarding lives," he interrupted. "They were a threat, whether or not they wanted to be. And now I'm left with you as the sole survivor, a suspect who has endangered Jocelyn Breckenridge before. Someone who could stand to profit off of murdering members of the Council, prospective or otherwise."

"Then burn me, already!" I said. "Do you hear the whistling holes in your own theory?"

"Easy, Alex," Agni said, his voice both calm, but full of threat.

"Or what? You'll kill me? It won't save her, or stop him!"

The Sheriff sighed and clasped his hands behind his back. "You say this was Jesse's doing-"

"Yes!"

"Why? If he's avoided our detection so far, why risk himself now?"

"I don't know. He wanted zombies. An army. He wants a war!"

"Gunning down a restaurant will not get him anywhere near that goal. Think harder, Alex. Calm your thoughts."

I spat out a curse, but tried to do what he said. Images raced through my mind, punctuated by anger and fear. Jocelyn, Jesse, blood and screams and gunshots...

"They risked everything because he wanted Jocelyn. I don't know why. Because..."

They're close to whatever it is they want to accomplish, I thought.

Jesse wanted Jocelyn to bear witness. I remembered the naked hatred in his voice. He wanted her to suffer.

'I've got a date with godhood,' he'd said.

I rubbed my jaw, trying to make sense of it. Godhood. Cults. Loa. Stig. I could see a pattern. "Agni, Ascension is for very old, powerful mages, right?"

"I don't see what-"

"Can you speed up the process?" I asked.

It took him a moment, but I saw the realization dawn on him. "Under certain circumstances, spiritual energies can bolster magic. But the Edict of Sanctity-"

"Enough to Ascend?" I asked.

"By exploiting the Untold? He would need the spiritual essence, the raw magic, of hundreds of people."

"Or zombie astrals," I said. "Bottled souls. Bottled faith? Is there a difference?"

"The process would kill them," Agni admitted. "This kind of magic has been taboo longer than the Society has existed."

"It fits." I said. "And if he's acting so brazenly, he's getting ready to try."

"It would never work," he insisted.

"You think that will stop him?"

He stared at me for a long minute, then shook his head. "Alex, if I believed this outlandish scenario, which I have only your word to go on-"

"Oh, come on, Agni! You can see the patterns! He's been selling these drugs for months! He already has what he needs!"

"Even *then*," he continued. "If I knew where they were, I would be there. There are limits to my power."

"What?" I said. "You can't hunt someone without proof? You find me easily enough!"

"Because you are a suspect," he warned. "I could follow you anywhere you wished to go, because your hex is a beacon for me. The moment you, Alex Fossor, commit an act that breaks the Edicts, I will know. I will be there faster than you can blink. And you will burn substantially less quickly."

The darkness faded around us, and we materialized outside my house. Rain pelted us as I took a second to orient myself.

"Remember what I told you before, Alex," Agni said. "You are the accused. It is on you to prove your innocence, just as it is my duty to prove your guilt."

Then he vanished.

"Flesh and blood, bone and breath," I snarled at the empty air. "What's the point of having laws you won't enforce, of power if it only benefits *you*? What was the point of *magic* if it makes you goddamn cowards *so fucking useless?*"

The words boomed over the rain, but no answer came. I wanted to punch Agni's face in. I wanted to find Jesse and break him so hard he'd have to eat with a straw through his nose. I wanted to squeeze my fist and watch the whole stinking lot of them rot to death before my eyes, squealing and pissing themselves like-

Fog curled around my body, and my breath came in cold puffs. I closed my eyes and let myself calm down. Satisfying as it would be to show those scheming pricks what pain was, it wouldn't fix my problem.

Jesse had Jocelyn. The Brothers wanted godhood. Maybe they'd leave enough twisted cultists behind to start a proper religion. One based on drugs and pain that fed on the weakest and lowest in society. It was a horrific thought.

But how could I stop them before they succeeded?

I headed for the house, hoping that Madelyn had some answers for me. If not, then I was gonna put that cockroach bullhorn to Samedi's ear and scream at him until he answered.

The front door was bent inward, and dangled from a single hinge.

Fresh fear joined a crowded party in my guts. The interior was dark. It could have been an ambush, or a trap. I wondered if my gun was still sitting on top of the fridge, and if I could reach it before someone got the drop on me. I shouldered my way into the room, took three giant steps to the fridge, and grabbed the revolver's box.

No one attacked.

I peeked into my room, knowing the layout by memory. The computer was in sleep mode. There was no sign of Madelyn. I pulled the magic wristwatch off and tossed it on the ruins of my bed. My clothes turned back into my jeans and denim jacket.

Aside from the busted front door, the house looked untouched. The terracotta pot with Madelyn's soil sat where she'd left it, by the front door.

"Madelyn?"

Nothing. Every survival instinct I had was flashing klaxons. I dug my revolver out of the box and stuffed it in my pocket. A wild scenario of Madelyn hiding in my basement spurred me towards my trap door. I flung it open and peeked into the darkness.

"Madelyn?"

Silence. I descended the ladder, dread knotting my guts. There was a familiar smell in the air, thick and cloying. Breathing hard, I flicked the light switch at the bottom of the ladder.

Cigars, matches, apples, and Papa Williams' flask of goat pepper rum were arranged like a shrine on my slab. Syrettes of Stig and chicken feathers had joined the arrangement.

A body lay under the shrine, covered in a white sheet.

TWENTY-THREE

For a terrible moment I thought it was Madelyn, and my heart froze. I yanked the sheet aside, and dread turned into confusion.

Josh Wilkes was stripped to his waist, and painted with what I hoped was the chicken blood from the fridge. The symbols looked like a Loa's veve, but twisted somehow. More anarchic and snake-like.

His eyes were closed. I put two fingers to his forehead and felt the whirlwind of Stig and necromancy in his brain. Not dead, then. But still a zombie.

Something was tucked under his tongue. I pulled it free, and found the veve of Baron Samedi I had printed out. Someone had written *'Run!'* on it with a pen.

No way Jesse had time to hit my place before attacking the restaurant. But I didn't remember seeing Kincaid during the attack. If Jocelyn hadn't taken me to dinner, he could have kicked in my door while I was napping on the couch.

So where was Madelyn? Had she run? I feared what would happen if Jesse got his hands on her, too. But why leave Josh?

The pieces clicked together. Panic rose in my gut as I grabbed the flask, cigars and matches, anything that had my fingerprints on them, and stuffed them in my pockets. I climbed the basement ladder and hit the back exit before I stopped myself.

No. They'd be looking for the van. I ran out the front door and saw a convoy of police cars heading my way. I bolted across the street and dove into the bushes behind a house.

The patrol cars surrounded my place. The plucky rookie Runner and his valkyrie partner Loresndottr led the charge through the broken front door. A moment later, she emerged.

"We need EMT's!"

Police tape and tarps cordoned off my house. An ambulance arrived, and they hauled out Josh's body. A small army of forensics analysts moved into my house. They snapped pictures, dusted surfaces, bagged evidence and gathered everything into a truck.

A flurry of emotions stormed through me. Anger, betrayal, frustration, despair, fear, and a sense of defeat that made me want to lie in the frigid mud and scream. I was no longer Alex Fossor, person of interest, I was Alex Fossor, murder suspect.

I leaned against the fence, soaked to the bone. My life—structured to balance the legal and illegal, the real and unreal—was over. Even if I could evade the drag net, I'd be ash the second I set foot outside the city, or the Society caught wind of it.

The more I thought about it, the angrier it made me. I wasn't a good person. I did things that people would hate, or fear. If that got me killed one day, then so be it. But I wouldn't be the patsy for some asshole cult who wanted to spread poison and murder.

I emptied my pockets to see what I had to work with. The cigars and matches, my burner phone, Jimmy Runner's contact card, Papa Williams' flask of spicy rum, and my revolver with six rounds.

I watched the cops for a while, and a desperate plan took form. Risky, stupid, but no one was around to stop me, and the clock was ticking.

Lorensdottr barked orders and went over everything with a pair of gloves. She carried herself like a warrior-queen after a conquest, which would have been hot as hell if it weren't *me* she was stepping on. Still, I could respect that sense of victorious sadism. I was almost flattered.

Runner stood off to the side, the collar of his duster pulled up against the rain. He chatted with the forensic team, but otherwise kept out of their way with his hands in his pockets.

Keeping low, I darted across the street to Runner's blue compact. Perhaps it was the weather, darkness, or blind luck, but I reached the vehicle without being spotted. The rear passenger door was unlocked, and I slipped in. I pulled out my burner phone, and saw a message from my landline.

Madelyn.

My finger hovered over the button, but I stopped myself from listening. I hoped she'd made it to safety, and had called to let me know she was okay. But I couldn't spare the time. Instead, I dialed the number on Jimmy's card.

Runner pulled his phone from his pocket and tapped Lorensdottr's shoulder. She waved him off, content to tear my place apart.

"Detective Runner." He said through my receiver.

"Guess you decided quid pro quo wasn't good enough," I said.

Runner's eyes scanned the street, but there was nothing to see in that rain. He reached for his partner again.

"Don't do it, Jimmy," I warned. "Start making noise, and I'm a ghost."

He frowned, but took a step away from the other cops. "We found your little chop shop. You're a sick man, Fossor. And there ain't no one to help you now."

"You want me? Or do you want the people giving us both problems?"

He frowned. "What are you talking about?"

"Time's wastin', Jimmy," I said. "The body you pulled out of my house? He's the first of hundreds. Every junkie who's ever taken Stig is at risk, and not from an overdose."

"How?"

"I want to meet. Alone. I don't have many people left to trust, and I can't afford to go to prison. Not until I stop the bastards responsible."

He exhaled, looking angry. "How am I supposed to trust you?"

"What does your gut tell you?"

"That you need to be behind bars."

"Goodbye, Jimmy."

"No!" He sighed. "Where?"

I considered it. "West-Side Noodles. Where I was first arrested. You know the spot?"

"Yeah. I'll be there."

"Ten minutes," I warned. "Or I'm gone."

I hung up. Runner looked at Lorensdottr, then shoved the phone into his coat and headed for his car. I kept low as he got into the driver's seat, and when he dug into his pocket for his keys, I pressed the barrel of my revolver against his neck.

"Hey Jimmy."

He froze. It wasn't the panicked, goose-honk reaction I was hoping for, to satiate my mean side. He took a long breath.

"You got balls, Alex. I'll give you that much."

"Yeah. Big swingin' brass ones. Start the car."

"You're kidding, right? I so much as honk my horn and you'll have two dozen cops ready to take you out."

"I'm sorry it had to be like this Jimmy, but the bad guys made my job a lot harder by pushing you in my way. Shut up

225

and listen for a few minutes, because this is going to take a long time to explain, and I need you to keep an open mind."

"Yeah? About what?"

"Magic," I said. "The real thing. And the worst kind."

"Magic." His hands tapped the driver's wheel. "What? You *magicked* that kid into your house?"

"No," I said. "The Brothers did. They already tried to take me out tonight, and if they're making a double-play like this, they know I'm close to finding them. They need me out of the way."

"For what? Is Pulling rabbits out of hats a felony in Magicland?"

The conversation was already circling the toilet. Jimmy was still young, but he was a cop. That training can make people callous to ideas that don't fit the norm. Then again, he'd reached across the table first. Maybe he still had a place in his heart for fairies and warlocks.

So I gave him a push. I put a bit of my power into my hands and poked Jimmy's head. He jumped so hard he hit his head.

"Wh-what?" He gasped.

"That's the first spell I ever learned," I said. "How to ramp up someone's fear. I'm a necromancer, Jimmy. And I need your help to stop the others of my kind before they kill a lot of people."

And I get the blame for it.

In the rearview, I could see the confusion, fear, and a million questions flickering in his eyes. "I- what-" He swallowed and wiped cold sweat from his brow. "What is going on?"

"Like I said. Long story. I'll explain everything I can on the way."

He started the engine but didn't put it in gear. "Is this real? How do I know you didn't drug me?"

"You're gonna see more than that tonight," I said. "Get us moving."

He didn't take his eyes off me through the rearview mirror, but he turned the car west.

"The body at the Arlington, where'd you take him?" I asked.

"What? Uh, yeah. Jefferson- how did you-" He sighed and shook his head. "You were there, weren't you?"

"Yeah. I saw the people behind all this. To find them, I need the corpse."

Jimmy frowned. "There ain't much left of him, man."

"It will be enough," I said. "I hope."

☠

"The origins of magic aren't a mystery," I explained. "Magic is everywhere, in everything. The weather, the rocks, the plants, barbeques, fountain soda, and rock n' roll. But humans have a certain *something*. Maybe God made us in His image, so we have a bit of that potency in us. There are a thousand and one theories and each one could be right, or each could be wrong. Whatever it is, wherever it comes from, it's tied into the soul. You've known about magic all your life. When you read about Hercules, Merlin, jackalopes or vampires. All of them were mages, or the byproducts of magic. Creating things, changing things. Living like gods when they thought they could get away with it. Hiding the evidence when they realized they couldn't."

"So where are they now?" Runner asked. "If they were so godlike?"

I smirked. "Most died. A mage can live centuries, but they're not immortal. Not on this plane of existence. Some really powerful mages ascend to their own planes, where they have almost complete power. A real taste of godhood. And I think the Brothers want to- *watch the road!*"

He swerved away from an oncoming car. The driver leaned on the horn as it roared past.

"Shit! You better keep this shit to Basics One-Oh-One until I can get my head around it. Let's talk about these guys you're after. The Brothers?"

"One is Samuel Kincaid," I explained. "A Haitian. Excommunicated Vodou priest. Another is a white guy, brown hair, named Jesse Kendall. He's a necromancer like me, and he's here selling Stig. It makes people into zombies, the mind-controlled kind, not the brains-eating kind. It lets him tap into their souls for power. With it, and a little extra juice from a cult he's formed, he's going to do something bad."

"Make himself a god?"

"Or the closest thing to it," I said.

"So how'd you get involved in this?"

"The mages in charge of this city want the case solved."

"In charge? How many- Can't they help?"

"They don't see what's going on," I said. "Or they don't care what happens, as long as it doesn't disrupt their laws."

"Isn't enslaving people with magic drugs kind of that?" Runner asked.

"Yeah, but they don't see enough 'evidence' to do anything about it. They think I've been killing people with intent to raise them as zombies. The modern kind."

"You can do that? Like flesh-eating zombies?"

"If I wanted to."

He gave me a long stare. "So your 'superiors' won't help because they think you're responsible."

"Until recently I was the only necromancer in the city," I said.

"I gotta say, this isn't painting you in the most innocent of lights," Runner said.

"You're not the first one to think so," I said. "And I don't care what any of you think. I've got to stop them. The moment the Society thinks they have enough evidence on me, they'll flip my kill switch and I'll be dead before I finish this sentence." I waited, then exhaled with relief.

Runner shifted away from me. "So, you need to prove you're innocent? Expose the real culprit before you're executed?"

"And then there's no one to stop them. Not before they succeed at what they're doing."

"So what's this dead body going to tell you?"

"I need it to talk to the Loa, entities tied to the Vodou faith. It didn't work for me the first time, I think that's because I'm not a priest. But the dead guy used to be. I can use him to help boost the signal. Make them hear me."

Runner frowned. "This is all too crazy for me. You better not expect me to dress up and do a tribal dance or something. My family has been Christian since before the Emancipation Proclamation."

"Your family were slaves?" I asked, then flinched. "Sorry, stupid question."

He glanced at me. "No shit. But we didn't stay that way. Hiked from Louisiana to Ontario. My great grandma said the Underground Railroad gave us the surname 'Runner.' Badge of honor, I guess."

"Like your coat."

He smirked. "Yeah, like my coat."

"If it helps, I'm Canadian."

Runner rolled his eyes. "Right. Are you here legally?"

"C'mon man, gimme a break."

He snorted a laugh. "Between keeping a body in your basement torture dungeon and holding a cop hostage, you're building one hell of a rap sheet, Fossor."

"Not torture," I said, and paused. "It was a shrine. I wanted to talk to the Loa, but my first attempt didn't work."

Runner snorted. "I've lost it. Twenty-eight and I've already lost my damn mind."

"You ain't seen nothing yet."

He pulled into the 8th Precinct garage. "Listen, you've still got half the city's cops looking for you, so if you are legit, I'm gonna put my neck on the line. But if I think you're playing me, even for a minute? I'll arrest you, and put a bullet in your head if you try to stop me."

"You drive a hard bargain."

The garage was empty of police. He parked near a set of doors marked 'Restricted', and cut the engine.

"Let me go in first. I'll make sure the coast is clear."

"How do I know you won't decide I'm crazy and call for backup?"

Runner turned around to look at me. "I'd be lying if that thought hadn't crossed my mind. But I've been willing to hear you out so far, Alex. I'm showing you trust. Time to show me some."

He was right. Not that I liked it, but Runner—despite his dedication to sticky notions like the law—had been honest with me since I met him. I nodded.

He slipped out of the car, straightened his big detective's duster, and pushed through the Restricted door. I waited, nervous and exposed, unsure whether Jimmy would come back alone, or with enough backup to cook my goose.

The door opened. Runner poked his head out, looked around, then waved me over.

"So what now?" He asked.

I got out of the car. "We talk to some gods about a thing."

TWENTY-FOUR

Runner led me to the morgue, but we took an erratic route through a supply room to avoid getting caught in the main corridor.

"The EMT's took the body from your place to Grace Hospital," Runner explained. "So our pathologist is there for the time being. No telling when he'll be back. Make this quick."

"I hope he doesn't cut into him," I said. "Josh isn't dead."

Runner frowned. "I'll call 'em. Ask them to hold off on an autopsy."

While he got on the phone, I surveyed the morgue. It was small for such a large precinct, with six cadaver lockers and an examination table with lots of space. Like any good doctor, the pathologist kept the place immaculate. It felt as clean as the funeral home I worked at.

Or used to work at, I assumed.

Runner ended his call, then gripped the handle of the top-middle locker and pulled it open. The body lay inside, zipped up in a black cadaver bag. "You may want to prepare yourself."

I looked at him. "Think about who you're talking to."

He shrugged and unzipped the bag. The smell hit me first, the unmistakable stink of burned flesh. I was ghoulish enough to think about food when it hit me.

The body of the Haitian was a mess. Fire had scoured his left side, the muscle scorched to the bone in places.

"I feel like I'm gonna throw up," Runner said.

"Smile. It suppresses the gag reflex. Help me get him onto the autopsy table."

Runner's forced his million-dollar grin onto his face, but it stretched into an almost comical grimace. "Uh, can't you like, magic it over?"

"What happened to your guts?"

"My gut thinks it's a bad idea to play with dead people."

"So hard to get professional help these days."

I hefted the body. The legs and left arm hung at an unnatural angle. He must have fallen through the floor during the Arlington fire. "You're keeping him at a negative temp?"

"No ID on him," Runner said. "No idea what the cause of death is yet. He's gotta stay cold until we find out."

"He's Haitian. Smuggled into the country with the rest of the Brothers. You should check him for tetrodotoxin."

"What?"

"Pufferfish toxin. One of the key ingredients in Stig."

"Fish? The aquariums." Runner nodded. "So now what? Sacrifice a goat? Wear one of those weird masks? You need to charge your mana or- *shit!*"

The corpse sat up and waved at him.

"Hi Jimmy, welcome to the world of magic!" I said in a mock circus announcer's voice.

The look on Runner's face was worth it. I ended the spell, and the body went limp.

Runner heaved, but kept his dinner down. "Please don't do that again."

"Sorry," I said, but my grin suggested otherwise. "We take our stress relief where we can find it."

"So what now?" He asked.

"Now is the easy-ish part." I took out the cigars, matches, and Papa Williams' flask of goat-pepper rum. I opened the pack of cigars and took one out. "I'll need you to look some stuff up for me on your phone. I need the Veve for Baron Samedi. Vee-Ee-Vee-Ee."

Runner took out his phone. "They keep magic stuff on the internet?"

"Vodou isn't 'magic stuff'," I said. "Lots of people still practice it. That's why I had chicken blood in my fridge."

"Chicken? It was chicken blood?"

"Yeah. Got it from the butcher at Kent's. Did you think it was human?"

"It *is* unusual to find a bucket of blood in a suspect's fridge, yeah," Runner said.

I snorted. "Found the Veve?"

He showed it to me. "Like this?"

"It'll do. Hold that steady." I traced the pattern into the air above the body with my magic, as if I were drawing a mage-mark. Blue-green light shimmered over the body.

Runner looked the design over, his revulsion replaced with curiosity. "You know if you wanted to prove magic was real? You could have just done this."

I smiled. "Sorry. I'm a bit of an asshole."

"A bit."

"Okay," I said. "Samedi won't appear on his own. He needs to possess, or 'mount,' a body, and I don't think he wants to ride me, so our Haitian friend will be his horse. Since he's bokor, he's got a link to the Loa, so that should cover the steps I'm missing or skipping."

"Cheating at magic?" Runner said. "Oh yeah, this'll be great."

"Point is, he's gonna be angry, but I'll try to bribe him with rum and cigars. Then he'll answer my questions and leave. I hope."

"And if not?"

I shrugged. "Least case scenario, he won't come at all. Worst case, he kicks my ass six ways 'til Sunday."

Runner smirked. "That would make this all worth it. Just the same, I'll be over here." He moved to stand near the door.

"While you're there, find me some Vodou banda music," I said. "Drums and chanting."

Runner did his internet search and played a sample of rhythmic music.

"That's the stuff," I said. "Crank it."

The music echoed off the hard concrete walls. I opened the rum, breathing its scent in deep, and sipped it, then set the flask beside the corpse's head. The rum was sweet and cloying on my tongue, which turned to spicy heat that made my eyes water and throat burn. I lit a cigar and puffed smoke into the air to hover around the Veve symbol. With the offerings prepared, I sent my magical pulse into the Layered.

C'mon, you bastard, I thought. *Do something! Fix this mess you helped make! Tell me what I need to know!*

After a few minutes of concentration, I still sensed nothing. No uncomfortable sense of being watched. The body before me didn't so much as shiver.

I grabbed the sides of the table and got in the corpse's face. "Goddamnit, answer me!"

Nothing. The music clip ended on Runner's phone, and my mark fizzled out.

"Is that it?" He asked. "You better not tell me to dance."

"How about *'freeze'*?"

Detective Lorensdottr entered the morgue, sidearm first. She regarded us both with cold fury. "Hands over your heads," she growled. "Do it!"

Runner took a step forward, hands beside his chest. "Loren, easy now, partner. This ain't what it looks like. It's, well, shit, it's as crazy as it looks. But not the *bad* crazy. Sort of."

"Shut it, Runner," she said. "Save the bending-over-backwards for a judge. Right now I see a murder suspect and an accomplice tampering with evidence. So hands up!"

"She's charming," I said, raising my hands.

"Shut up, Fossor. Loren, you gotta roll with me here. This shit is bigger than cops and bad guys."

"I said shut it!" She dug into her coat for her phone. In a second she would have every cop in the building on us. But her fingers stumbled, and the phone dropped to the floor.

Loren's eyes bulged as she stared at me. "You wanted... what?"

There was panic in her voice. She took a shaky step forward, hissed, and then flopped onto the floor. Her gun slid out of reach.

"Loren!" Runner cried, but he hesitated to approach.

Lorensdottr's body shook, as if locked in a seizure. Then she spidered forward on her hands and feet and slammed into the autopsy table. She gasped, back arched, and grabbed hold of the table to haul herself up. Her blond bun untangled into a mane of scarlet curls, and her sapphire blue eyes shifted into emerald green.

Her lip curled into an angry snarl. "Ye stupid, rat-fuck, piss-sucking, cockwagging, *self-righteous fuckwad of a mage! Y'fuckin' gobshite! Y'absolute shitheel!*"

Runner blinked. "Loren?"

"No," she snapped, then grabbed my jacket collar and yanked me off my feet. "Y'thrice-damned self-entitled white prat! Y'really made bags o'this!"

The Loa dropped me on my already bruised tailbone and I let out a shout. She flexed her shoulders and paced the room,

235

firing off a rant of insults and foul language that would make a smack-talking videogamer break down in tears.

Runner circled around her to help me to my feet. "Is she okay?"

"It's the Loa," I said. "Samedi's family, the Guede, enjoy colorful language."

"Oh toss it you fucking thick *pisser*," the Loa spat. "Like you know a fucking thing!"

Her eyes fell on the rum and snatched it up to her lips.

"Woah easy," I said. "That stuff is-"

She held up a finger, as if to say 'hold that thought', and took four big gulps. "Okay. Okay, I think I'm okay."

"Baron?" I asked.

The Loa looked at me in disgust. "Fuck off, boyo. You think he'd wanna ride a girl?" She paused, then snorted. "Poor choice of words, isn't it?"

"She uh, doesn't sound Haitain," Runner said. "She sounds *Irish*."

I blinked, going over what I could recall of the different Loa. "Maman Brigitte?"

She gave me a smirk. "Was I that obvious? Oh, you're deadly. Sharp as a round brick!"

"Who's Maman Brigitte?" Runner asked.

"Samedi's wife. One of the few Loa who doesn't trace back to Africa, but Ireland."

Brigitte smiled. "Haven't been to the Island in donkey's years." She took another swig of rum. Then two more. "Alright you fuckin' chancer, what am I doin' in this kip, and why am I mountin' this fine thing?"

"I was trying to talk to the Baron."

"Well, he ain't here," Brigitte said. "He sent me 'cause he's too angry, wantin' to smack the shite out o' you. Fucking necromancers acting the maggot. Look at this disgrace! You buy these cigars at the corner shop? You think he's gonna pop

236

by for a visit 'cause you can toss shapes with magic? If any o' us appeared every time a couple college floozies painted their faces and cracked a bottle o' pink wine, not one of us would get a fucking thing done!" She jabbed a finger into my chest. "You ain't one o' the faithful, you ain't *houngan*, you're some entitled white boy who thinks havin' magic makes it okay for him to stick his fingers in shite he doesn't understand! Am I wrong?"

I swallowed. "No."

"So why am I here?"

"Why are you? Why answer at all?"

"Fucking hell, dumb as two flat rocks." She hopped onto the slab next to the body, and her eyes softened. "Oh Wesley, y'poor bastard. You won't have to wait long. My fella is diggin' your bed right this moment. Don't you worry about Jesula. Won't be one of us who isn't watching over her, 'til she can be with you. Someday."

I recognized a wake for what it was. "Respect for the dead? Even for bokor?"

"Everyone makes mistakes. You saw him at the end, gravedigger. Did he look like a man proud o' himself?" She kicked off the table. "Know this, Alex Fossor. It ain't this pissy excuse for a shrine, it ain't your shite magic that convinced me to come. It was him. Wesley put in a kind word. Says you brought him out o' the zombie. For that, you get two more minutes of my time. Ask those questions you think are so important."

I cleared my throat. "Okay. What are the Brothers Midnight after?"

Brigitte shook her head. "Ascension, obviously. Samuel and Bettany were after money, but then along came a serpent with some real dark magic. He promised them something greater, and oh, ambition got the better o' them. They wanna be Loa, like us. And won't that be a lovely greet? A pack of infants with

237

our sort of power, and not a scrap of wisdom to temper it. Bondye, spare us."

"Why not stop them, then?" I asked. "Don't you have the power?"

"Power to what? Intervene? Make the world a better place? That's not how this works. Consent, boyo. All Immortals live by that rule above all others, including the Ascended. It was law even before the *Edicts* existed."

Shit. So that explained a lot about why the Loa hadn't acted, and why Papa Williams had been loath to ask.

Brigitte's emerald eyes flashed. "One minute, boyo."

"Can you intervene?" I asked. "I'm asking, and I'm living."

"We're not some army you can raise to fight your battles. Besides, we've already helped more than you realize." She shook the flask. "Papa Willy. Sly old bastard."

"He told me not to."

"He knew you'd try regardless," Brigitte said. "Feckin' white boys. It's why I went black."

Runner snorted behind me. I sighed. So much for the direct approach option.

"Okay," I said. "Where do I find Jesse?"

Brigitte smirked. "You already know that."

"I do?"

"Yes, ye thick twat. Have y'checked yer messages yet?" I patted my pocket. She touched her nose and then drank the rest of the rum, setting the flask beside the body. "Time's up, boyo. Don't go calling us again, especially not with this Google Rituals shite!" She shivered, then blinked. "Oh. One last thing."

Her presence *filled* my perception. I felt like I did back in my basement, watched by something too vast for me to comprehend.

"You. You made Madelyn. Her blood has a forgotten history, Alex Fossor. Count your shadows as you walk that path. The fourth will be the end."

Before I could process what she said, Brigitte shuddered and collapsed. Runner and I caught her, and her hair faded to blond as we laid her down.

"She's out cold," Runner said.

"Don't know how long she'll stay that way. But she'll be out of our hair for the time being."

"What do we do now?"

I tugged out my burner phone. The message from Madelyn.

"Hey, uh, don't know when you'll get this, but I got a hit from my friend," she said. "Tyler's selling at a rave tonight. Pier Seventeen on the south end of the river, at the Bodega Street Marina. He-" Something banged, like the sound of a door being kicked in. "Oh shit! Who the fu-"

The message ended. I stared at the phone in my shaking hand. Madelyn. The bastards had pulled her into the shitstorm with me.

"Pier Seventeen?" Runner asked. "I can have every cop in the city there in a half hour."

"No," I said. "Runner, I know you want to ride in and do the cop thing, but there could be a lot of people there. It'll be a bloodbath if someone starts shooting. Besides, the tip she got was for a dealer, not the leaders. I can get the info out of him."

"How?"

I smirked. "Think about who you're talking to."

"Okay, okay," he said. "What do I do?"

"Keep close to your phone. When I know where they are, I'll call you. This has to be precise, Runner. Those zombies are under someone else's control. They'll obey any command they're given, but they're not responsible for what they're doing. Shooting them means killing innocent people."

"Shit," Runner sighed. "Is it always like this for you people?"

"This is one of the worst, for sure."

239

TWENTY-FIVE

Lorensdottr's car had boxed in Runner's cruiser. The keys were in the ignition.

Guess you're my ride. I sank into the seat, and a panic attack hit me. My sweaty hands shook on the wheel as I tried to control my breathing. It was bad enough that I hadn't gotten a full night's sleep in days, that I was living off caffeine and adrenaline, or that I'd cast more magic in a week than I ever had before in my life.

But I had just gotten schooled by something so powerful I couldn't process its true form. I doubted many people could keep themselves going after all that.

And my night wasn't over. I had to storm the gates, take on the Brothers, save Jocelyn *and* Madelyn, and stop a murderous ritual intended to grant Jesse easy-bake godhood.

I thought about my mom, my childhood, my teens, and the family she'd built while I grew distant. Of the Visatori, and the community I had with them. The Gallows, and the uncertain future they faced. My mind lingered on Madelyn, how her horrible luck had brought her to my door, and how she'd been dragged into my fight.

I'd lost my home, I was being hunted by cops, Keepers and asshole cultists. The people I cared about were under attack. My empty, lonely life was being torn to pieces just as I was pulling it together.

Anger boiled in me. I was a mage, goddamnit. The Society were assholes, but they had given me one bit of wisdom. They'd shown me how far down the totem pole I truly sat. Yet they treated me like I was a *bomb*. Like I could do greater harm than I believed myself capable. They didn't see some plucky nobody, content to wile away his days in obscurity. They saw me as a threat. Something to fear.

Maybe I could find it in myself to become that nightmare. To pay back Jesse for all the shit he'd put me through. Yeah. They fucked with the wrong necromancer.

Assuming I didn't get my damn head blown off.

I huffed, shook off the last of my anxiety, and put the car in gear. There wasn't anything between me and Jesse but rain. I hit the brakes on the edge of Bodega Street and turned the car off. The rain would help mask my approach, but not if I arrived in a police car. I jogged the rest of the way, leaning into the storm.

☠

Port Bodega specialized in boat construction and repair, but the area smelled of fish guts anyway. I was used to the smell of decaying people, but seafood always made me queasy, so I had to breathe through my mouth. Weird choice of locations for a rave.

I spotted movement on Pier 17. Men in raincoats huddled under street lamps, dressed like dockworkers. Groups of young people, three or four at a time, passed them, heading for my destination, a dry docked cruise liner called the *Caribbean*

Sunset. I recognized it from when Jocelyn and I crossed the Center Street Bridge into Downtown, days before.

The guards gave me stern looks, but none of them stopped me as I walked to the ship. The music from within was audible as I ascended the boarding ramp, a rapid-fire blend of styles that didn't go well together, but was full of lively, directionless energy.

A single guard waited at the top of the ramp, leaning beside an open doorway.

"Hold on," he said. I could see a polished chrome .50 caliber stuffed into his waistband. "A stamp is twenty bucks."

I didn't have a dime on me, so I just smiled, sighed, and punched him as hard as I could. He bounced off the wall with a grunt of pain, but put up his fists, ready to shout for help.

So I hit him again. And again, and again. He finally went limp.

It wasn't clean, or nice. I shook a kink out of my wrist and dragged his body out of sight, then tossed his piece over the side.

Wouldn't the good guys knock a thug out with a judo chop? Hadn't he actually gone limp after the third hit? Maybe I was more angry than I realized.

"Sorry," I said.

I put it out of my mind and entered the ship. The music got louder as I descended two flights of stairs and followed the direction markers to the ship's ballroom. All around me I could see signs of damage and repair. A battered cruiseliner in need of some renovation and a fresh coat of paint offered plenty of places to smuggle drugs. They could have stuffed the walls with whatever they needed, hidden contraband all over the ship.

When I reached the ballroom, the noise was almost deafening. Two hefty-looking bouncers in hoodies stood guard, staring at me over their sunglasses.

"Who goes stag to a rave?" One asked. He had to shout to be heard.

I shrugged. "I'll find a friend inside. If she's out of it, she's up for it, right?"

They exchanged looks. "Yeah, whatever."

He opened the door, and noise, light, and smells bombarded my senses. The rave was in full-swing, a wall-to-wall mass of thrashing, leaping bodies that lost themselves to the chaos. The smell was heavy with weed and sweat, sex and blood. I took a deep breath and shouldered my way into the mass.

I wasn't so old that I didn't see the appeal of a rave to someone like Madelyn. It was mindless escapism, where the music sets the tone, drugs steal your worries, and all you have to do is float on an ocean of oblivion. A waking dream.

On the other hand, it was nonsense noise at ridiculous levels. Bunch of filthy, drugged-out, stomping-child nonsense. They could read a book if they want to get lost in something. It'd save them money and their eardrums.

Seriously, it was stupid how loud it was.

I had no idea where Tyler would be. Did underground raves have concession booths? A souvenir pavilion? I hadn't seen any dealers on my way in, so they had to be somewhere people could duck out, get a hit, and return to the crowd.

Higher ground had to be the answer. I could see balconies connected by spiral staircases. I drifted towards one, head low so they wouldn't notice my approach.

A man crashed into me, skinny and topless, wearing headgear that was a mix of alien antennae and diving goggles. He bounced off me into another with a cry of slurred joy. A woman no older than Madelyn followed him, with tattered neon clothes and a vacant-eyed smile. Her hands fondled my chest and reached below my belt, and I twisted out of the way, putting a man screaming at the top of his lungs between us. They became entwined and were swallowed by the crowd.

A hefty-looking guard blocked the stairwell, but I relaxed my limbs and tried to look half-baked. When I got close, he gave me a firm shove. Getting trampled would have sucked, but I stayed on my feet and made a gesture like I was trying to prick both my wrists with a needle.

He nodded and stepped aside, then held off three or four others who tried to crowd in after me. He wasn't shy about throwing punches either, to make sure the addicts knew he wasn't playing around. I didn't want to tangle with him if he could control a group like that.

I ascended the stairs, where another guard grabbed my shoulder and herded me down a side corridor. We entered what looked like a private dining area, and he shut the door behind us. It muted the noise from deafening to annoying.

Mr. Handy—Madelyn's dealer, Tyler—sat behind a table with his feet up and a distracted grin on his face. An open suitcase behind him overflowed with blue and red syrettes of Stig.

"You need a hit, then I got what you-" The words died in his throat as he recognized me.

"Heya, Tyler," I said.

I cast my fear at the guard holding me, and while he let out a shout of panic I turned and slugged him. His head bounced off the wall and he dropped, satisfying my desire for a one-hit KO. I drew my revolver on Tyler before he'd gotten out of his chair.

"Easy," I said. "Keep those wandering hands up."

Tyler raised them. "Hey look, this don't have to be a thing. If you're mad 'bout your girl, it wasn't personal, you know? Just checkin' for a piece."

"Shut up," I said. "You've got something I want, and it ain't the shit you're pumping into these kids. The Brothers. Kincaid, Jesse, that little old lady who looks like a shoe. Where are they?"

He blinked. "Sh-shit, are you for real? What are you, like a cop or something?"

"Or *something*. Finger's getting twitchy, Tyler."

"Alright, alright! Damn, you loco man. Fuck it, I ain't gettin' greased over whatever spat you got."

"Then spill." I cocked the hammer.

Tyler flinched. "They're here! All of 'em! Doin' their Vodou shit upstairs!"

Here? I thought. *I'm giving Madelyn a raise.*

"Show me."

"Yeah, yeah, this way." He pointed towards another set of doors. "Right through there leads to the kitchen, with stairs. The boss has his freaky-ass garden in the lounge, at the end of the hall."

"Start walking." I paused, wondering if I should grab the unconscious guard's gun, or tie him up. When I looked back, Tyler had bolted. He hit the doors to the kitchen and shouted a warning before vanishing out of sight.

So much for subtlety. I rushed after him, entering a kitchen full of chrome shelving and custom cooking surfaces for sea travel. Tyler was gone.

Cursing, I dug out my phone and dialed.

"Runner. That you, Alex?"

"It's me," I whispered. I spotted a flight of stairs on the far side of the kitchen and headed for them. "I'm on board the *Caribbean Sunset*, a cruise-liner at Pier Seventeen. I've got a semi-reliable source that tells me the Brothers are here. You need to surround this place. But be quiet about it. There are a ton of people here. A lot of-"

A door burst open. The hag rushed into the kitchen, shrieking and swinging a pair of flensing knives like maracas. I ducked a slash and deflected a second with my pistol. The hag spat in my face, which made me retreat with a roar of anger, and definitely not a cry of squeamish disgust.

As she closed in I threw my phone at her, but it smashed against a cupboard. I didn't want to shoot a crazy old woman, but she was more than prepared to stab me, so all was fair in bloody murder. I aimed for her face.

She jabbed a crooked finger, hissing a curse in Haitian, and her pain magic skewered me. Every nerve ending fired in my ribcage, and I screamed. The hag huffed and snorted, and the pain dug towards my heart. It drove me to my knees, and my gun fell from my grasp.

But through the agony, I sensed a flaw in her magic. It was potent, but a pain spell was a low effort for someone of her advanced age, who should have been wielding power near that of the Archmage.

Unless she wasn't as old as she appeared.

My senses attuned to the raw, bleeding energy in her spell. She was peeling her own soul away to boost her power. If a soul was a fruit-bearing tree, and mages gathered the fruit to fuel their magic, then the hag was cutting down an entire branch away to get at all of the fruit at once. A bounty of power, but the branches wouldn't grow back. One day, the soul would no longer bear fruit. It would *die*.

I'd never felt such a thing before. Even *sensing* the mutilation made me recoil in sympathetic pain. I could have been fighting a woman no older than myself, left decrepit and withered by flaying her own soul. But maybe she didn't care, when the goal of living forever through Ascension was within her grasp?

Facing any other mage, it would have given her an edge. But a grim, sadistic realization brought a smile to my lips. She was tearing her life-energies away from herself, leaving them vulnerable. Against a necromancer, she may as well have been attacking me with a Philly cheesesteak.

I fought through the agony, bound her spell with my will, and *pulled*. The woman gasped and redoubled her efforts, realizing too late what I intended. With a snarl, I slashed at the tattered soulstuff bound to her magic. It fell away like a severed limb, and sank into my flesh.

A rush of sensations overwhelmed me. Pain, shock, and jumbled memories tried to force themselves into my mind. I only got a few momentary flashes, a child in an empty room, a knife, a body lying on its stomach, a cacophony of drums and chanting, angry faces and cruel words that weren't in English, but I could almost understand. I didn't know what significance the memories were to her, but they were part of her magic, and that meant they were important to who she was.

I shook off the stolen reverie. The memories blurred and faded, like dreams forgotten when we return to consciousness. I hoped that was where they'd stay.

The hag's attack had stopped. Her arm hung limp and shriveled, like dried meat.

She screamed in pain, and I punched her in the face. I wasn't proud of it, but tact was for sweet old ladies who had never hurt a soul in their life, not a crazy witch who traded people's lives—including her own—for power. She dropped like a sack of grain.

I grabbed my gun and broken phone. One down, and a bunch more to go.

TWENTY-SIX

I ascended the stairs to a hallway lined with passenger cabins. As Tyler promised, a lounge waited for me at the end, near the ship's stern. The interior was dark, and rows of aquariums had replaced the tables. Each held three or four pufferfish the size of my fist.

An exit at the rear opened onto an outdoor patio. Planter boxes crowded the deck, white and purple Devil's Trumpets bloomed within. Not as big as a weed grow op, but the Brothers didn't need a long-term investment. In the center of the garden was a small shrine of skulls, flowers, bottles of rum, and various bones.

Samuel Kincaid knelt before it, with his back to me. He breathed in tobacco smoke from a clay bowl and put his hands together in prayer.

"Come forward, Alex Fossor," he said. "I am relieved to see you got my message."

"You left the note with Josh?"

"I have ensured the Society cannot find us. But I wanted you to, if you were able."

More curious than cautious, I approached. "Why?"

"The Loa speak your name," he said. "They say a gravedigger comes for me, a promised rest after months of troubled dreams."

"I can imagine. What you've done to these people is sick."

"You know nothing. When we came to this city, we believed in our cause. We believed *him*. He told us we could combine our knowledge to become like the Loa. To be Loa."

"That's breaking the Edicts," I said.

"I care nothing for these things. I care for my homeland. Every hardship, every disaster that affects Haiti, there are those who blame my faith for it. They say our magic is not real, yet condemn us when disaster strikes. You know a little of this, I think. To be outcast for who you are."

"Yeah," I said. "You turned the city against me. Did you think I'd come running to join you after that?"

He turned to face me, and his intense eyes were like two white pearls in the dark. "Bettany and I saw a kindred soul in you. An outcast. I wanted to approach you as a friend."

"You picked a hell of a way to do it."

"That was not my decision," Samuel said. "*He* forced all of our hands."

"Jesse?"

He nodded. "And now he prepares his end game. My brothers, the Loa, they all spoke, but I did not listen. Now I am the only one left. Even Bettany has lost herself to his madness. They warned me about this man, but all I heard were his promises."

"Ascension? Cheat your way to godhood?"

"Ascension is not a guarantee," Kincaid said. "Only a few mages have the potential, and it takes centuries to grow into that power. Most die long before it can manifest. Haiti, Vodou, and all I hold dear could die before then."

"So you'll murder hundreds to skip a step or two? How noble."

"It is a chance to serve my people. To become Loa who do not sit idle and ignore the plight of their servants. To spread the faith, and to teach them how to take the reparation they are owed. I would have seen my homeland thrive, my beliefs flourish. The debts of the past repaid, in full! As a man, I am a heretic and a criminal. But who is the Society to tell a Loa not to speak to his people? Not to serve them?"

He took a calming breath. "None of that matters now. Jesse's lies have led me on a blind path, and now there are only two deaths before me. One at his hand, or one at yours. Either way, my grave is waiting."

I frowned. "I would rather not kill you, but I won't let you do this."

He rose to his feet. "It is not your choice to make."

A gunshot went off, like the clap of an angry god. Kincaid collapsed on the shrine, scattering its implements.

I whirled to face Jesse, who stood at the exit with a smoking pistol in hand. Behind him were two of his blank-faced zombies, holding a bound and gagged Jocelyn and little Eddie Breckenridge. The two-year-old was startled awake and began to cry.

"I guess it was *my* choice to make," Jesse said. "Drop it, Fossor."

I put the gun on the ground and raised my hands. "In five minutes, the police will have this place surrounded. And once the Society realizes you're here, they'll come in force."

Jesse smirked. "Don't know how you found this place, but it doesn't matter. You can't stop what I'll become."

"A god?" I asked. "What'll they call you? 'Jesse, Loa of Raves'?"

"Loa," Jesse sneered. "Did Sammy give you his little 'pity-me' speech? I sold him bullshit, and he bought it for the sake of his cause. Oh, he saw the writing on the wall, but by then all his bokor buddies were nice and obedient." He gestured at the zombie holding Eddie. "Now it doesn't matter what they be-lieve. I've got a ship full of addicts, and a gaggle of zombies. All ready to slit their throats and help me Ascend."

"They aren't worshipers. They're slaves."

Jesse shrugged. "What's the saying about tomatoes? A soul is a soul, all I need is their power. That little spark of magic that exists in all of us, but most people can never tap into."

"How?" I asked. "That magic I felt in the old woman?"

He nodded. "The darkest of dark magic. The kind that was forbidden before the Society ever existed. Hell, they *created* the Society just to bury it."

"How did some punk like you get your hands on it, then?"

"Well, funny thing. Would you believe it came to me in a dream?" He paused, then snorted. "What's it fucking matter? I've got it. And the ritual is almost ready."

I gritted my teeth. "So what now? You kill me?"

He smirked. "Me? Nah."

Hands locked around my wrists from behind. I twisted my head to see a gaunt young woman in punk-goth garb, staring back with empty eyes.

"Madelyn," I grunted. "You're a real bastard, Jesse."

"I never knew my drugs could control a wight. But we know now, don't we? C'mon, sis, destiny's waiting." He pointed at Madelyn. "You. Kill him."

With inhuman strength, Madelyn flipped me onto my back and planted a knee on my neck. Chuckling to himself, Jesse and his captives disappeared into the ship.

I tried to wrestle Madelyn off, finding it absurd that a scrawny little girl could overpower me.

'Alex!'

The zombie hadn't spoken, but I'd heard Madelyn's voice.

'Alex! Up here!'

The air swirled, and Madelyn's incorporeal soul appeared above her body, transparent and glowing with pale blue light.

Kid? I thought. *You gotta help!*

'I can't stop it!' She shouted in my brain. Her spirit clawed at her physical form, but the zombie didn't so much as flinch. *'The drugs are keeping me out of my body!'*

It was up to me, then. I remembered how to breach Jesse's control and charged my magic. But he must have briefed his zombies in self-defense, because Madelyn grabbed my arm and twisted it away from her.

My lungs were being squeezed, and my vision turned blurry and dark. I was going to meet my end from a rotten-luck girl while her own disembodied spirit watched. But dying like that wasn't so bad. Suffocation is kind of like falling asleep. You start to just drift away...

Besides, I thought. *How many people could say they died with a woman straddling their chest?*

Madelyn's spirit choked and snorted through tears.

Hey, you made her laugh.

Madelyn's ghost-light shimmered when she laughed, reflecting off a shape beside her, the scattered bones and other implements from Kincaid's shrine to the Loa.

Waitaminute. I didn't need that physical contact for my usual brand of death-raising. I kept my eyes focused towards the shrine and made a clawing gesture with my pinned hand.

Samuel Kincaid's body jerked, shifted, and twisted towards us. The Madelyn zombie didn't see him coming until he yanked her off of me. I rolled away, gasping for air.

Madelyn kicked and thrashed, but I had Samuel's corpse pull her into a full-nelson. Her spirit watched the bizarre sight with a grimace.

'This is too much,' she sighed. *'Alex, are you okay?'*

I nodded and sucked in more air. "Oxygen deprivation sucks."

'Can he hold her? Me? Fuck, this is confusing.'

252

"For now," I said. "But if I stop concentrating, the corpse will stop moving."

'You mean he's not like me?' She asked.

"Kincaid is dead. I'm just moving his corpse around." I pushed myself onto my hands and knees. "His grave is dug."

'What?'

"Nevermind." I got to my feet. "How are you *that?*"

'I don't know! When he kicked in your door, he took one look at me and did something. Next thing I knew, I was floating over my body! I couldn't get back in, so I followed it. I didn't know what else to do!'

I pressed my thumb against Madelyn's forehead. The hurricane of Jesse's power waited for me within. I fought through it to the center of her mind, the eye of the storm.

"Try now."

Madelyn's spirit touched my outstretched hand and rushed *through* me—talk about a strange sensation—into her body. When her consciousness appeared in the center of her mind, I pulled her to the surface.

Whole again, Madelyn gasped and touched her face. "I'm me. I'm alive!"

"Sort of," I grunted.

Dizziness hit me, and I dropped to my knees. Samuel's body went limp and collapsed over Madelyn.

"Hey!" She shoved the corpse aside and shuddered. "Gross!"

"Sorry," I panted.

She winced. "I can still feel him in my head. It's like he's squeezing my brain."

"Try to hold it together until the drugs wear off."

"What about you? Alex, you don't look so good."

I shook my head. "Jesse's got Jocelyn, Eddie, and all the people on this boat. He's gonna kill them all, Madelyn."

"How do we stop him?"

"We kill him first." I found my gun on the floor, and we hobbled back to the lounge. "Any idea which way he'd go?"

"You're asking me?"

"You must have seen something," I said. "Or were you not paying attention while you floated around?"

She winced. "I was scared, okay? Bite me!"

"Then we try to distract him," I said. "Find a fire alarm and hit it, then go to the bridge and start hitting buttons. Maybe it'll cause a problem they have to fix."

"What about you?"

"I'm gonna find Jesse."

Madelyn took a breath. "Okay, okay, I can do that."

"You can do it." I offered my fist.

She bumped it with hers and grinned. "I can do it."

"Don't go zombie on me again. It was pervy."

"You're the perv." She rolled her eyes and headed towards the kitchen. I took a port-side exit, which led into another hallway of passenger cabins.

If I were a heartless megalomaniac looking to become a god, where would I do it? I wondered. The ballroom? Or somewhere more dramatic?

A door at the end of the hall swung open, and I hurled myself into an unoccupied cabin. Three of Jesse's goons—Tyler among them—emerged from a door at the end of the hall. Tyler carried a crying Eddie at arm's length.

"Man, how do you shut this stupid kid up? I'm about to pistol-whip it!"

"You hurt him, and Kendall will kill you," said the first thug.

"Whatever."

"You'd suck as a dad," said the second.

"Don't mean I ain't one," Tyler snickered. "Let's put it downstairs."

"Think that motherfucker is dead?" Thug Two asked, as they passed my hiding place.

Tyler snorted. "I was about to whack that sucker. Comin' at me with that little popgun. Almost wasted him myself."

"Yeah, it was impressive the way you pissed yourself and ran," said Thug One. Thug Two laughed.

"Fuck you both, man," Tyler groaned.

I didn't want to leave Eddie with them, but no one was safe as long as Jesse was still free. When the coast was clear, I crept to the door they'd exited, marked 'Lido Deck'. Sounded like a good place for a raving madman to execute his diabolical plans. It opened into another stairwell.

How high does this stupid boat go? I thought. Between physical exhaustion and vertigo, it was a rough climb.

A swimming pool dominated the lido deck, overflowing with murky water. Wooden crates, loaded with tools and re-pair supplies, offered plenty of cover. The sky was heavy with black clouds, broken by the occasional peal of lightning, but the bone-chilling rain had slowed to a trickle.

Jesse knelt next to a shrine of his own. It was bigger than Kincaid's, and a monument to cruelty. He'd hammered dead snakes and human skulls to a wooden pole that dripped with layers of melted red candle wax. Large glass jugs, full of scor-pions in filthy yellow brine, sat at the base of the grisly totem.

Hundreds of bottles surrounded his mockery of a shrine, like mementos from the victims of a massacre. Leather cords bound paper and coins to the glass. Zombie astrals. There had to be hundreds. A thousand. Souls packed together like cheap wine.

Enough to make a man a god? I wondered.

I had six rounds, and almost no magic left. He still had his pistol, the whip at his belt, and his necromancy was souped-up on drug-induced worship. Worse, as I got closer, I saw Jesse's loaded assault rifle set against a crate.

No room for errors, then.

I didn't trust my aim, so I closed the distance, using the crates for cover. Jesse checked the bottles, tightening their corks or the leather cords around them. He didn't notice my approach until the lightning cast my shadow against the shrine.

As I leveled the gun at his head, I felt like saying something badass.

"The Lido Deck is closed."

Whatever. It had been a long week.

TWENTY-SEVEN

Jesse's lip curled as he turned. "Fossor. You truly are a pain in my ass. Should've shot you."

"Dumbass badguy mistake," I said. A wave of fresh dizziness hit me, and I had to lean on a nearby crate.

He smirked. "Running on empty, are we?"

"Shut up. Toss the gun in the water."

He drew the pistol with two fingers and underhanded it into the pool. The smile never left his face.

"My life was real cozy before you showed," I growled. "And you gotta go piss all over it."

"You lived in a box," he spat. "You squandered your power. A home? A job? You're Versed, for fuck's sake. Act like it."

"Like the Archmage?" I asked, and he winced. "Like the Society? Like you? Lording power over people? Turning them into puppets?"

"It's how power works. Ask that pack of wights you keep in the sewer. That zoo."

I thought about the Gallows, and the quiet fear they'd shown as I justified Max's execution. "It's not a perfect system, but it's better than what you offer."

He snorted and took a step forward. "So what now? Arrest me? Should I surrender and clear your name for you? Or do you wanna kill me?"

I grinned. "Yeah. Figured I'd shoot you."

"And break poor Jocelyn's heart?"

"Whoever her brother was, he never came back."

The smugness vanished. "You don't know a damn thing."

"I know she wanted to spare your life. But how many Edicts have you broken, Jess? Consent, Life, Sanctity. To say nothing of how you've pissed off the Loa. The one I talked to wasn't too keen on you joining the club. From what I've read, they have strong opinions about slavery."

He spread his arms. "If they don't like it, they can strike me down where I stand."

I aimed the revolver at his chest. "Poor choice of words."

Jesse took another step, then dove behind a crate as I fired, missing him by inches. He reappeared with the assault rifle and opened fire.

I dropped flat as bullets tore apart crates and dug gouges into the floor. When his weapon clicked dry I scrambled to my feet, but he ducked before I could return fire.

"You're screwed, Fossor! How many bullets have you got?"

Five, I thought.

"Plenty," I told him.

"My boys are gonna hear the gunshots and come runnin'. Just give up and die!"

"Fuck you!"

Jesse dove and rolled, like some kind of Hollywood commando. I took the bait, firing two rounds that flew wide. He returned fire with a burst that drove me behind cover, and I lost sight of him.

He had a better gun and stronger magic. I had three rounds left and was seeing double. Some distant, sane part of my mind chastised me for being such an unprepared fool.

We stood at the same moment, drawing a bead on each other. I fired first, but the bullet hit a support beam to the side of Jesse's head. He sneered and squeezed the trigger, and I dove out of the way. The crate was shredded, spilling sheets of metal siding over the deck.

Jesse kept his finger on the trigger, twisting the gun my way, but it clicked dry again before it could perforate me. He cursed, and dug into his pockets for a fresh clip.

I charged. It wasn't a game-winning football tackle. I screamed like a scared, angry, crazy person and smashed into him at full speed. My left knee twisted under his weight and we both fell. Jesse grabbed my gun, so I went for his. He yanked the revolver from my hand, aimed it at my face and pulled the trigger.

Nothing happened. For a heartbeat, we stared at each other. Confused, he pulled the trigger twice more to no effect. With a sneer of amusement, I pulled the rifle from his hand and flung it behind me. He clubbed me with the pistol, then battered me with a flurry of punches and kicks until I had to let him go.

I went crawling for the assault rifle, then I heard a crack and something stung my chest. Blood stained my shirt.

Jesse had drawn his whip. He flicked his wrist, and a furrow opened in my thigh. The denim I wore did little to protect me from its bite. He worked the weapon like a master, each hit precise and torturous.

"C'mon, boy!" He cackled. "Take your lickin's like a man!"

Holy shit, you are a dick, I thought.

I pulled myself into a ball, but that gave Jesse new angles to attack. The whip cut the flesh over my left shoulder blade, opened a bicep, then struck my face and I screamed. The left side of my mouth hung in ragged scraps of flesh.

Finally he relented, and inhaled the scent of my blood like a man savoring a grilled steak. I shivered on the ground like a beaten dog.

"I could do this all day, Alex. I could." He knelt and grabbed me by the hair. "But you shoulda taken the fall like a good patsy."

"*You* walked the zombie out of the morgue." I slurred my words through the slash in my lips. "If it weren't for you, I would still be in jail."

He let out a breathless chuckle. "You think I'd leave you for the cops? You could walk through them like they were paper. I wanted the *Society* watching you. Kincaid could mask us from them, but we knew they'd catch on. So I put you on a hook and dangled it. They went for it like the out-of-touch shitheels they are."

Speaking of out-of-touch, where the hell *was* the Society? Kincaid had been dead for at least half an hour. I doubted his magical smokescreen could keep their auguries from finding us, so where the hell *were* they?

Jesse checked his wristwatch. "Playtime's over. Time for lessons."

He slammed a fist into my face and the world went dark.

☠

I came to with a groan, groggy and blurry-eyed.

"Hey boss, this clown's awake."

I was hauled onto my knees. My body felt like chewing gum after the fact. Every wound throbbed, and my head pounded in rhythm. Tyler held my revolver against my temple.

The rain had died. The city was quiet, broken only by the rumble of distant thunder. Everyone from the rave—everyone in the *city* with an ounce of Stig in their veins—stood on the lido deck. They surrounded the pool on the ground floor and crowded the balcony level above it. Hundreds of blank-faced, motionless addicts.

Madelyn's zombie was with them, on the opposite side of the pool. The Stig must have reclaimed control. Her soul floated above her body, unseen by everyone else. Her wide eyes pleaded with me for help, but she couldn't seem to move or speak.

Jocelyn was bound to Jesse's totem by her wrists. Her good eye was focused on Eddie, who rested on a thin mattress at Jesse's feet, swaddled with blankets. Despite everything happening around him, he looked to be asleep.

Jesse stood before his collection of bottled souls, which glowed with dim light. The bastard looked none the worse for wear from our brawl. A horde of drugged-out cultists chanted and drummed around him. The number of worshipers had tripled since I'd last seen them. The old hag, Bettany, stood nearby with her basket of flowers and Stig. Her face was a bloody ruin, and her left arm a crippled twig, but she was on her feet.

"Back with us?" Jesse laughed. "I'll give you this much, Fossor. You're a tough man to keep down. Maybe Sammy was right, we should have offered you a place with us. It wouldn't have changed the outcome, but it would have saved me a headache."

"Fuck you," I groaned.

He smiled and slugged me. It almost put me under again, but he followed it with a slap. "Focus, Alex! Eyes front! I don't want you to miss this."

"You gonna play god by killing all these people?"

"This ain't about godhood, Alex. I told you that."

"So what is it, then? Mass murder the only way you get hard?"

He grabbed me by my hair. "It's about *freedom*. Freedom from the Society. From the Edicts. Freedom from all the people who want to shit on our lives!"

He dragged me towards the altar and threw me in front of Jocelyn. "Why not tell him, sis? Tell him about the life I had to live. The life you *provided* for me."

Jocelyn gave Jesse a pained look, her eyes welling with tears.

"No? Allow me, then." Jesse put his arm around Jocelyn and gave her a rough shake. "After mom died, and dad fucked off, it was just us twins, yeah? Two Versed without a home. Then the Society finds us. Ol' Walter Breckenridge, ain't he a fine Yank? Tells us about the Society, said ol' Joce here had 'so much potential'. You could see how he wanted her. Was grooming her. But Joce was so into that, wasn't she? Nothin' ever opened your legs like a rich prat with a fat purse. Oh, the Society would be a sweet life for you, wouldn't it? But me? I was the problem."

He pointed at me and him. "You and me, we ain't people, Alex. We're the skeletons in their closet. We're fucking plague rats. I didn't get a mentor. I got told off for being what I was. I got ignored. I got *blamed*. And a man can only take being called rotten so long before he starts *being* rotten, can't he? You know a bit about that, don't you, Alex?"

He dug into his deep pockets and pulled out Jocelyn's teleportation bracelet. "See this? It's my shackle. When Walter decided I was breaking the Edicts, Joce begged him not to execute me. He needed her, so he buried me. Fourteen years, I lived with this fucking thing on my wrist. In a prison behind a bookshelf. I'm told you got a taste of it. The soul-sucking power in that room? That was how they kept me. Fourteen years! Think about what it's like to be trapped in your own goddamn mind, by your own blood, while she fucks the bastard that built your cage!"

I tried to meet Jocelyn's gaze, but she looked away.

Jesse snorted. "Oh, she tried to be kind about it. Every birthday she'd sing for me. Colored lights at Christmas. Sit with me for hours and reminisce about the good old days." He twitched, his face twisted with anger and pain. "All I could do was sit there while she rubbed my nose in her sweet little life. I couldn't even beg her to kill me!"

Jocelyn tried to offer some kind of denial, but it died behind the gag.

He dropped to one knee and looked me in the eye. "Unable to move, or speak, or *scream*. Gettin' fed soup and IV injections. Havin' my goddamn *diapers* changed. Do you have any idea what it's like?" He flinched, and the anger boiled over. "Then when he's got me locked away, and she's wrapped around his finger, ol' Walter says she's ready. Sponsorship into the Council. But only if she'll make a few concessions. Marriage, babies, the usual Society crap. Make yourself a lovely little broodmare and look at the fine barn you get to live in! Whoring herself to an ancient old bastard!"

He shook his head, and his face softened again. "But little Edwin, *he* saved me. Getting pregnant distracts you. Momma can't be looking in two directions at once. It took every ounce of magic, all my hate, and maybe a few years off my life, but I got out. I broke free. I ran as far as I could. For a while I was happy. All I wanted was my life back, but Joce was always two steps behind me. I knew I'd never escape her, or them. She'd never do me the mercy of killing me, because she 'loves' me. No. She'd pack me away in that box again. So I decided to run somewhere she and her stud would never find me."

"Ascension," I said.

"Think about it, Alex, and tell me you'd do it differently in my shoes?"

I didn't answer right away. My head was a murky swamp of exhaustion and shock. Jocelyn's shoulders shook as she cried. But I looked past her, past the Society bullshit, at the people

263

around us. The dregs. I didn't know any of them, but addiction and pain had made them prisoners, too.

I saw Madelyn up in the stands, a scared spirit watching her one shot at a second chance being torn away from her to serve Jesse's goals.

"Yeah, you're tugging my heartstrings," I said. "Ask these people how they feel about being trapped in their own heads. How they feel about being sacrificed on your altar."

Jesse shrugged. "They'll be free, too. These people had nothing. I offered them an escape from their shitty lives and they drowned themselves in it. What I'm about to do is a mercy."

I bowed my head. Pain, dizziness, and disgust thrashed inside me like angry snakes. "You're a psychopath."

Jesse paused, his expression less certain than before, then he smirked. "Won't matter in a few minutes."

The worshipers rose their chant to a fevered pitch. Jesse went to stand before the bottles. The light within them had grown brighter, like bottled lightning.

"You gonna kill the kid too?" I asked. "That's some uncle."

"Oh, nah," Jesse said. "No, no, Eddie's my hero. I'm gonna take him with me. When he wakes, he'll be like Adam. He'll be a king in my world." Jocelyn tried to scream, and he backhanded her. "Shut it, sis. I'll show him more care than you ever gave me."

Bettany took a mortar and pestle from her basket, and painted Jesse's body with blood mixed with Stig. Binding his power to the souls of the people around him. As he did, the zombies began to emit a deep-throated, toneless chant.

Jesse's necromancy pulsed from him, a hot wind that felt like poison. It was the bite of the rattlesnake, the sting of the scorpion. It made me nauseous, and my wounds itched.

A shadow spread outward from the totem, like a pool of black ink. Snake-like tendrils rose from it, hissing and thrashing. Whenever the black energy licked at the glass bottles, the

life-force inside recoiled and faded. Bottles cracked and im-
ploded with each one devoured. A body crumpled to the
ground among the zombies. Then another.

I had to do something. But what did I have left? No gun, no
magic. I could barely throw a punch. My head lulled.

'Alex!' I saw Madelyn's ghost being entangled in Jesse's spell.
It wrapped around her like barbed wire, digging into her ethe-
real flesh, pulling her towards Jesse's shrine. 'Help!'

She wasn't the only one. The worshipers, Tyler and the
other thugs, and even Bettany had been ensnared by Jesse's
spell. They groaned and gasped, eyes wide with pain and
shock. Jocelyn's eyes rolled into her head as her chest erupted
with light. Her soul was coming unmoored.

The magic hissed against my flesh like acid. My consciousness slipped in and out of my body, and I could see myself,
head thrown back in pain as Jesse's ritual tore the life away
from me.

The skies above the boat split and cracked like glass. The
way to another realm opened, an entire world spreading out
before me, so close I could touch it. I saw sun-bleached deserts
dotted by black, jagged mountains, and lush oases with deep
shadows. Mile-long centipedes crawled across the sands, and
bat-like predators with scorpion tails soared amidst the
mountains. I could even see people, primitive and cowering in
the few areas of safety, helpless before the merciless heat and
poisonous predators of their world.

A newborn dimension, and a perfect reflection of Jesse's
cruel, twisted soul.

'Alex! ALEX!'

I tore my eyes from the alien world. Madelyn was almost to
the altar. She screamed as Jesse's black tendrils pulled her into
a bottle, where she could be devoured, her face distorting and
twisted. The scream reached a pitch that rattled me, in body
and spirit. It was full of fear, pain, sadness and...

Holy shit.

The screaming. A scream that could buckle windows and shake dirt from the ceiling, a scream that came from the soul?

Her blood has a forgotten history.

Madelyn wasn't an ordinary spirit.

A desperate plan formed in my brain. I fought against Jesse's power. Anger gave my weakened magic a boost, and I pulled until my soul felt like a peeling, bleeding piece of overripe fruit. The tendrils tore free and recoiled. The pain I felt made the color wash out of my vision for a moment, but I grabbed my pistol from Tyler's limp hand.

Jesse didn't look like himself anymore. With each soul consumed, he glowed brighter from within. It illuminated his heart and ribcage. His face was transparent and skeletal. He smiled at me with insane, lidless eyes.

"You can't stop it!" He held out his arms. "Take your shot, you worthless nobody! Try to kill me now!"

Madelyn, can you hear me? I thought.

Madelyn was almost half-way into a bottle. The black magic had almost engulfed her.

I need you to scream, Maddie, I thought. *Scream as hard and as loud as you can. Scream!*

She didn't respond.

On three. One, two-

I fired. The bullet ripped through Madelyn's bottle, and it exploded. Seconds stretched out like hours as nothing happened.

Then Madelyn MacLaith—wight, zombie, *banshee*—erupted from the bottle.

She threw her head back and screamed.

Every bottle on Jesse's altar shattered into a cloud of glass. And then every window within half a mile splintered and cracked. Ears and noses bled as the living heard the cry of the mournful dead. Several women broke free of Jesse's control and screamed with her, compelled by the banshee's keening to share their grief. It was the agony of a mother who had lost her children. The wail of a wife who would never see their husband again. The cry of a daughter whose parents would not come home.

Jocelyn cried out through her gag. Bettany's face paled, and she dropped dead where she stood.

I sensed Madelyn's pain, the trauma of a girl whose life had been ripped away, and a twisted mockery left in its place. How scared and hurt and utterly *alone* she felt deep down, made worse by a cruel and uncaring death among strangers. It made my pain seem petty by comparison.

Her keening became a storm that broke the spell of drugs and black magic. Jesse fell to one knee, hands pressed to his ears. The screams of his victims drowned out his own. The zombies and thugs collapsed around us like dominoes, their souls ravaged by his magic. Freed spirits returned to their bodies, or faded from sight.

Madelyn's keening ended, and she disappeared. Her body collapsed.

Above us, the dimension forged in Jesse's image blurred away to nothing, swallowed by the darkened skies. The lido deck fell silent as a grave. Eddie began to cry.

"No! No, no, no!" The light in Jesse's body evaporated into the empty air, dulling him back to mere mortal status. He clawed at the shattered glass around him, shredding his fingers in an effort to snatch the evaporating power.

I pushed to my feet. "It's over."

Jesse's eyes blazed. He snatched the assault rifle and aimed it at me. "Die!"

"Stop!"

Jesse convulsed. His body twisted as he strained against the sudden command.

"*Stop*, Jesse." Jocelyn had freed herself, and pulled the gag from her lips. Her voice was cold but gentle. I could hear the lyrical notes to them, the hymn of her magic.

Jesse's eyes bulged. He strained against her so hard his face turned red. "I won't!"

"Stop, Jesse." She approached, taking the teleportation bracelet from his pocket. "It's time to go home. Let's go home."

I shook my head. "Jocelyn, get away from him."

Jesse screamed, and Jocelyn's hold on him shattered. He knocked her to the floor and wrapped his hands around her throat. "I'm not going back! *You can't make me!*"

I took aim, but Jesse was faster, and opened fire with the rifle. I hurled myself into the pool, curled into a ball as bullets zipped through the water. A few heartbeats later, the gunfire ceased.

Empty, or waiting for me to surface? I wondered.

I needed something to fight with. A dry gun, a bit of magic, anything. I closed my eyes and tried to think. The answer was waiting in the air above me.

I swam to the edge of the pool and peeked over the side. Jesse had Jocelyn in a two-fisted choke.

"Die! *Just die!*" His scream was hysterical.

I let myself relax. The spell I was about to try could make me pass out, or it could kill me. I'd sapped too much of my magic, but I knew where to get more. The rotten power of Jesse's failed apotheosis, all that stolen life-force, still hung in the air. It was directionless and dissipating, but there was more than enough for what I needed. I reached out and took hold of it.

The energy crackled with that familiar, angry feedback. Pain rippled up my arm, but I held firm. Our wills—my own and Jesse's—competed for control, but he had focused his wounded psyche on his sister.

I calmed my mind and swirled the magic in the air. I thought of rest, and comfort, and the cool, damp soil of a dark grave. There is no peace like it. The magic shivered in my grasp and changed. Dark shadows turned to wisps of fog around me.

I could have closed my eyes in that gloom and slept forever. But Jocelyn's face had turned blue, so I pinched at Jesse's mind with the magic I'd wrested from him.

"Wh-what?" He recoiled from the fog like it was a snake. "Get away! Stop it, Alex! What are you doing?"

I crawled out of the pool. "Digging your grave, Jesse. Feel free to rot."

He screamed, and the fog flowed down his throat, into his soul. He gagged, choked, and fumbled over incoherent words. Then he collapsed onto his side, and curled into a ball.

Jocelyn gasped for air and crawled to Eddie. She hugged the wailing toddler close, cooing and rocking him, but never took her eyes off her brother.

"What did you do?" She croaked.

The effort had taken almost everything left in me. The vertigo wouldn't stop, and my entire body shook. "Fear is the mind killer."

"Is he dead?"

"No." I aimed my pistol. "But he should be."

"No! Don't, Alex! You've done enough!"

"He's too dangerous, Jocelyn. You can't control him anymore."

"I can't let you," she said. "He's my responsibility. Put the gun down."

I felt her words settle over my shoulders like a warm blanket. Everything she said sounded like the best idea I'd heard all day.

But my mind said *no*.

It was her magic. And it was *familiar*. Friendly, warm, and flirtatious. I had been so eager to help a beautiful woman with a problem that I hadn't recognized it before. Her magic had

269

made blunt commands sound like pleading hopes that tugged at my sense of compassion. But now that I knew the real Jocelyn? The person behind the mask of charming smiles and vulnerable tears? My mind shivered at her touch.

Who knew how long she had been using it? Using *me?*

I let the revolver drop from my hands. Maybe I could have fought Jocelyn, resisted her. But I was too damn tired. Of everything.

"Lady, let him go."

Madelyn stepped in beside me. She was in her own body again, but her hair stood on end. It shifted in the air as if she were underwater.

Jocelyn frowned. "I'm not-"

"Bitch, I broke your brother's *godmode*. What do you think I could do to you?"

Jocelyn glared at her, then shut her eyes and turned away.

"Everything he's done, everything he might do? That's on your hands." I told her. When she didn't respond, I shook my head. "C'mon Maddie, let's get out of here before-"

Fire erupted from my chest. It surged out of me like a sun. It was pain, like nothing I'd felt before, which, given my past few days, was a surprise.

Sheriff Agni stood between Jocelyn and I. "Alex Fossor, for your breach of the Edicts, I sentence you to death."

And then my world was fire.

TWENTY-EIGHT

Death smelled like sterile bed sheets and medicine.

My everything hurt.

Light peeked through my eyelids, and the buzzing of some nearby fluorescent light grated in my ears. I tried to will it all away, to dive back into that blessed unconsciousness, but the ache grew too insistent.

I opened my eyes in surrender. I was alive, somehow, in a windowless hospital room. A security officer sat on a bench just outside my room, reading a newspaper.

My face itched, but when I tried to scratch, I found my arm was cuffed to the bed. The rattling alerted the guard, who sprang to his feet and spoke into his shoulder-mounted radio before vanishing out of sight.

I took a moment to inspect my skin, what I could see of it under my various bandages, and saw that it was intact. The flames hadn't even singed the hair.

A short time later a doctor came in, flanked by the guard. He checked my eyes and pulse.

"Mr. Fossor, can you hear me?"

"Yarp."

He went down a list of questions about what I could and couldn't feel, where the worst pain was, what I could remember, and all the while he checked and rechecked my vitals. I was cooperative about everything but the memory, lest I incriminate myself in something.

"Very well," he said. "You twisted your leg and there are multiple contusions and cuts, but our X-rays showed no fractures or deep tissue damage. You can focus and answer me clearly, which is good."

"Blerf," I agreed.

Then he gave me some painkillers and left me alone, so he was my new favorite person in the world.

I let the numbness take me under for a while, and when I woke the doctor took some more tests. It went on like that for a while. Sometimes there was a nurse, sometimes a different doctor. The security guard didn't change. I named him Bob. He looked like a Bob.

My pain progressed to where it was just annoying and not torturous. Then a skinny nurse sat me up and fed me soft food in little trays and made me drink about a gallon of water. Hospital food is nothing to write home about, but after my week, it was a feast for the senses.

I had just finished a breakfast of oatmeal and scrambled eggs when my two favorite detectives arrived. Runner had his big smile and anachronistic duster. Lorensdottr wore her sharkskin suit and a scowl in her stunning blue eyes. She did not look happy to be deprived of a meal.

"Mr. Fosser, how are you feeling?" Runner asked.

"Good as I look, I imagine."

"Then you must feel like shit in stitches," Lorensdottr said.

"I know you've got questions," Runner said. "But we've got more important ones."

They grilled me for nearly an hour. My whereabouts over the past week. What relationship I had with Josh Wilkes, with the Brothers Midnight, if I'd ever taken Stig, the nature of the setup in my basement, and how Josh had ended up there, 'unconscious'. I fed them a lot of confused uncertainty, and Runner did his best not to smirk when he knew I was lying to his partner. Then they started over, asking the same questions with different context or perspectives, trying to peel the real details from the bullshit I fed them.

"I barely remember any of it," I insisted for the fourth or fifth time. "The last memory I have is buying some chops from Kent's. Then I woke up here."

"This is such horseshit," Lorensdottr muttered. "If you expect us to believe any of it-"

Runner put a hand on her shoulder. "It's okay, Lo. Mr. Fossor just needs to gather his thoughts. Why not grab some coffee?"

She stared at him for a moment, then walked out, fists at her sides. Runner watched her from the door, then looked at me and mouthed 'ouch'.

"What does she remember?" I asked.

"Nothing," he replied. "I brought her upstairs and sat her on a couch in our break room. She woke up assuming she'd returned from your place and fell asleep."

"She still suspects."

"That's who she is," Runner replied.

I remembered Maman Brigitte's presence, when she wanted to impress on me just how big an entity she was in comparison. It had put me on my knees. Lorensdottr brain-meat might not register something like that, but her soul would remember when they had shared a body.

"Maybe," I said. "But do you remember what Maman Brigitte said about Consent? Even a Loa can't force itself into your body if you don't give it permission. On some level, Loren understood what was happening, and allowed it. I think Brigitte offered something in return."

"Like what?" Runner asked.

"Dunno. She might not even know herself. But if she ends up winning the lottery, I'm calling it now."

He exhaled and made the sign of the Cross over his torso. "This crap is a bit too heavy for me. I never stopped believing, but circumstantial evidence is more than I ever got from Sunday Mass."

I shrugged. "You're toes deep. Look at what I have to deal with, and it's at my ankles."

He took another peek down the hallway. "So, what about the real details of what happened?"

I told him what happened on the boat, but not everything. No reason to pull Runner in any deeper than he was.

"After I blacked out, I woke up here," I said. "So, it's your turn. What happened?"

"We found your friend Madelyn onboard," Runner said. "She was leading the survivors off the ship."

I felt a touch of pride. "She needs to be near her gravesoil. The pot in my house."

"She told me," Runner said. "It took a bit of convincing, but when I realized we had a mutual 'friend' I got her released from the hospital. So what is she, like, a zombie or a vampire or something?"

"No. It's complicated. Let's leave it at that for now. What about the Brothers?"

"Forensics is still going over the ship, but they found aquariums full of fish, and a grow-op for datura metel, a poisonous flower. Between the fire at the Arlington and the stuff we found on board?" He shook his head. "The consensus is that they were a cult, using drugs and religious iconography to twist addicts into followers. Most of their gang—the ones who had guns on them—were all dead. We figured it was a 'drink the poisoned punch' moment."

"Close enough," I said. "How many people died?"

Runner looked at his feet. "There's still people in intensive care with unidentified trauma, and a lot of the junkies fled before we could do a proper head count. Current toll is seventeen, not including the cult members."

There was no way of knowing when they'd died, or if I could have prevented it if I'd been faster. And Runner's count didn't include those killed at Aubergine's.

I had set out on a mad quest to save my own skin, but there were people who would never go home, never see their loved ones again. It made me question every action I'd taken, every mistake I made. Every scar became penance.

"What about me?" I asked.

"Far as we know, you got dumped outside the hospital. The doctors thought you were a hit-and-run. When they tagged your ID, we had them hold you, but since the Wilkes kid was found alive on the ship, we can't exactly stick you for murder, so no homicide case, again. No idea when or if they'll let you keep your scary ass Vodou shrine. That's all you were using it for, right? Please don't tell me you were trying to make Frankenstein's monster."

I didn't have the heart to tell him, because he would have arrested me. "I was trying to summon Samedi."

"And the mortuary slab?"

"My boss was getting rid of it."

"That's morbid, you know?"

I let myself smile. It hurt my stitches. "Yeah, but for me it's Tuesday. Anything else I should know?"

He shook his head. "As far as the law is concerned, the case is closed. I heard Jefferson is getting a parade."

I frowned. No doubt Agni had gotten Jocelyn and Eddie off the boat. But what about Jesse?

Runner checked the hallway. "She's on her way. Put your game face on."

"One question," I said. "*Loren* Lorensdottr?"

275

He grinned. "Her first name is Olga, but she's touchy about it. Picked on as a kid, is my guess. It's not even on her driver's license. You say it out loud, or tell her I said it, and I'll make sure she guts you first."

"Your secret is safe with me."

"Ditto."

Lorensdottr entered with a styrofoam cup of coffee and pushed it into Runner's hand. "Tastes like shit," she said. "Like his story."

Runner tasted it and winced.

"I could make you some later," I said. "Assuming my coffee grinder isn't also evidence."

She glared. "Everything about you is evidence, Fossor. Every thread I pull on you stinks like death. I don't know when or how, but one day, I'm going to find out where those threads lead, and when I do? I'll bury you."

She badgered me with a repeat of a few questions, but halfway into her third question she got a call on her phone. "What?" She listened for a minute, then tucked the phone away. "Let's go, Runner."

"What's up?"

"Come on!" She gave me one last glare and left. Runner shrugged and followed.

I watched them go. Another homicide, I figured. Someone dies all the time in most big cities. Believe me, I'm in the business.

Agni was standing at the foot of my bed.

I jumped, and it made every part of me hurt. "Don't *do* that!"

He sipped Runner's discarded coffee, indifferent to its flavor. "Only when it stops being immensely funny."

I sighed. "So, what? Come to finish me?"

He smirked. "Who do you think brought you here? All things considered, you did well, Alex. Sloppy, but for your age and skill, few could have done better. Co-opting the energies from the ritual was impressive, though I was about to kill you for it. If it weren't for Mrs. Breckenridge's intervention, well…"

"Where are they?"

"Safe, at home."

"Jesse's too dangerous. He's broken free before, and with his knowledge he could try this all again."

"Mrs. Breckenridge has assured me that Jesse will remain secure," he said. "A pity he may never awaken from what you did to him. It would have benefited us to question him on where he learned his ritual."

I frowned. "He said he learned it in a dream."

Agni's eyebrow piqued. "Curious. But if you wanted him dead, why not kill him yourself on the boat?"

"I didn't have a choice," I said. "Jocelyn wouldn't let me."

He nodded. "Suffice it to say, the case has been dropped. Mrs. Breckenridge has spoken in your favor, and between your service and the evidence collected, the Council's vote has swayed in your favor. The Archmage has removed the hex. You're a free man, relatively speaking." He gestured at the handcuffs.

"Of course, there is the matter of your own actions over the past few days. Allowing unsanctioned wights to run free, leading to a fatal attack. Creating a wight of your own from the victim, one that possesses an unforeseen amount of power in her own right. Interacting with the Ascended. Exposing your abilities to the Untold, and *police* for that matter…"

I glared at him. "I did what I had to. You didn't care to notice, but I've been getting my ass handed to me left and right to fix a mess that you and your Society could have solved with a hand wave!"

Agni smiled. "But-?"

"But, uh," I stammered. "If you knew the Archmage was involved, but didn't stop it… you didn't want to?"

The smile vanished. "Or those of us who wanted to, could not."

A chill settled in my gut. "Kincaid's ward wasn't keeping the Brothers hidden. *You* were. You and the Archmage. Why?"

"Because that's the nature of what we are, Alex." He leaned close enough to whisper. "There are always bigger fish, and they control the Society. They make the rules and they like things quiet. When one of them tells us we're forbidden to intervene, we are quite literally incapable of doing so."

I took a long breath. "Walter didn't want the rest of the Society to learn about Jesse."

"He already had a considerable record in Europe when he was first arrested. The Council believes Walter executed him, but for the sake of his recent marriage, he contained Jesse instead. The Society doesn't jail lawbreakers, Alex. Execution may seem rash to you, but Versed grow in power as we age. The resources needed to hold a single person are astronomical, as I'm sure you realize."

"But he still got out," I said.

Agni nodded. "His escape threatened to expose the Breckenridges. The Archmage could have weathered the scandal, but his wife's sponsorship would have been forfeit. Thus, when Jesse attempted to frame you, the Archmage saw an opportunity to intervene. He took steps to assure *you* could deal with the problem."

I frowned. "That's why he let me go. He wanted me to sweep up his mess, while making it look like you were dealing with me."

"And you performed as needed," Agni said. "The Brothers are dealt with and Jesse is back in custody. I'm told this affair has lent the Society considerable negotiating power in bringing Haiti's Versed into our fold. That's all the Council needs or wants to know. If you think it's unfair that we used you in this manner, then I suggest you cry into your pillow."

I flipped him off.

He grinned. "Archmage Breckenridge may be a bastard, but be happy he finds you a useful resource. His rivals would make your life a much shorter, far more hellish one, if they were in his place. Remember what you did to your friend Max. Understand how the people who make themselves responsible for us will react if we don't walk the line they draw. We all have swords to our necks."

It was unfair, and pragmatic. It was bullshit, and it was smart. Jesse proved that even a young mage could do unspeakable damage if he had a will to. The only way to prevent that was to have another, stronger mage ready to stop them.

Detente. The Society's whole purpose was *detente*. A unified front to cow dangerous mages into walking a straight, narrow line. It was a horrifying, sobering thought.

Agni nodded as he saw me connecting the dots. "Puts the world in perspective, doesn't it?" He brushed off his coat and returned to stand near the foot of my bed. "While your services can't be officially acknowledged, you are expected to keep the details discreet. As far as anyone is concerned, you fought and killed a coven of rogue Versed from Haiti, who had violated the Edicts. Neither Jesse Kendall, Jocelyn Breckenridge, nor Walter Breckenridge was involved. I don't need to remind you what the consequences will be should anything contrary reach the Council's ears."

I frowned. "You're welcome, asshole."

Agni shrugged. "If nothing else, consider this ordeal a way to expand yourself. Jesse was right about one thing, Alex. Intentionally or not, you've been keeping yourself in a box, ignorant of your potential. You would do well not to squander it. It will be necessary in the future, should the Society have a need for talented agents again."

My anger boiled over. "Fuck you. You didn't do this for *my* benefit. Necromancers don't get to expand ourselves. We don't get a seat at your table. We get treated like garbage 'cause our magic scares you! You bully us, threaten us, you beat the rules into our heads and kick us for every mistake! You stuck us in that box!"

Rage wafted off me in a cold fog. "Don't you tell me what a 'good soldier' I am for your crooked little clubhouse, when you put a gun to my head and told me to fix your fucking mistakes! Jesse Kendall is the monster *you* created. All those people suffered for your fucking *careers*. You, Walter, Jocelyn, you can all jump on your golden thrones and go fuck yourselves!"

Agni's face was unreadable. I waited for him to lash me with another potent reminder that he was in charge, that my life was something he could snuff out if I didn't bow my head and grovel for it.

Instead, he nodded, once. "Until we speak again."

It took my eyes a moment to grasp that he'd vanished. I laid back and tried to calm down. Thinking over my life until that moment, I realized that being the world's most unobtrusive necromancer, a bottom-feeder too weak to notice, was more appealing than ever, and the stupidest thing I could do. It was only a matter of time until another mage with an agenda saw me as an easy mark, and the insanity would start all over again.

I had been the pawn in all of it. Jesse's patsy. Jocelyn's bloodhound. Walter's gravedigger. I hated the feeling, the sickening knowledge that they had used me, that I was just a tool for people's schemes. And that I never had a choice.

Sort of like Max.

If the week had taught me anything, it was that the city—the entire world—was crawling with assholes, wielding a power that was leagues above mine. But there was no way I would let them throw me under the bus again. That meant spending the rest of my life preparing for the next time someone tried to stick his nose in my business. A magical arms race, one that I and every other mage on the planet were playing, and had been for centuries.

No peace. Just detente.

Like I said. Horrifying.

I closed my eyes and tried to sleep. I didn't want to think about it for a while.

TWENTY-NINE

I used the time cuffed to my bed to catch up on the sleep I'd missed. No one else came to visit, and after two days Bob the hospital guard stopped by to remove my cuffs without a word. I hobbled into the bathroom to check myself out in the mirror.

Days after the fight on the boat, I still looked like a moldy onion; gaunt, and covered in deep purple bruises. I had enough stitches for a closed casket funeral, and each cut would form a nasty scar. The one across the left side of my lips would get me a few gawkers. People would assume I repaired a cleft palate with a staple gun.

When I came out of the bathroom, I found three people waiting. Philip Wilkes, his cousin Josh, and a small, elderly woman who radiated the warmth only a loving grandmother could.

"There's the man." Philip stepped forward and clasped my hand tight. "I owe you big."

"Glad to see Josh is okay," I said.

"Whatever." Josh looked haggard, and a lot less cocky than the last time we'd spoken. "Why are we here?"

Philip patted his shoulder. "Gran wanted to share a few words with the man."

"Why? All he did was a job."

"Joshua," the old woman admonished.

"Yeah, yeah," Josh said. The deference he showed, quiet and patient, proved she was the woman who owned that pleasant-looking yellow home on Lincoln Street.

Philip gave me a sidelong glance. "Hey Josh, you mind givin' us a few minutes? We'll hit the road in a few."

"Fine," Josh said, wandering out.

Philip shrugged at me. "Sorry. He doesn't remember anything."

"Not as dead as either of us thought," I said.

Philip made a sign over his head that reminded me of the one Papa Williams had made. "The boys would have lost it if they'd found out. But I'm just glad Gran didn't have to come home to a funeral. Thanks."

I shrugged. "I think I made it worse."

"That's not true," the old woman said. "Not all situations are clear from our perspective. But those with a loftier vintage can sometimes point us in the right direction, even if we don't see it ourselves."

"This is my grandmother, Roseline," Philip said.

"Hello," she said, smiling. Her mere presence was a kind of comfort. Not magic, just the very human strength that comes from love. I could see how a group like the Mambas would do so much for her.

"The whole sitch was sideways," Philip said. "When I heard you got arrested, I thought my world was about to explode, and I didn't see a way out of it. I had to do some praying, but eventually he showed me the way."

"He?"

He smiled, rolling up the sleeve of his jacket to show a tattoo on his arm. The same veve I had painted to summon Baron Samedi.

283

"My daughter never cared for it," Philip's grandmother said. I could make out a hint of Haitian in her accent. "But Philip here came to me for guidance before he enlisted."

"There ain't no atheists in foxholes," Philip agreed. "And hey, who better to pray to than the man who'll dig your grave?"

My mind drifted to Maman Brigitte's words. "Small world."

The grandmother frowned. Everything about her demeanor shifted, from a kind grandmother to a colder, business-like matron. "Is it true? Was the man who poisoned my grandson, who was killing my boys, Dinclinsin? The slave-driver? The Loa of Wrath, who keeps everything he can put in his pockets?"

I shook my head. "He was just a bastard. Evil like you can't imagine. But mortal."

Philip nodded. "I hope when you put him down, you made him suffer for it."

I didn't respond to that. Instead I asked, "What's next for you?"

He sighed. "Got some shell-shocked boys still dealing with all the hits we took. I'm hoping with Josh on his feet, and this sitch dealt with, they'll ease out again. But there's turf to reclaim, respect to re-earn. Streets gotta know the Mambas aren't on their backs anymore. Time will tell."

I nodded. Philip was a good sort for the leader of a street gang. But who the hell was I to judge?

A question occurred to me, unbidden. "How'd Josh get his hands on the Stig?"

Philip looked at his grandmother, who turned that stony gaze on him. "The truth? The Haitians were always bringing it into our turf. Just leaving it in plain sight. Waiting for people to find it and try it. I knew something was up with it, and told my boys to flush any of it they found. But Josh..."

"That boy," Roseline sighed. "I told you not to leave that poison anywhere near him!"

Philip bowed his head. "I know, Gram. If I'd have known he had it- I should have been watching him closer."

"Don't be too hard on him, or yourself," I said. "I've seen families fall apart, squeezing too hard."

Roseline smiled at me. "Very true, young man. But let's go find Joshua before he gets in more trouble."

I shook Philip's hand again. "Take care out there."

"You too."

"Thank you," the woman said, holding my hands in hers. "Thank you for helping me and mine."

I gave her hand the gentlest of squeezes. "If you ever speak to Maman Brigitte, tell her 'thank you' for me."

She smiled, almost knowingly.

☠

I was allowed to leave the hospital the next day. They tried to prescribe me a king's fortune in painkillers and antibiotics, but I was used to the pain by then, and only had enough insurance for one. Antibiotics it was. Either way, I'd be paying off my hospital stay for a while. Big pharma, they're the real crooks. Real swell of Agni to skip the bill. You'd think my ex-tortionists could at least cover my *expenses.*

Between my jigsaw puzzle scars and torn up clothes, I got plenty of stares on the bus ride home, but the guy who stared hardest had inch-long fingernails. Weird is relative.

Someone had replaced the front door of my home. It smelled like fresh paint, and it had a peephole. My key worked in the lock, so I went in. Inside, it smelled like coffee and frying eggs.

Madelyn was working over my stove in her underwear.

"Oh shit!" She was halfway into my bedroom by the time I noticed her. "You should have called!"

"It's *my* house." I sat on the couch and noted the nest of blankets and pillows she'd made for herself. "Where'd the door come from?"

"Your landlord," Madelyn said. "I told him I was watching the place while you were in the hospital."

"Did you meet him naked, too?"

"Shut up!" She emerged from my room in one of my shirts. It hung down to her knees.

"Making yourself at home, I see."

"Nice to see you too," she replied. "You look like shit."

"You're welcome. Where have you been?"

"After that cute detective let me out of the hospital, they called my mom. I had to admit I was a junkie. She was bouncing off the walls. Tried to get me into a clinic, but I told her... *you* were my therapist. So uh, do some reading on addiction treatment for when she stops by."

I exhaled. "Great."

"Then I went to the Gallows to let everyone know what had happened and get some things before I ghouled out again." She loaded a plate with scrambled eggs and sat down. "You want an egg?"

"I want to sleep. For a million years."

"Listen." She stabbed at her eggs. "I wanted to say thanks. For saving my life."

"Which time?"

"Every time. I mean... fuck. This is me, now. I still don't know how I feel about that. But, after everything that happened? I'm glad I'm still here. If not technically alive. I mean it. Thank you."

"Glad I did. You saved the day."

She smiled. "Yeah, I guess I did, huh? How?"

"Good question. Banshees come from a specific bloodline, you know. Old, old Irish."

"I'm a banshee?"

286

"And a wight. And you were a zombie. We call it a hat trick in the biz."

She nibbled her eggs. "Banshee. Can I kill people with my scream?"

I thought about Bettany. "Uh, maybe? Don't go testing it around here, eh? I'll see what I can learn."

"I should start a band. I'd make a killing." She flinched. "Was that a bad joke?"

"The worst. You're terrible."

She threw a pillow at me. "You got some mail. And I listened to the messages on your machine."

"Do you want to borrow my wallet while you're going through every facet of my private life?" I asked.

"It could have been *important*," she argued. "Don't be such a prude. Some people hire house-sitters."

"The ones that don't get paid are called 'squatters'," I muttered. "So lemme guess. Bills, bills, 'you're fired, Alex'."

"No," Madelyn said. "Well, yes, to the first two. No one called to fire you."

"Will miracles never cease?"

"Oh, and this Indian guy showed up in an old taxi and dropped your gun off. I put it on your nightstand. And the cute detective called to say that you can get your truck from the impound lot on Riker's Street."

"Great. Let me get a shower, and we'll go get it. You can drive, right?"

"Yes, duh."

I made a face at her. Then I showered, shaved—carefully around my stitches—and put on some fresh clothes. As I came out of the bathroom, I felt almost normal again.

"Have you seen my cell phone?" I asked. "I need to find out if I broke it on the boat."

When she didn't answer, I went into the living room. Madelyn had backed into the kitchen with a scowl on her face. Jocelyn stood in the open doorway, dressed to the nines in an expensive ivory outfit. A wedding band of diamonds and platinum had appeared on her finger.

"Hi," Jocelyn said. "Um, do you have a moment?"

"Sure." I grabbed the silver watch off my bed and put my shoes on.

"Alex?" Madelyn asked.

"It'll be okay, kid. Eat your eggs."

I shut the front door and walked Jocelyn to her car. I could see Eddie inside, strapped to a child's seat.

"I guess I have you to thank for not being executed," I said.

"I told you I would. Thank you for not killing Jesse."

"I helped you get him," I said. "Just like you made me."

She bowed her head. "I know. But Jesse was my responsibility. We both failed each other."

"Where is he?"

"Away," she said. "Far away from anyone he can hurt, even if he wakes up. What did you do to him?"

I shrugged. "Hell is what you make of it."

She nodded. "Alex, I-"

"Don't," I interrupted. "After all this? Don't try to justify yourself to me."

"I was *desperate*. Walter thought getting involved was too risky, but when I learned he and Agni had set you against Jesse, I knew I had to get close to keep you from killing him."

"Wasn't hard, was it?" I asked. "The right words, the right magic, and I'd go along with anything you said. I wouldn't even know it."

She closed her eyes. A tear started down her cheek. "You know that my magic doesn't work right if the person doesn't want to do what I tell them. You wanted to help."

"You didn't *ask*," I said. She flinched away again. "You put a leash around my brain. Like your brother. You took what you wanted. And it worked. You got it all. Wealth, power. And blood. Don't forget all the blood. Every life Jesse ruined? It's on you, Jocelyn. Not that anyone will care what some lowlife has to say about it."

"I know," she said. "I wanted to- I'm sorry."

I nodded. "Is that all?"

She met my gaze. "I guess so."

We both hesitated. Heaven help me, I still wanted to reach out to her, despite everything she'd put me through. She wanted the same. To grab hold of my hand if I offered it, like I had at the restaurant.

But why care about someone like me? She wasn't on the Council yet, but she had more power than most Untold humans could ever dream of, and she'd never have to face the consequences of her actions, no matter how awful she claimed to feel about them.

I stared into those beautiful, sad, lonely silver eyes, and I knew... it hadn't been worth it.

I could only guess what her life was like. The life she and Jesse had lived before their powers developed. How early had Walter gotten his claws in her, grooming her to take her mentor's place on the Council? Building a cage with her own ambitions? How long had it taken her to come to terms with what she was doing to her brother? To everyone else?

In the end, she had all the power in the world, and it hadn't earned her an ounce of freedom. Walter had woven the perfect trap for her, one that she would always lock herself in, for fear of losing everything.

But maybe it wasn't too late? Jesse would never forgive her, and her marriage was a farce, but she'd been testing the waters with me. Asking about dating and romance, seeing if I was the person who would look beyond the power and care about Jocelyn, the person. Then, no matter how hard life was in her tower, when the pain, guilt, and loneliness threatened to overwhelm her, she could reassure herself that I was on her side.

She wanted what I wanted. A place to belong. I'd be her rock. She'd be my island.

All I had to do was reach out.

I took a step back.

Jocelyn hugged her arms. When she opened her eyes, they were flat mirrors of cold silver. "Mind yourself out there, Mr. Fossor," she said. "Your actions served the Society this time, but if—and when—you cross the line, there won't be anyone to help you."

My scarred lips twitched as I tossed her the wristwatch. "Go tell your husband, he's welcome for saving his worthless ass. And yours. And your son's."

Jocelyn caught the watch and stared at it. Then she shook her head and dropped it on the dry grass. "He won't miss it."

When she left, I reclaimed the watch and went inside. Madelyn sat on the couch, with an untouched plate of scrambled eggs on her lap.

"You knew?" I asked.

"When she showed up that night, she started talking and you did everything she wanted. It was weird. You were like a robot."

"You didn't think to say anything?"

"I tried! But you weren't listening."

"No. I guess I wasn't." I went into my room and closed the door, sat at my desk, and tried to bury my feelings in a mental graveyard.

☠

Since I had a wight for a roommate now, and no new gravedigging jobs, I visited the Gallows to grab some more rations. The atmosphere was quiet as I arrived, and I found the wights sitting in a circle of lawn chairs and stools near the kitchen.

I was curious, but felt like an unwelcome eavesdropper, so I went to the freezers and bagged a few things. Deb and Jeb broke away from the circle to join me as the rest of the wights departed to their rooms.

"What's all that?" I asked.

Jeb shrugged. "I thought it would help us to talk about what happened as a group. Each of us was treating our existence as a 'me' problem. Hearing about Madelyn's perspective and sharing our own... it helped us bridge gaps we'd left between us. So we don't feel so much like strangers around each other."

I glanced at him. "Dr. Jeb? Sounds like a great talk show."

"I think it's opened up some doors between us." Deb patted Jeb on the shoulder. "He's very talented as a counselor."

He shrugged. "It was one of my goals in med school before... all this."

"We were isolating ourselves from one another, not just the surface. It was turning into resentment. I wish things hadn't turned out like they had," Deb said.

Her lip quivered, and I saw a line of black form in her eyes.

"I crashed into your world like a bully," I said. "If I had just stayed away-"

Deb stepped forward. "We'd still be living in squalor. Dreaming of a life we'd never have. I feel horrible for what became of Max, we all bear some of the burden for his decisions. But he chose to take that anger out on an innocent. If you had not been here, Alex, it would have been Ichiro, or Norton, who would have put him down. And Madelyn would have *died*. Being a wight is a bleak existence, but she is still here. That matters."

I forced myself to meet her eyes, and nodded. "I've been thinking about that. I think we've been squeezing them too hard, Deb."

"What do you mean?" Jeb asked.

I put the bag on top of the freezer. "I mean, have you ever thought about going back to school, Jeb? Finishing your doctorate?"

"Sometimes," he admitted. "I keep telling myself, if I'd kept learning, and stayed in school, I could have helped Madelyn. Maybe saved her. But I froze up." He stared at his hands. "Doesn't matter."

"Sure it does. And knowing what could have been... it's more important than ever that we do more than hide ourselves."

"Hey Jeb, you done with your pow-wow?" Donnie appeared from the side corridor. He met my gaze and froze. "Uh, nevermind."

"C'mere, Donnie," I said. It wasn't a command, but then most of the wights had taken to seeing it that way. "Have a seat."

He, Jeb and Deb all sat, looking tense.

"We haven't been out," Donnie said.

"I know." I dug into my coat and brought out a bottle of chili-infused rum, which had been sitting in my fridge since my first failed Loa summoning.

I poured four glasses as I spoke. "I know I was hard on you. I don't deny it. And I won't stop being hard, because too many lives are at stake to leave it to chance."

Donnie frowned. "Easy for you to say, you don't have a leash."

"Donnie-" Deb started.

"It's alright," I told her. "But you're wrong, Donnie. Last week I learned I've got a leash around my neck too. I've been very, very blind about the world. We all suffered for it. Situations we should have prepared for, we weren't. Trust we should have shown each other, we didn't."

I pushed the drinks out in front of them. "Someone gave me the advice not to squander my potential, so I intend to stretch out a little. Improve myself. And you guys deserve the same."

Both men perked up.

"Yeah? How?" Jeb asked.

I shrugged. "Depends. You could finish school. Find different jobs than the ones I give you. Get a place that isn't an old sewer. Maybe even try to reconnect with your families." I looked at Deb. "Whatever's reasonable. As long as you—as long as we—take it one step at a time, trust each other, and don't put each other at risk..." I took a glass and toasted it. "What's the point of living if you never leave your coffin?"

Donnie took his drink, but hesitated. "I know what happened, happened. Had to happen. Max was my friend. But he didn't get mean, he started mean. I thought letting him out more would help, but I think I just made it worse." He shook his head and wiped a black tear from his eye.

"Blame me, if you want," I said.

Donnie shook his head. "No, no. I'm tired of seeing it like that. I wish it hadn't- that it didn't happen the way it happened."

I sighed. "Me too."

Jeb toasted his glass. "Max."

We clinked glasses and drank.

"Ugh," Jeb said with a wince. "That burns like a motherfucker."

"Jebidiah Rainsford!" Deb admonished. She took a dainty sip from her shot glass. "Oh, tits! That's hot as hell!"

"Don't you dare make this come out of my nose," I told her.

Donnie chuckled. "Pussies. You gotta learn how to live."

I smiled, and poured him another. "Don't we all."

Note from the Author:

Alex's tale is far from over. If you enjoyed this novel, I encourage you to leave a review on Amazon, and sign up for my newsletter over on the website. You'll get updates on the next release, my other writing ventures, random foibles, and free short stories that tie each book in the Alex Fossor series together.

As a novel, Death Dealers represents a labor of blood, sweat and tears. Not all of them were my own. I'm a storyteller, no more or less, and getting myself to this point has taken the support of very good friends who may never understand how daunting all of this felt to me, even as we overcame obstacles that another writer might find effortless.

To those who helped make this book a reality, you have my undying gratitude. And to you, the reader, thank you so much for giving me this chance to tell you a story.

mggallows.wordpress.com

Printed in Great Britain
by Amazon